ABYSSINIA, Italy and the Secret Service form the back-ground of this fast-moving novel of action and suspense, of strange and violent adventures in the post-war years, in search of lost Government documents and resistance-money.

ROGUE'S GAMBIT

by

ALAN CAILLOU

toExcel
San Jose New York Lincoln Shanghai

Rogue's Gambit

Published by toExcel
an imprint of iUniverse.com, Inc.

For information address:
iUniverse.com, Inc.
620 North 48th Street
Suite 201
Lincoln, NE 68504-3467
www.iuniverse.com

Originally published by London: Peter Davies Ltd

ISBN: 0-595-00703-1

Printed in the United States of America

Prologue

The report was written badly, shakily, at times almos
illegibly, on two ragged pieces of paper. It began in ink, and was
clear, precise, detached, almost cold. And then after the ink had
run out and the soldierly dispassion had turned to hatred and
despair, the rough pencil had trailed into loneliness, incoherence,
and death. It began:

LAKBAR, ETHIOPIA,
June 10th, 1941

ON the morning of June 9th, my patrol, consisting of
myself, the Ethiopian guerrilla leader Ras Aklilu, and
seven irregulars, made contact with a party of twelve
Italians of the —— Regiment. They opened fire on us,
and in the ensuing engagement Ras Aklilu and five of
his men were killed, as well as four of the Italians. The
remainder surrendered to me; one Lt. Franconi, a
Sergeant Ricci, and six other ranks whose names I do
not remember. This was about a mile and a half south-
west of the bridge that spans the Lakbar ravine. Both
the Italian lorry and my own truck were damaged by
gunfire and rendered useless, so we camped at this
point. I was not able to receive H.Q. on my radio, and
therefore sent a report blind, informing them of these
events; I do not know if it was heard. My own activities
were limited by a bullet wound in my right hip, and
consequent loss of blood. I took the precaution of tying
the wrists of the prisoners for the night and of posting

guard over them, the two remaining Ethiopians taking turns at this.

I regret to report that these precautions were insufficient. During the night I awoke to hear gunfire and to find the camp firmly in the hands of the Italians, who had somehow contrived to release themselves; both the Ethiopians and one Italian had been killed in the process. The remaining seven Italians under Lt. Franconi were fighting among themselves, and I was beaten over the head with a rifle butt; it was daylight before I recovered consciousness. By this time it was clear that my equipment had been rifled and that the previous contention had been about the disposal of my funds, still intact as received from H.Q. on behalf of the Lakbar guerrilla groups, to whom I was to deliver them. My truck, which was loaded with rifles and ammunition for the same groups, was at this time being burned, and I heard a suggestion that the money should be shared out and hidden. I then realised that these men were deserters from their regiment, and I heard them discussing the problem raised by the presence of a British officer prisoner; I heard one man say (I think it was the sergeant), "*I morti non ci disturbarano*". Sergeant Ricci then walked over to the cot on which I was lying, pointed his revolver at me, and fired three times. The first round misfired, the second struck me in the neck, and the third entered my chest below the left lung. I lost consciousness.

Here, the writing in ink, shaky but precise, ended, and the narrative was taken up in pencil, unsteadily, as though the recollection of these events had in itself weakened the writer.

When I awoke, it was dark, and I fell from the bed while trying to reach the water-bottle. I was not able to get back or to reach the first-aid kit which was . . . (*there followed an illegible line. It went on*) . . . that I have lost a lot of blood and I do not expect to live throughout the night. The man who shot me was called Ricci—Ricci, I think his first name is Gianni; he speaks very good English, about 35 years old, and talks like a Sicilian. His name is Ricci, Gianni Ricci; this was the deliberate murder of a prisoner. If this paper is found, please tell my wife that I was killed in action. I have nothing to leave her except my love. I do not think I have time to write to her now. Please tell her that I am sorry to leave her. It is dark and I am finishing this in the darkness. Send a replacement to Lakbar with a repeat consignment of the arms and money which have been stolen. This is urgent and important.

JOHN HEWITT, Major, K.A.R.

When the patrol reached the little camp, Major Hewitt's note was found wedged under a stone; the hyenas had dragged away his body.

Chapter One

In the tall red-brick building overlooking St James's Park, Metcalfe was looking for a lost file when Claire, Sir John's secretary, rang through. She said: "Ian? Straighten your tie and come on in; the Colonel wants to see you."

He found the Colonel sitting back in his swivel chair behind a completely empty desk, the smooth glass surface deflowered only by a yellow bronze ash-tray. Everybody believed that the ashtray concealed a microphone, and the Colonel encouraged this pleasant little deception, believing, and probably with some correctness, that it encouraged coherent lucidity. And the empty desk was meant to indicate to visitors that he didn't really work there at all, but had been brought in from some other office. He said:

"Sit down, Ian, and listen to what I have to say."

"Sir."

"Have a cigarette if you want one. I suppose you're tired of sitting at your desk all day, are you? At least, I hope you are. I have a job for you which I think you will like; I want you to go to Ethiopia for me."

One of Sir John's minor, and most irritating, idiosyncrasies was a penchant for assuming that his staff would only be happy in some other place; not any particular place, but in some spot where they did not happen to be at that moment. So that the men in London and Moscow, Chungking and Rio, were always urgently changing places. More strictly, he liked to give this impression, though in actual fact he believed that the operations officer in the wilds of China should get his daily pint in The Feathers once in a while, and that the man who strolled to work across the park every day should have a chance to see the distant mountains into which he sent his weekly instructions and reports. And perhaps his enemies would have said (and he had plenty of enemies) that he liked to play with his staff as though they were chess-men. But he believed, very rightly, that the arm-chair man who can send a cable saying "Go to Timbuctu and contact so-and-so" should occasionally be sent there himself just to see how easy or how hard this was; and vice versa. He knew that so mechanical a device as transportation should do no more than add to his efficiency, and he had the rare ability to conduct his very important branch of the Foreign Office as a business machine, with results as the only criterion.

He was quite an important man; he was tall, and handsome in the grey-at-the-temples sort of way, most impeccably dressed, and his manner was urbane and convincing. For all his debonair elegance, he was quite ruthless; and he looked exactly what he was—a highly paid executive doing a skilled and sometimes dangerous job. He said:

"I think it's time you got away from the office, don't you?" Smiling, as though the point were moot.

Metcalfe said, genuinely pleased: "I always did want to go back to Abyssinia."

Sir John corrected him gently. "Ethiopia. If you study your etymology, you will find that Abyssinia is not a very courteous word to use. I sometimes wish they were called *Amharim*; 'people of the mountains'. Their language is very prettily named *Amharic*, and yet they call themselves Ethiops; as though there were no other sun-burned peoples in Africa."

Metcalfe said, startled: "Sun-burned?"

"The Greek, I believe, is *Aithiops*—'burnt faces'. Abyssinia has a faintly Arabic connection, and means, if anything, 'mongrel'. And yet a purer race than the Ethiopian would be hard to find anywhere; Semitic, of course, right back to Solomon, though their religion is Coptic. An interesting and delightful people."

Sir John stood up and wandered over to the window, and, hands in pockets, stared thoughtfully down at the broad, green grasses of the Park. He waited a long time before speaking.

"Broadly," he said at last, "the job is simple enough. I want you to go to a village called Lakbar and pick up an Italian named Franconi, who is held there rather against his will. Loosely, I suppose you would call him a prisoner, though the word he uses is *slave*. A left-over from the war, but a man we badly want to talk to."

He turned, and said: "They do have slavery there, you know, although not in the accepted sense. They still buy and sell bodies for work, in the remoter areas which are too far removed from the Emperor's influence, but it's not really as vicious as it always sounds. After all, most Africans and a lot of Arabs, Indians and Chinese buy their wives and their concubines. In some places they buy men as well, and that is supposed to be the difference between legal marriage and illegal slavery. I suppose it's a question of prejudice, really. However, that's beside the point. Franconi has been in Lakbar since the war, unable to get out, and has just managed to get a message to us by the hand of an Armenian trader. Claire will show you the file, which I want you to study well, but I will put you briefly in the picture. So listen carefully.

"During the East African offensive of 1941, there was, as you know, a lot of moving back and forth, advancing

3

and retiring, before the Italians gave up and surrendered; you may remember that during this period the natives there were well organised into guerrilla bands under their various leaders and did us excellent service. We had a man out there called Hewitt, Major Hewitt, whose job was to help organise these bands, arm them and keep them supplied and informed on the progress of the war. When he went out, he took with him a fairly large amount of money for this purpose—well over a quarter of a million pounds' worth of gold, banknotes and the silver Maria Theresa dollars which were the official currency of the country—and still are, in some parts of it. Now, Hewitt was captured by a group of Italians and he was murdered. It's fair to assume that in the chaos then prevailing, the Italians thought they could get away with the money he was carrying by killing him and burying the loot, and by then going back after the war (they thought it would be over, you remember, in a very few months—in their favour) to recover the spoils. There were actually several cases of this sort of thing happening during the war—in France, Yugoslavia, Austria; everywhere, in fact, where the underground movements attracted not only the brave and the patriotic but also the criminal and the cowardly. But some of those Italians fell into our hands later on, and after a very long period of silence the truth, or part of it, eventually came out. And since then other little bits and pieces have been jig-sawed together, and the very energetic Italian police, who for reasons of their own are interested in Hewitt's death, have made out a *prima facie* case against two of their countrymen who now happen to be in America. They have applied for extradition, but the State Department has rejected the request on the grounds of insufficient evidence. You may have read about this aspect of the case in the papers.

4

There were seven men involved in the murder, as far as we know. Two of those are in jail in Italy (the source of most of the news we have), two are in America, one died in a prisoner-of-war camp, and the only remaining one we know about—named Franconi—disappeared. And that, up to a few weeks ago, was the *status quo*."

Sir John tapped a cigarette delicately on his thin silver case and lit it. He was walking soundlessly up and down the thick red carpet on the long oak floor. He placed a dead match carefully in the centre of the big ashtray and went on:

"Now see what happened. Remember that the Italians want Franconi, the Americans want his testimony for their pending extradition case, and *we* want to know a bit more about what happened to Hewitt." Metcalfe watched the Colonel's long slim fingers, as delicate as those of an Indian dancer. He noted in the Colonel's tone a hardness that was quite frightening. "It was thirteen years ago that Hewitt was murdered; we've been waiting a long time to find out what happened. We want Franconi. And now I think we can get him. Look at this."

He opened the door and spoke into the outer office. He said: "Claire dear, let me have that Franconi file, will you, please?" He came back with it and handed Metcalfe a piece of ragged khaki cloth, torn, perhaps, from an old army shirt. He said, quite inconsequentially, "Pretty girl, Claire. Very efficient, too."

Metcalfe smiled and nodded, and examined the piece of rag. Heavily scrawled across it, in what appeared to be charcoal, were the words: "*Aiuta me, sono schiavo, priggioniero, Lakbar, Franconi Giuseppe.*"

Sir John translated, thoughtfully: "*Help me, I am a slave, a prisoner, in Lakbar, Franconi Giuseppe.*" He laid the opened file on the smooth red desk-top and said:

5

"This piece of cloth was handed to an Armenian trader named Hadkinjian, in Lakbar, by a man he thought was a native. He just caught a glimpse of him in the market-place before he hobbled away. Hadkinjian deals in hides and skins, in myrrh, incense, that sort of thing, and makes frequent trips into Lakbar, where a lot of incense is produced. A risky business, because the power in these more removed parts of the country is most despotically in the hands of the local chiefs, but I suppose that's an occupational hazard." He looked at Metcalfe quizzically. "How well," he asked, "do you know that part of the world?"

Metcalfe said: "I have a vague idea of where the Lakbar range is, though I've never actually been there. I know the route up from Djibouti to Addis Ababa, of course, and the Ogaden border fairly well. The plateau is not too far north of that, is it?"

"About three hundred miles north-west. Well, this fellow Hadkinjian had to leave Lakbar in a hurry—had some sort of trouble there and lost all his stock-in-trade. He went down to Somaliland and told the Brigadier there that someone had slipped this piece of rag into his hand in the middle of the market square. He saw the man for a moment, and says he looked like a native—black eyes, dark skin—but *could* have been a European."

"You said, sir, that he *hobbled* off. Was he an old man, then?"

"That's the point. There are quite a lot of East African deserters out there—Swahili drivers, mostly, from the East African forces. They were usually stopped on the tracks by couriers from the various petty chiefs, offered large sums of money in cash for their services and their arms, and then escorted off to these mountainous redoubts where local force is the only law. On arrival, the money paid out was at once recovered and the poor ignorant deserter was hamstrung so that he couldn't ever get away again. Just a matter of cutting two of the tendons at the back of the knee—enough to stop a man from walking too far, but not to hinder him too seriously in his ordinary work. This was quite a common habit out there. We can only suppose that this is what happened in Franconi's case, and that as a result he has been there ever since, awaiting the chance to get a message out. Which, at last, he has now done."

"I see. And you want me to go in and bring Franconi out."

"Precisely. Normally, of course, this would merely be a question of cables between Addis Ababa and London, but unfortunately Lakbar has been in a state of semi-revolt for so long now that the arm of the law simply has no effect there whatsoever. All this area"—Sir John spread a delicate hand over the map on the desk —"all this area is quite inaccessible from the military point of view, and the local chief, an excitable desperado called Ras Guggla, recognises no authority but his own. If the Emperor were to demand Franconi's release, then Guggla would undoubtedly kill the man at once just out of sheer pig-headedness. So the only answer, I'm afraid, is for you to go in and buy him. You will have to regard Franconi as a goat and make an offer for him. It's simple enough, really."

Sir John paused, and Metcalfe said:

"Does the Italian Government know about this?"

The Colonel smiled and said carefully: "They do not. As a matter of fact, I was wondering if you would ask that. It's a very good point. Well, we shall inform them in due course, naturally; they've been very helpful over the Hewitt case. But for the moment we will handle this ourselves. We want to know particularly what happened to the papers Hewitt was carrying. I expect they were destroyed by the Italians at the time of the murder, but they may have been hidden together with the money—though no mention has ever been made by the Italians of any documents. These papers are not exactly incriminating, but we would not like them to fall into anyone else's hands. You will remember that certain Communist organisations in Italy were on our side in those days. Nowadays the Western world is not as favourably inclined towards these gentlemen, and among Hewitt's effects was a lot of information about the Communist cells in Africa that we are very anxious to get hold of. If these papers are still extant, they must be recovered. It's quite important. There is also the question of the money, which we would naturally like to recover if it can be found—and that will be the subsidiary part of your job. First, get Franconi and the papers, and then, if you can, get the money. Franconi should know where they are hidden, since the Lakbar plateau is where Hewitt was killed and Franconi was then the lieutenant in charge of the party which made the capture; the loot will almost certainly be hidden in one of the caves in the side of the mountains there, and the only difficulty I can foresee is that after so long Franconi may not be able to locate it. Once you mention the murder to him, he's bound to feign ignorance of the whole affair. But if you study the file before you go, you will learn enough about the case to convince him that we know all about it. Let him know particularly about the depositions of his two friends in the Italian jail—you will see copies in the file. But the important thing is Franconi himself. I want him brought to London at all costs. Is that quite clear?"

Metcalfe stood up. He said: "Quite clear, sir."

Sir John said: "Sit down; I haven't finished yet."

8

He went on: "You won't be able to do this alone, so I've got some good help for you, two very good men. You know Harry Pender of the Queen's African Rifles?"

"Oh yes, indeed. A very good fellow. We were good friends out there. I saw him last night, as a matter of fact."

"Officially, he's on leave from his regiment. I thought he might be useful to you. He did a lot of work for us out there during the war. A bit lackadaisical, but a very reliable man, I think. The other man . . ." the Colonel hesitated, "is Dinesen. I believe you know him too."

Metcalfe said: "Yes . . . I know Dinesen too, sir." He said diffidently: "Do you think he will agree to take orders? There can be no dispute about who's in command on a job like this."

Sir John smiled. "Handling Dinesen will probably be your biggest headache. But he knows who is in charge; I made that quite clear to him. He'll be a useful man to have. He knows the area well, and he knows Ras Guggla. In spite of his somewhat lurid past he's a handy man to have around. He's quite clever, you know, under all that bombast; and to be frank, if I thought we could trust him a little more surely, I would have probably sent him on this job alone. But there's the question of the money; a quarter of a million pounds is quite a lot, and," said the Colonel mildly, "if it can be found we'd rather like to have it. I fear that Dinesen by himself might put the money before Franconi. Of course, I may be doing him an injustice. But by and large, I think the team is a good one as it stands. And if there should be any trouble—any violence or fear of violence—then he will be worth more to you than a company of troops. We've brought

9

him back from Somalia to brief him for this and he's quite keen on the job. You'll have to keep a firm hand on his exuberance or we shall have a major war on our hands."

"Somalia?" said Metcalfe, frowning. "What's he doing out there? The last I heard of him, he'd gone off to Budapest."

"Oh yes? Well, he's been along the Red Sea coast for the last few months. Trading, he says. I suppose that means smuggling. Anyway, he's in London now." Sir John looked at his watch. "Two minutes to eleven. At this moment he is undoubtedly trying the door of The Duke of Buckingham, waiting for it to open. I've arranged for you all to meet at Harry Pender's flat this afternoon at five. You know where that is, don't you?"

"If it's still in that mews near the Oratory, then I know where it is."

"Good. Now. Claire will let you have the file to study, and then you'd better go and see Reynolds about money and supplies. Leave your passport with Claire and she'll get the necessary visas for you. You can pick up most of your expense money at Aden—Maria Theresa dollars, I'm afraid, which will be a bit heavy to carry. And they've arranged for the Military at Hargeisa to provide you with a civilian truck. Our chap in Aden is a fellow called Withers, and he'll meet you there on arrival. As soon as you have handed over here, you'll be ready to go; that should be in a couple of days or so at the most. You'll be away about three months, I expect, so hand over to Reynolds any worries you have here now."

"Well, sir, there's only that Austrian thing I'm working on at the moment, and Major Reynolds knows all about it, anyway. I must say, sir, this is a very welcome change. It'll be nice to see Africa again."

Sir John said pleasantly: "Well, don't underestimate the difficulties. But I want Franconi back in London within three months. At all costs."

Metcalfe said: "I'll get him, sir."

"I think you will. See Claire first, then Reynolds. Come and dine with me on Wednesday—eight o'clock at the Bagatelle. All right?"

"Yes, indeed, sir. Thank you very much."

Metcalfe went into the outer office, where Claire was reading through a bulky file. "Here you are," she said, "all the dope. I've put in some maps, but if you want any others, let me know. You'll need an hour or so to study that lot, but you can't take it out of the office, so sit down and make yourself comfortable. I've told Ops. E. that you'll be coming over for some kit at two o'clock, and they'll have everything ready for you—tropical clothes, compasses, rifle and pistol, camp kit, medical box, emergency foodstuffs, all that sort of thing, and money from Major Reynolds. What else is there?"

"The efficiency of the woman," said Metcalfe, "Come and have a pink gin; they've just opened."

Claire said placidly: "Don't be damn silly; you know I can't leave the office now. I'll have one with you at lunch-time."

"All right. That's a date. Let's have a look at all this bumph. Where do I find this fellow Hadkinjian? Ought to have a talk with him, really, when I get out there."

"Apparently he lives in both Berbera and Djibouti. Want me to try to find him for you? I can send a cable."

"What do you think? He'll have a lot of background information, but I don't know that we ought to advertise ourselves too much."

"Well, I'll find out just where he will be and when, and I'll let you know at Aden. Of course, he may be up-country, but if he's available I think you'd be well advised to see him. He won't go with you, of course. He obviously got into some sort of trouble the last time he was there. Probably sold them some dud ammunition or short-changed them."

"Harry and Dinesen. Have they been briefed?"

"Yes, they've both been in. You have to see them today at five. Harry's place."

"Yes, I know." He added: "The cagey bastard! I ran into him last night—he didn't say a word about this."

"Well, of course not," Claire said primly.

"And, what is more, he tried to sell me some tickets for Wimbledon; no wonder he wanted to get rid of them."

Claire laughed, showing her beautiful, even teeth. Metcalfe thought, *The old man's right, she's a damn pretty woman.* She saw him looking at the smooth curve of her body under her grey sweater. She said: "Now then, keep your mind on your work."

Metcalfe said: "I'll drink that bastard's cellar dry tonight. Wimbledon indeed. And why should I keep my mind on my work when I'm with you? Come and have dinner at my place tonight."

Claire smiled her secret smile. "All right. Now get on with your reading." Metcalfe picked up the file, leaned back in the leather chair, made himself comfortable, and started reading. From time to time he looked up and watched Claire at her work.

The clock on the spire of the church at the end of the mews struck five as he raised the big brass knocker on the door. He heard footsteps cluttering down the stairway, and the yellow-panelled door was thrown open. Harry Pender stood in the cheerful little hall, beaming, a pewter mug in his hand. He said, grinning: "Come to collect those tickets for Wimbledon? Come on in."

They shook hands. Metcalfe said: "Every time I come here I like this place a little more. But I'm damn sure you don't keep it like this yourself; the woman's touch is all about us. Is our friend here yet?"

"Just arrived a few minutes ago; he's barely had time to finish off my last bottle of Scotch, but he will. Come on up."

As they entered the living-room at the top of the short white-painted stairway, Dinesen climbed languidly out of his chair and stood up, grinning affectionately.

Dinesen was tall and straight and strong as an ox. He might have been twenty-five or forty, but there were fine lines about his pale blue eyes, at the corners; and his mouth, wide and expressive, showed in repose a certain harshness, an intolerance, the indefinable impatience of an older man. His features were fine and delicate, but there was a high-cheeked mongoloid frame to his face that belied the light colour of his eyes and hair. He made you look twice to see whether he was perhaps of Tartar origin and not Nordic, as you had first supposed. His lips were somewhat too thin, but very flexible; his chin was long and firm, and his forehead broad. He had the head of a very intelligent man, a head that made sculptors pause and ponder; and he had about him the air of a man who knows that he holds the centre of the stage. When you met Dinesen, you knew that you would not easily forget him. It occurred to most men that he would make a very bad enemy; though not many of them sought him out as a friend. People were very often afraid of him; and he was in great demand by the ladies.

He had been born in London, the son of an out-of-work actor of indefinite nationality who had once been a popular matinée idol, until the police found that he had entered the country illegally. The father had been a huge and powerful man, and his only offspring, the son of a young Polish ballet-dancer who had befriended him, carried from birth all the signs of the strength of body and mind that were to be his in years not yet come. He knew he was a bastard from his very earliest youth; he was passionately devoted to his mother, and in his childhood he had known his father only as a broken-down tramp, a sad and bitter giant of a man who sometimes came to his mother's room for a meal. The child grew up in the streets, and at twelve, when his mother died, he had been supporting both of them financially for more than three years; he stole on the streets. It was a long time before he recovered from the shock of his sudden loneliness; for a day and a half he had sat beside her still, cold, white body, silent and filled with a sad and lonely hatred of everything that lay outside the shabby, untidy room, with the dust on the window-panes, and the broken floorboards and the chipped and shattered plaster ceiling, and the soiled and sordid wallpaper, and the cinnamon-coloured patches of damp that seeped in and brought with it the pneumonia that kills. At last the neighbours took the body and the child away. Within a few years the scars had healed and the sickness of poverty had gone for ever. At fifteen, Dinesen was wearing tailor-made clothes; at twenty, he drove a Daimler. At twenty-five he was the owner of a flourishing art-dealer's place in Kensington and was well established in a comfortable flat at Notting Hill; a quarrel with his *patronne* changed his residence and he moved to France till the outbreak of war; he always seemed a jump or two ahead of the police, always just within the law. He made frequent trips to Rome in these lush days, driving a long red Maserati; and he had a villa in the hills above Rapallo. In Rome he lived in a beautiful old house near the Tevere, and his consort was a titian-haired actress from the studios in Cinecita. One of his friends once made this point: if you see a red-headed woman and a long red road-racer waiting outside the Louvre, go inside and you will find Dinesen, just a little bit drunk, trying to buy the Mona Lisa.

By the time the war broke out, Dinesen had learned what he wanted; and he had acquired it. "My tastes are simple," he said. "All I want is the stuff that money will buy." He spent six months of the year in Italy and six months in France and England; and there was no income-tax collector who had ever heard of him.

It was not until the war that Dinesen really came into his own, and then he quickly became a legend. As soon as the Germans marched into Poland, his half-forgotten blood stirred (or perhaps, for a moment, he recalled that white and beautiful cold face, still and silent as alabaster, and his long and tearless vigil in a shabby room) and he disappeared overnight. He was heard of in Warsaw at the height of the fighting; news came through of his outstanding heroism and he was decorated by Sikorsky. He turned up with the maquis in Paris, with the underground in Vienna; he dropped twice into Germany; for a time he was, unaccountably, attached to Scotland Yard's Special Branch as an adviser on Polish affairs—until somebody discovered that (a) he was officially a deserter from the Polish Army of Liberation and (b) that he spoke practically no Polish at all. He was in Morocco and Yugoslavia, and

Ethiopia and Spain, and in Greece; he was always in some sort of uniform, though no army ever seemed to own him. And he was always either about to be court-martialled or had just been decorated. The truth is, of course, that nobody *owned* Dinesen, except, perhaps, Dinesen himself.

As he stood up, unwinding his long form lazily, he held out his hand and grinned. Metcalfe said: "Hullo, there. Glad you're going to be with us. Should be a good trip."

Dinesen said: "It's a cup of tea. Take a week to get there, two months to get out." He smiled quickly, a frank, open smile. "Did you come across this fellow Guggla when you were out there?"

"No. I hear he might be a problem."

Dinesen shrugged. "No. No problem at all. We can either buy friend Franconi with a handful of gold sovereigns or fetch him out with the help of a few hand-grenades, whichever you like. You're the boss."

"The accent," said Metcalfe deliberately, "is on trade; no blowings-up."

"As a matter of fact, that will be the easiest way. It's never worth fighting for anything at all if you can buy it. A handful of gold will buy all the Franconis in the world, black or white, male or female. Besides, Guggla is a very reasonable man; I must confess to a grudge against him, because we quarrelled last time I was there. But he will listen to reason." He helped himself to half a glass of whisky. "Any idea where the loot will be?"

Metcalfe settled back on the divan. "Oh, in some cave or other nearby," he said. "There's a good chance we shall find it, I think, but the main thing is to get Franconi out first; we can tackle the problem of the cash and the documents afterwards."

Pender said, passing round the beer bottles: "I read the depositions of those Italians they have in jail. They described the place pretty thoroughly. Did you notice that?"

Dinesen said: "Quite. Precisely what I would do under the circumstances. It was a hell of a lot too precise, in my opinion."

"It doesn't really matter," Metcalfe said. "Franconi was the lieutenant in charge of the party, and he's the one man who is sure to know the right spot."

"And we can soon find out from him," Dinesen said. "That bunch of bastards invented a lot of amusing devices to get the truth out of uncooperatives. Franconi was a Blackshirt officer; one of the élite. A lesson in manners wouldn't hurt him, anyway."

Pender said: "I wonder if it has occurred to you that, as the Italians know just how much money is hidden there, they may have sent a party out to look for it?"

"Not a chance of it," Dinesen said. "They will know as well as we do that their prisoner friends will not have told the truth about the hiding-place; and Ethiopia isn't very healthy for Italians even today—especially that part of it. Unless they know that there's a better guide, to wit, Franconi, waiting on the doorstep for them, the trip would simply not be worth their while. Franconi is the magic word, and without it Sesame stays shut."

Metcalfe nodded.

Pender said: "I wouldn't be too sure about that. A quarter of a million will attract a lot of flies. Once buried gold gets talked about, unlike the aureate dust, a lot of men want it dug up again, pretty damn fast. There have been far wilder treasure-hunts than this one inaugurated on a mere rumour; this, at least is a fact. I wouldn't be at all surprised to find that we had competition."

"Well, we'll see. No hints of that from the office. Anyway, here's the route." Metcalfe drew a map from his inside pocket and spread it out on the polished parquet floor, kicking the rugs to one side. They slid from their seats and gathered round it. Stubbing a thick finger in the Red Sea, Metcalfe said: "Fly to Aden. By dhow to Berbera. Truck to Hargeisa, Jig-Jigga, the Madar Pass and Harrar . . ."

"Best coffee in the world," Dinesen said. "We might pick up a truckload."

"From Harrar we turn north-west, off the main road, and keep going for about three hundred miles. Right?"

Dinesen said: "Right. There's a fairly good track for most of the way, till we get about a hundred and fifty miles south of the edge of the plateau; then it's pretty rough going, but a good truck can make it. We shall need axes and shovels most of the time."

"Lakbar is here. We barter for Franconi—without," he added, "using our hand-grenades. We bring him out, and as soon as we are well clear (he'll be under arrest, so to speak, anyway), we tell him we know all about Hewitt's murder, quote some of the evidence already known, and find out where the loot is hidden." He looked up at Dinesen, "We persuade him," he said, "by sound argument and nothing more. Is that understood? If he's anxious to get back to civilisation he's bound to talk."

"Of course," said Dinesen. "In any case, moral suffering is much more effective than physical torture; and less offensive to the hypocritical mind." He added blandly: "I beg your pardon; I mean, of course, the *hypercritical* mind."

"The only possible trouble," said Pender quickly,

"can arise if they find out we are carrying all that money and decide to take it from us; might be advisable to leave it outside and arrange for cash on delivery, say twenty miles or so away."

"I don't think so. We shan't be carrying as much as all that. After all, we're only buying one solitary slave; I don't doubt that that's a very small piece of business by their standards."

"How much shall we have?"

"Five thousand Maria Theresa dollars. That's about three hundred pounds. Not very much, actually, though it's worth a lot more on the open market, of course. It's going to weigh a ton. Why the hell they can't accept paper money, God alone knows."

"Well, they won't," said Dinesen. "Speaking as a trader, I can tell you that they won't look at anything else out there. That problem is one of our biggest headaches—how to transport the damn stuff. And, what is more, the Ethiopian Government is withdrawing all silver dollars and replacing them with paper money, so you can't get fresh supplies at the banks. The old stuff's out of circulation, and up-country they won't accept the new. So we have to barter. And the moment you start offering copper wire instead of silver dollars, they start offering their surplus wives instead of leopard skins. It's a headache."

"Well," said Metcalfe, "is everybody happy?"

"Clear enough," Pender said. "We can face any snags when they arise. Best to keep an elastic plan."

"Dinesen?"

"I could do with another drink. Was that your last bottle again?"

Pender laughed and said: "Let's go over to the Crown."

Chapter Two

THE rear wheels of the big green-and-yellow Ford spun round savagely in the hot red sand, sending a spray of dusty earth and sharp grey rock-chips spitting into the air behind them. The truck sank deeper, drunkenly, into the hot valley floor, while the dust hung heavy in the stifling air and settled slowly on their perspiring bodies. Metcalfe stopped pushing; he took out a soiled handkerchief, wiped the sweat off the back of his neck and spat the dry, bitter dust from his mouth. He said: "Leave the bloody thing. The hell with it."

Pender said: "They can't be very far behind us, you know. Can't imagine what's keeping them."

"They probably think we are too heavily armed."

"Don't you believe it. I have no exaggerated liking for these bastards, but guts is one thing they're not short of. And they outnumber us ten to one. And they have horses and are mobile. And we have a truck and are stuck with it. If you want my opinion, we're about to be slaughtered."

Metcalfe grunted. He said: "Let's try again. *Aiyah, sukuma!*" As he leaned his great bulk heavily against the door-jamb the others gathered round again to push; there was Ali, the Egyptian cook, Yussuf, the young Sudanese boy, and a motley collection of six ragged, dirty, unkempt, simian thugs who constituted "The Army". They were led by a half-caste giant named Mfupi, a cut-throat gang recruited as a bodyguard in Aden from that hybrid gutterful of half-contented derelicts that can be found in any port of the

Red Sea or thereabouts: Arab, Somali, Lascar, Nubian, Levantine, Galla, Ethiop, Bantu, Indian and cast-off European—the blood of a hundred races was scrambled in this magnificent hotch-potch of roguery. When Metcalfe had hired them, he said to Withers, the Army type at Aden: "Make sure we don't get only one tribe, or they'll gang up on us—they'll soon find out we're carrying money. Just as long as they're tough and can use a rifle; it probably won't be necessary, but if there should be any trouble we may as well be ready for it." Withers had said: "Sounds as though the jail will supply the men you want; I'll have a word with a pal of mine in the Police here; if he can't find what you want, nobody can." And in the jails and in the gutters he had found them.

While they strained against the hot metal body of the truck, Ali and Yussuf, long accustomed to the mechanics of lorry travel in those remote parts where a truck can go only as far as it can be pushed, were stuffing twigs and branches under the spinning back wheel; two of the Army were scooping sand away from the front wheels; and the others were chanting rhythmically, "*Aiyah, aiyah, aiyah, aiyah.*" Metcalfe, the perspiration dripping from his face on to his thick brown arms, was forcing his heaviness against the door-jamb, an unheeded cigarette between his lips. Pender, the lightest (and who always got the easiest job, anyway), was in the driver's seat, revving the engine up, methodically slipping and engaging the clutch so that the wheels spun round in fits and starts in time with the chanting and shoving, and inch by inch the truck eased forward, climbed out of its own ruts, and suddenly shot clear as the Army yelled its jubilation, clapped its hands, stamped its great splayed feet into the hot earth, grinned and shouted and laughed and danced; the delight of achievement is no less ecstatic in more primitive places. The burning rubber of the over-heated tyres filled the air with a sweet and pungent smell. The hills in the distance were blue and grey, shimmering softly in the heat of the mid-morning.

It was out there, in those purple, red and green hills, that the shooting had started. The first surprising volley screamed viciously over their heads, and as Pender started from his grimy lethargy and shoved his foot hard down on the floorboards, sending the truck violently bouncing forward, half a hundred yelling tribesmen rose out of the bushes and charged towards them, shrieking and waving their ancient rifles. They were small, brown, wiry men, incredibly light and supple, clothed in ragged khaki, with double bandoliers slung across their chests; tough little men with close-cropped beards and crinkled black hair frizzing up high above their high-cheeked faces. Their eyes were sharp and black, with the dull yellow whites of the bushman, and their great wide feet were bare as they raced down the slope towards the track and the lurching, speeding lorry.

Long before the first shots thudded into the sides of the vehicle, Pender had swung it savagely off the road, wrenching the wheels round viciously, so that it lurched, staggered, then leaped over and down the edge of the embankment, heeling over at a crazy angle, but moving fast away from the dirt road. Metcalfe yelled above the hullabaloo, "Keep to the road, you bloody fool!"

Grimacing as his head pounded against the hot, bouncing roof of the cab, Pender shouted back: "There'll be a road-block round the bend somewhere ahead of us." (There was.) "Get the Army cracking, for Christ's sake!"

Metcalfe was struggling to get his Luger free. He

22

swung round to shout an order, but the Army, rubbing the sleep from its eyes, was already firing back. Its leader, the grinning, toothless giant Mfupi, was wedged into a corner against a sack of maize flour, firing and reloading with a smooth and quite surprising efficiency, stopping only to bellow dreadful imprecations at the enemy. As a bullet smacked to a sudden stop in the flour sack beside him, he looked down in surprise and yelled with laughter. The others were struggling to take up strategic positions, standing, lying, kneeling, falling, struggling over each other and swearing and firing at the same time, in a dangerously deadly medley of arms and legs and rifle barrels. Metcalfe breathed a prayer that all the rifles were pointing roughly aft. Through the open back of the truck he saw that the running tribesmen were falling behind, still firing, and he leaned out of the window and emptied his long-barrelled pistol at them. The truck was careering on down the slope almost out of control, while Pender hung on to the wheel with all the strength of his wiry arms, slewing it more and more away from the valley ahead of them till they were running almost parallel to the road which wound along five hundred yards above them. They saw the barrier on the track now, a crude pile of stones piled up and manned by a dozen more tribesmen, now breaking cover and firing wildly into the valley. Pender said: "See what I mean?" Metcalfe winced instinctively as a round crashed into the seat beneath him; he heard the sharp whine of it as it split its way through the door and buried itself in the seat beneath him. He said, calmer now: "Keep going; we're almost out of range."

Pender grinned. "I wonder if we can get back on the road as easily as we left it. And I wonder how the hell I knew that barrier was going to be there? Instinct, I suppose. Sound military training."

"We'll have to get a long way clear before we try. We don't want to get stuck in the sand now." He was aware that he was shaking. He said nonchalantly: "I shall be annoyed if they've damaged the truck."

"This won't do the springs any good, but otherwise she seems all right. And I think we'll have to go on down a bit before we try for the road again; won't take them long to catch up if we stick now."

The firing, except for a few sporadic shots ("More in hope than in anger" said Pender) had stopped. Metcalfe called to the back of the truck. "Ali! Anybody hurt?"

"Two men wounded, *effendi*."

"Coming." He climbed out on to the lurching running-board and swung himself unsteadily into the back. Mfupi, grinning happily, was binding a filthy piece of rag round a bleeding forearm; on the floor, moaning and rocking to and fro, one of the men was holding a piece of shattered jawbone against his face. The others were watching, staring black-eyed and silent, waiting for praise or blame. The truck bounded steadily onwards. A mile or more away, the tribesmen had stopped running and were gathered round the road-block. Metcalfe said: "Get the first-aid kit and fix this man up."

Ali slithered out from under cover and pulled out the medical box. He took out bandages, iodine, a piece of gauze.

"You all right, Mfupi?"

Mfupi braced himself and said, "I kill six. Ten maybe. Maybe more." He roared with laughter, his great moon face, pugnosed, unshaven, alive with hilarity. "Next time, I kill fifty, eh?"

"Better keep an eye on your pal here. They've made a nasty mess of his face." Metcalfe was carefully winding a long bandage over the bloody gauze.

"Is nothing, *effendi*. He not die. Tomorrow he get drunk, you see."

Metcalfe took the hint. "Ali," he said, "pass out a bottle of brandy. One drink each, mind you. God help anybody I find drunk."

The Army caught the word *brandy* and its face lit up. Metcalfe said: "Understand, Mfupi? Just one small drink each. We'll stop in an hour or so and fix this man up properly. And you'd better put some iodine on that arm of yours."

Mfupi said: "*Ndio, effendi*," and Metcalfe knew by the ease with which he agreed, that he would rather lose his arm than burn it with disinfectant.

He felt the truck turning left again, and heard the engine labour as it started to climb the hill. He clambered back into the cab and said: "What gives?"

Pender explained. "We're getting back on the road again, but there's a ridge up there we'll have to cross. They'll have to get out and push."

He crashed the gears down, and the Ford climbed steadily upwards, obliquely, with the cuneiform valley below them and the road growing nearer above them on the left. The heat and the dust were unbearable. Metcalfe squinted through the haze, screwing his eyes up against the hot sun. The road-block was out of sight now, a couple of miles and more away. The front wheels of the truck lifted high in the air and the back wheels spun round savagely. Pender shouted: "Now, you bastards, all out and push!"

The bodyguard and the servants tumbled untidily out, and leaned into the truck, bare feet pushing into the dusty ground. The lorry shot forward and lumbered over the hump on to the road. Yelling and laughing, the Army chased after it and pulled itself clumsily into the back, falling over itself in a tumbled mass of brown limbs and ragged clothing. Pender called out: "All aboard?"

"All aboard, *effendi*."

"Hold tight, then."

They shot forward and gathered speed. Metcalfe took out two cigarettes, lit them, and passed one across to Pender. He said: "Lucky we've got a good truck, or we'd never have got out of that one alive."

"I wonder if that was just ordinary banditry?"

"Surely it was. There's plenty of it in these parts."

"As well organised as that? I don't think so. If they were just ordinary bandits, they would have stopped us at the road-block before opening fire; that looked to me like a rather more organised effort to stop us."

"What's on your mind?"

"Oh, nothing in particular. I suppose they must have just hoped we were carrying something worth battling for. On the other hand, with all those dollars lying around in Hargeisa waiting for us, neatly packed up in heavy wooden boxes, I suppose it's possible that word of our safari has gone out ahead of us. If that is so, every petty chief within a hundred miles will be after them."

"I wonder if we're in Ras Guggla's territory yet?"

Pender said decisively: "No, we're not. We have to cross over a narrow ravine—you remember Dinesen mentioned it. We should get there by tomorrow morning. I've never been there, but I know more or less where it is. Should be quite a sight—there's a broad flat plain that stretches for miles, and just as you reach it there's a damn great crack in the ground; it's a sort of volcanic fissure several hundred feet deep that stretches to left and right and finally joins up again, enclosing the whole works like a moat. Bang in the middle there's the volcano crater, and the whole area is thick with game and vegetation. Well, Guggla hangs out there, perfectly safe from interference, because the moat is too wide to bridge (it's a couple of miles wide in parts) except at just one point where the two lips of the valley, so to speak, are only a few feet apart. He simply has a village at this point; if any unwanted bodies turn up—raiders, or police, or the Emperor's men—someone from the village will notice it, and a couple of hundred guerrillas turn out to hold the bridge. Horatius could have held it against a couple of battalions. Anyway, that's how things go out here: law and order on the highways, more or less, and complete despotism by the local chiefs the moment you get into the hills. We'll be all right as a trading outfit, of course, provided we can get that far. Once we are there, we shall see what happens."

Metcalf said: "What do you know about this fellow Ras Guggla?"

"Only what I've heard—mostly from Dinesen." He added briefly: "He's dangerous."

"Well, apparently he did very good work against the Italians during the war."

"Quite. And with its usual bungling finesse, what did the British Government do? It supported his brother as paramount chief and sent a good and brave ally into exile. So, when the brother got himself conveniently bumped off, Guggla came back and set up house once more. Only now he doesn't like us very much. That's what comes of making ministers out of thirty-bob-a-week railway clerks. Democracy!"

"Pity. They did say that his men were well trained and comparatively disciplined. Seems he makes a living now by raiding over the border into Somaliland

and the Ogaden: you know, cattle, goats, skins, women; there's plenty to steal down there."

"Well, don't make the mistake of regarding him as just another bandit. He's intelligent, tough and by local standards you'd call him educated. Speaks good French and Italian and tolerable English. According to Dinesen, he's quite a character; drinks too much *tej*, eats too much raw meat, sleeps with too many women. Bags of guts, tremendous personal dignity and completely ruthless. Thumbnail sketch of Ras Guggla."

"His name sounds like indigestion."

"And we will still treat him with the greatest respect."

The going was easier now. The dusty track stretched out ahead of them into the hazy distance, and on both sides high sandstone pinnacles balanced great precarious boulders atop their heads, rising out of the hot green shrub in awful, silent, imposing majesty. Partridge scuttled into the bush at their approach, hyrax scurried anxiously about the rocks; somewhere a leopard coughed.

Metcalfe said: "I'm sorry for that poor bastard in the back. A bullet smashed his jaw. We'll have to pull up as soon as it's safe and take another look at it."

"We're far enough away now. Might brew up at the same time. I could do with a cuppa." He slowed the truck to a halt.

Metcalfe called out: "All right, ten minutes' stop. Ali, *fanya chai!*"

The Army and the servants tumbled out of the back. Tadessa, the wounded man, was red-swathed in his loosely tied bandages. Pender walked over to him and said: "Let me have a look at that." He pulled the blood-soaked bandage away and carefully felt the wound with practised fingers. He put on a new dressing and bound it tightly. He said to Mfupi: "He'll be all right. But he won't be able to eat very much."

Mfupi shook his head, showing his toothless mouth. "No trouble, *effendi*, I eat his ration for him." He patted his enormous belly under his dirty grey shirt. "Plenty room here, *effendi*." He shook with laughter.

The men were lighting cigarettes, quite oblivious, as always, of the leaking petrol-cans about them. Pender sighed. Yussuf was making a fire of thorn-twigs, while Ali stood by with the huge billy-can full of water, staring silently at the hills behind them. His face was inscrutable. In a few minutes the water was boiling and he threw in a careless handful of tea-leaves, taking the pot off the fire at once. They drank out of mugs, squatting on the cool earth under the shade of the big thorn-tree, Metcalfe and Pender together, the two servants a little on one side respectfully, the Army under their own tree on the other side of the track, chatting in a quite incomprehensible mixture of Galla, Swahili, Arabic and Amharic, boasting of their prowess with a gun and with women, telling of the men they had killed in the battle. One of them wandered across to the truck and took out an empty fuel can and started to bang a steady rhythm on it, pounding his feet into the earth in counterpoint. The others scrambled to their feet and took up the beat, stamping their great prehensile toes into the dust, clapping their hands and chanting. They made a circle and moved round slowly, clapping and stamping to the beat of the drum, Mfupi the giant took his place in the centre, head thrown back and arms flung out like a crucified monster. Only his feet moved at first; then the rhythm slipped up to his hips and to his belly till he quivered like a jelly to the rhythm of the drum. Then suddenly his arms and shoulders took up the movement

and he leaped high in the air and threw himself forward,
stamping his feet together now, leaping up and down in
his own hot dust-cloud, pounding the dry and powdery
earth till the sweat ran down his great beefy face and
showed black through his unwashed and ragged shirt.
The circle widened and he began to sing, chanting in a
high falsetto voice, throwing his head back and rolling
his eyes in a sort of savage ecstasy. He sang:

> "The enemy came down from the hills and I slew
>   them,"
>   (*The others chanted: "Allah, Allah!"*)
> "They threw themselves on the bullets of the great
>   warrior,"
>   (*"Allah, Allah!"*)
> "They fell like goats before the onslaught of the
>   mountain lion.
> The vultures were waiting for the meat from their
>   bones,
> The vultures are the friends of the black-maned
>   lion.
> But the lion is not greater than the black-maned
>   warrior."
>   (*"Allah, Allah, Allah, Allah!"*)
> "The warrior slew the enemy that came down from
>   the hills."

Mfupi had seized a spear and was brandishing it
aloft; the earth itself was vibrating and the red dust
was rising to the bright green leaves above them.
Metcalfe coughed and said: "All right, Crosby, let's
go. Ali, Yussuf, *binimshi!*" The drum suddenly stopped
its beating and the Army broke its ranks, singing and
laughing, tumbling into the truck together. Ali emptied
the rest of the tea away and threw the scalding, heavy
pot on top of them all. In a few moments the truck was
on its way.

30

Pender said: "Camp about ten miles further on?"

"O.K. Shall we have to mount guard?"

"Hardly worth it. They'll only sleep. Light me a cigarette, will you?"

As they started smoking, Metcalfe said: "How do you feel about all this?"

"Oh, I don't know. Makes a change from peacetime soldiering. And they're paying me well enough."

"I mean Franconi. Think we shall ever find him?"

Pender shrugged. "Could be. But what then? Given time and patience all things are possible, but getting him out will be the first difficulty, and finding those papers will be a bigger one. If all that money is really there, Franconi will be very chary of showing us where it is."

"He's been a prisoner now for over ten years; I should think he'd do anything to ensure his safety and return to civilisation."

"Well, that's a point, of course. But once we mention the name of the man he's supposed to have murdered, he's going to get awfully coy and cagey. If he's got his senses left, that is. And even if we do find it, how the hell are we going to carry a quarter of a million pounds of loose cash out of the country? Look at the trouble we're having to get a couple of hundred pounds into it. Anyway, getting Franconi out is the first problem; and that, my friend, is your headache."

Metcalfe said stubbornly: "Well, we've got to get him out and that's all there is to it."

Pender sighed. "I shall obey your orders with the blind precision of the professional soldier." He added: "This is the sort of damn-fool caper I always seem to get into. Heigh-ho."

They drove on in silence. The valley closed in on

them and the air was cooling off. Suddenly one of the men in the back tapped twice on the top of the cab. Pender braked quickly. Metcalfe stuck his head out of the window and said quietly, "Where?"

Ali was standing up pointing away to the right. He said softly: "*Kudu, bwana.*"

Metcalfe was staring into the bush. He said: "I can see him. A beauty." He pulled his rifle slowly from the clamp, took aim and fired. The great beast started, stumbled, pitched forward on his knees, and rolled over dead. He said: "Go get, Ali." But one of the troops, a Moslem, was there first, slitting the dead animal's throat and bleeding it, thus making it (as Moslem-killed) fit for Moslem consumption. Mfupi and the other pagans were openly jeering their contempt at him; the men were grimacing delightedly. They dragged the carcase to the nearest tree, strung it up, expertly disembowelled it and stripped off the glossy skin. Metcalfe called out: "The skin's for the man with the broken jaw." Mfupi said unhappily, "*Ndio, effendi,*" then brightened up when it occurred to him that he would surely get the next one. The men stepped silently back from the carcase while Yussuf took out the fillet for the *effendis* and a leg for himself and Ali; and then they set about the rest of the beast with sharp daggers, slicing it rapidly into portable pieces, the Ethiopians among them gorging themselves at once on the rich warm flesh. The whole operation had taken twenty minutes. Then, belching happily, they dragged the rest of the meat to the back of the truck and climbed aboard with it.

Pender said: "Fillet steak again. Isn't it time we had some prime New Zealand lamb?"

Metcalfe said, grinning: "That wasn't a bad shot. Could hardly see the damn thing."

"In this sort of bush," said Pender, "you fire at anything moving and you've got your supper. If it had been a leopard, now . . ."

They camped in the evening well before dark, prepared the food and lit the fires. But there was a disgruntled uneasiness among the men. Metcalfe could sense it in the atmosphere; it was no more than a nervous tension, - a sullenness of spirit. He questioned the servants.

"*Simba, effendi,*" said Ali: "they fear the lions. Down there," he said respectfully, pointing, "maybe down there we keep fire all night? No one see there."

Metcalfe said: "All right, we'll move the truck down as soon as we've eaten. Tell the men. But no big fires, only small ones. *Fahim?*"

Ali grinned, "*Ndio, bwana,*" and hurried off to tell the others. Metcalfe wandered over to Pender and said, "Extraordinary thing how these people know instinctively when there are lions about."

Pender was shaking the sand out of his shoes. He said: "Instinct? You know how you can tell in England, out in the country, that a diesel lorry has been along the road even if it passed an hour before? It's the same thing here; they can smell a lion ten miles away. And the scent is just as strong, too; I can smell 'em at half a mile myself. Still, it's best to have a fire out here. Where do you want the truck?"

"Over there, under that clump of trees; we can have a couple of small fires there and we shan't advertise our presence if they're chasing us; they won't move at night, anyway."

"They won't be chasing us. We've come too far."

He climbed aboard and drove the Ford slowly off

2*

the road. It lumbered heavily, like a sick rhino, crushing the bushes ahead of it and thrusting its dusty hulk in among the thorns, crushing the dry scrub beneath its axle. They reached a sandy clearing, sheltered by tall green trees, and stopped. Yussuf put down the two camp beds, fixed up the mosquito nets, and filled the canvas bath from the forty-gallon drum which was slung under the tailboard. Metcalfe strolled over to where the Army was squatting round the hot red twigs of their fire. He said to the wounded man:

"All right, Tadessa?"

Tadessa nodded, his jet eyes gleaming in the firelight. "*Te'ena effendi*," he said. Mfupi was leaning against the trunk of a tree in the shadows, pin-pointed by a lighted cigarette. He said: "No trouble tonight, *effendi*. If they come tomorrow, I kill twenty more maybe."

"How was the kudu?"

Mfupi grinned happily and rubbed his great stomach. He said: "Good meat, *effendi*, make strong. Tomorrow I kill maybe fifty."

"Tomorrow we'll be a long way away." He went back to the truck. "*Ali! Geeb el beera!*"

Ali went to the back of the truck and pulled two bottles from the wet sack wedged under the spare wheel. They were ice-cold. He levered the tops off with his teeth, wiped the necks of the bottles with a dirty handkerchief to clean them, and placed them on the ground between the two men. Pender sighed and waited till the boy had turned away, then shook them gently so that the beer frothed over and washed the tops of the bottles. He said:

"I had a Galla servant once who saw my cook do that. He tried it himself, but found it easier to bite the glass top clean off. Never once saw him cut himself.

34

I've spent half my life in Africa and I've never ceased to wonder at the things these fellows can do with their teeth."

Metcalfe said: "The simple life. Plenty of sun, plenty of meat, plenty of oil. Vitamins in abundance." Not conscious of changing the subject, he said: "Any ideas about getting Franconi out? Here's health."

"Cheerio." Pender paused before replying. "Depends how far you're prepared to go. Force of arms, I mean. If we can just buy him, like a goat or a woman, well and good. If not, we may have to grab him and beat it like the bats out of hell. They'll be well armed and it won't be easy. But I don't see why they shouldn't sell him in the normal way. If we make it worth their while. After all, we can offer a very high price. I'm in favour of hiding our weapons a few miles before we get there and going in unarmed. What did they say about it in London?"

"Definitely no warfare; you know, the usual thing. Don't fire under any circumstances; but we want him out at all costs. Use discretion, old boy. In other words, the old, old game of passing the buck. I agree with you; it'll be best to leave our arms and go in naked and unashamed. Might hide our pistols in the truck somewhere, just in case of emergency. After all, he's bound to give us a fairly square deal—traders have been buying and selling in there for years. Look at it like that and where's the difficulty?"

Pender said quickly: "There's one difference. Traders come back for more; we won't. If he wants to give up his pet slave, he will. If he doesn't want to, he'll simply grab the money and throw us out; or cut our throats if he thinks it's worth bothering about."

Metcalfe said: "Well, that's a cheerful outlook." He

added moodily: "I wish to hell Dinesen were here. What a hell of a time to go sick."

"If the truth were known," Pender said, "friend Dinesen is the only man who could pull this thing off. They know him in there; he's traded with them before, and they'll play ball with him. And without him, old boy, this trip is a waste of time."

Metcalfe stood up and started climbing out of his clothes. He shouted: "Hey, Ali! Hot water!" He went on: "Right now Dinesen is having his appendix out, so we'll just have to do the job without him. And that's all there is to it."

Pender looked up sharply. "Appendix? Are you sure?"

"Why, of course. I told you so in London."

"You did no such thing. You said on the phone that he wouldn't be coming because he was in hospital having an operation."

"Well, it was acute appendicitis. The hospital rang me and said he'd be out of commission for two weeks. A hell of a time for a thing like that to happen."

Pender was studying the bowl of his pipe in the fire-light. He said carefully: "Who was it rang up?"

"The matron, I suppose, or one of the nurses; she just said it was the hospital. After that, the doctor 'phoned and said Dinesen was very anxious I should be informed about it, and did I know already. A Doctor Catelli or Cappelli, or some such; an Italian name, anyway."

Pender was silent. Metcalfe said: "What's on your mind?"

There was a long pause. Metcalfe said, "We might use his name in the village, of course. They know him well enough."

"Yes, of course. Good idea." Pender knocked the

bowl of his pipe out. "I'm for bed," he said. "Good night. Early start?"

"Crack of dawn. Good night."

Metcalfe finished his washing in silence. He rubbed himself down, wrapped the towel round his waist, and let the cool night air seep into his flesh. On his face was the puzzled look of a man who knows that something is wrong and knows also that his brain is not quite fit to cope with the problem. He walked over to Pender's bed and stood looking down at him. He said:

"What's the trouble? About Dinesen, I mean?"

Pender sat up under the mosquito net and scratched himself lazily. He said: "Shall we have another beer?"

In silence Metcalfe took two bottles from the wet sack and prized off the tops with the back of a hunting-knife. He handed one to Pender and said:

"I wish to hell you wouldn't be so damn mysterious."

Pender took a long swig of beer and wiped his mouth with the back of his hand. He said: "Are you sure it was appendicitis?"

"Of course. Both the doctor and the matron said so."

"You didn't think to check back with the hospital?"

"Well, of course not. It was just a few hours before we took off. Anyway, why should it be necessary?"

"Did you know Dinesen and I were in the Western Desert together?"

"I know."

"Well, I'll tell you a story. Just before the Alamein excitement, Dinesen was in hospital in Alexandria. As soon as the battle started and word got back, Dinesen was hopping mad that he wasn't there to join in the fun. You know how he's always itching to be up and at somebody." Pender was pushing tobacco into his pipe.

37

Framed above him against the dark blue sky, Metcalfe stood, arms akimbo, enjoying the play of the breeze on his broad chest. He said: "Go on."

"He went into hospital a few days before the fun started, when everybody was expecting the Jerries to move right into Alexandria; he was due out again about two weeks later, and would normally have gone off to Cairo or Luxor or some such for a few days' leave. But meanwhile the battle began. Dinesen stole a uniform, broke out of the hospital, and disappeared; there was hell to pay. A couple of days later, pale and weak but full of let-me-at-'em, he turned up with his unit, where I happened to be at the time. Said he had hitched a ride out to get in on the battle. He acquitted himself well, as always, and in a short time the whole affair was forgotten."

Metcalfe said impatiently: "Well, go on."

Pender's pipe had gone out and he lit it again, watching the cheerful flare of the match against the shiny, carbon-caked briar. He said: "Go on? My dear fellow, if I am to tell this story with the drama it deserves, you are supposed to say: 'What did they do to him in hospital?'"

"I'll buy it. What did they do to him in hospital?"

Pender said: "They took his appendix out. Good night."

It was some time later that Metcalfe stirred and said: "Hey, are you awake?"

"Uh-uh."

"I've got this figured out."

Pender grinned in the darkness. "Yes?"

"It's obviously a device for getting out of the trip at the last moment."

"Obviously. Have you figured out why?"

"Yes, I have," Metcalfe said complacently. "He told me when I contacted him that he knew where this village was, but said he hadn't been there for some years."

"Well?"

"So it's clear. The last time he was there he got into trouble. Probably swindled them over something—wouldn't put it past him. So now he's afraid to go back."

"Dinesen afraid?"

"Well, not exactly afraid, but . . . playing safe. If he got into some sort of trouble there he might well think twice about going back. Remember he said Ras Guggla was a very dangerous man? And on reflection he probably thought it wasn't worth the price he was being paid."

"If that's the case, we'd better not mention his name."

"Exactly. Don't you think that's what might have happened?"

"Yes, I suppose so," Pender said thoughtfully.

"So we don't mention his name. Agreed?"

"Agreed."

Metcalfe yawned and turned over. "Sorry if I woke you. But it was rather worrying me. Good night then."

"'Night."

A sweet, sickly scent hung around the thorn trees in the darkness. One of the soldiers stirred and kicked the embers of the fire into glowing life. In the shadows nearby a lioness sniffed, watching, alert, then turned and slunk heavily, silently away. Mfupi grunted and, sleeping, scratched at the tiny parasites crawling about his giant recumbent carcase. Pender lay awake in the

39

darkness and watched the smoke from his pipe curl slowly to the top of his net. Somewhere in the valley a hyena, finding raw meat, screamed; the frightening, hysterical arpeggio chattered through the stillness. Then the silence closed in again.

Chapter Three

"THERE it is," said Pender, passing the binoculars across to Metcalfe. They stood by the truck in the hot white sand and stared across the plain ahead of them to the shimmering mountain in the distance. Out of the vast immensity of the flat bush rose a tall, imposing mound, a green and blue Vesuvius of a mountain, heavily wooded in its foothills. There was a herd of wildebeest not far from the truck, wandering about quite unconcerned, some of them staring solemnly at this interruption of their peace. With a sudden squeal, a family of wart-hogs dashed from cover right beside them and scurried hastily into the deeper shade of a clump of bushes. The Army was tumbling out of the back of the vehicle, stretching its cramped legs and staring at the mountain. Mfupi said, showing off his knowledge to the others: "*Lakbar.*" Metcalfe turned to him and said: "Ever been there, Mfupi?"

The giant scratched his head solemnly. "*Ndio, effendi.* I go there one time, long time ago. Ras Guggla. Very bad man." He was not laughing. Pender noted that the boys were looking worried. He said: "You know, this adventure has all the flavour of Tarzan of the Apes. Now our porters are going to leave us."

Metcalfe said brusquely: "Nonsense." He turned again to Mfupi. He said: "What's the matter, for God's sake? There's nothing to be afraid of."

Mfupi said: "We go there, *effendi*, Ras Guggla take our guns, put us all in bottom of well. No come out."

"Mfupi, you're a fool. Tell the men that we are

41

leaving our weapons here—all of them. We'll leave two men here to look after the guns, and the rest of us are going to see Ras Guggla. I have a deal to make with him; there will be no trouble."

Mfupi cheered up at once: "*Ndio, effendi*. No rifles, Ras Guggla not steal. Not steal, no throw in bloody well. Is good. We make trade. Maybe stay few days, *effendi*?"

"I don't know. And if we do, lay off his women or *I* shall put you down the well."

"*Ndio, effendi*." Mfupi was laughing again. He shouted instructions to the Army and they started piling their weapons in the shade of the bushes by the side of the track. Pender said: "Better tell them they'll have to keep out of sight in case anybody passes. When we come back they'll see us' park here, and can rejoin us."

Metcalfe said: "Do you realise it's only a week since we left Aden? Ten days ago we were drinking in the Crown together in London."

"We've come a long way. A very successful trip, so far."

They waited till all the arms were stacked by the side of the road, then checked over the equipment. Metcalfe took back his own rifle and said: "I'll make a present of this to the Ras; show him we mean well. We'll strap your rifle under the chassis and keep our pistols in the tool-box, just in case. I've decided we ought to keep the money on the truck; if we try a C.O.D. proposition, he might easily take offence. After all, we're not the first traders to come to this place."

Pender said: "You're probably right. I don't think there'll be any trouble. God in heaven, I've spent weeks at a time in far worse places than this. Are we ready?"

Metcalfe said: "Come on, Mfupi. You and Aklilu,

Gabre and Eissa, better come along with us. Leave Tadessa and Dastar here. The two servants come with us. All aboard!"

Pender took his place at the wheel, looked back at the pile of arms, and started the truck. As they moved slowly off Metcalfe looked behind him; the two boys were taking off their packs, lighting cigarettes, and preparing to move into the bush, Tadessa with his bandage still showing brightly against his blue-black skin. He settled down in his hard seat and said: "Well, the last lap."

The truck bounced unsteadily through the bush, the heat shimmering up ahead of them, until they reached the sharp, sudden edge of the plateau. Pender said: "We're lucky; there's a bridge." As they slowed down to a halt, they all tumbled out again and stood looking down into the crevasse. It was a remarkable sight. The flat sandstone on which they stood, as smooth and as unobstructed as an unkept race-track, came to a sudden stop, and at their feet, as from the edge of a cliff, the land dropped suddenly and steeply away, deep, deep down into the depths of the earth. But it was not dark down there. Further to their right and to their left the gap was wider, and the sun poured its warmth down into the very bowels of the valley far below them. They could see tall and bright trees down there, yet the track continued across the flat red earth at their own level, on the other side of the rift, almost unbroken for another twenty or thirty miles. The chasm was only a few feet wide. They stared into the distance ahead of them. A mile or so away was a village, no more than a cluster of untidy huts of *mkuti* and adobe—rough-pounded mud sun-dried into bricks, and covered with

43

brown dry palm-fronds. Some of them seemed to be covered instead with grass. Already a few figures could be seen walking down the track towards them.

Metcalfe said: "Is that bridge all right, do you think?"

The bridge was a simple layer of thick logs laid across the four-feet width of the crevasse. Pender stood on it gingerly, staring into the depths below him. The bridge was firm, the logs solidly locked. He said: "Seems all right to me. Everybody walk over and I'll drive the truck across." He climbed into the driver's seat, started the engine, shifted the gear, and with his foot on the clutch, climbed back on to the running-board. He said, grinning: "I may have to jump for it. If I do, it'll take a long time to pick up the pieces of silver. To say nothing of pieces of truck. Here we go."

The truck lumbered slowly up to the logs, the front wheels moved on to them, the chassis rocked a little, staggered forward, and was over. Metcalfe said: "That's a good bridge. Safe as a house."

"I know. There's been another vehicle in here recently. Did you see the tracks?"

"I thought I did. Wasn't sure." He called to the back of the lorry: "Mfupi! When we get to the village, ask them how long since it rained here."

"Long time no rain, *effendi*," Mfupi called back.

"I suppose the tracks might be old. But nice if there's one of our trader friends in there at Lakbar: we can have a party. Were they coming or going, the tracks? Or both?"

Pender shook his head. "Too faint to tell. In any case, if there's been no rain, they could be six months old or more. We'll soon find out."

They reached the village and drove slowly through it. Little black children stopped playing in the dust to stare at them as they went past. A couple of young men, carrying ancient rifles and bandoliers, stood in a doorway and waved at them. A young girl, wearing only a small square of gazelle-skin, was carrying a water-jar of red terra-cotta on her shoulder. Metcalfe said: "Friendly place." He heard Mfupi shouting as they rolled slowly past the young men and he heard them answer. Mfupi climbed to the running-board of the truck and said: "No rain three months, *effendi*."

Pender said: "Shall we stop and say hallo?" Metcalfe nodded.

They pulled up under the shade of a huge mango tree in the centre of the village and climbed out, shaking the dust from their faces and their hair. A small crowd began to collect around them, staring at them with interest. There were several men, all armed, small and slight of build, with masses of jet-black hair combed up high on their heads. They wore a sort of uniform; some had off-white trousers, cut in the shape of tight jodhpurs, and loose blouses. Others wore only khaki shorts and shirts. The older men were dressed in clay-coloured cloth loinskins or wore a fold of cloth loosely wrapped about their middles, and they leaned on long, stout staves. The young women wore skins tied with string to the waistline, and their breasts were firm and widely spaced; they were slim and graceful to watch as they moved about, moving quickly, like children, their supple bodies glistening and smooth. Their hair was plaited into tight ringlets that hung down over their faces.

And then in the darkness of a doorway he saw two other women, dressed in long white gowns, loose and tied at the waist with a cord; they had their hair piled high, like the men, but more carefully, more precisely combed, with an obvious high regard for fashion. He

45

turned again to the bare-breasted young girls round the truck and saw that they had tiny, smooth brown marks on either side of the forehead, like little long-healed burns. He said to Pender: "See their slave-markings on their foreheads?"

Pender nodded. "They're probably Galla from over to the east. I see no sign here of the terrors we've been warned about."

All the crowd, now considerably increased, were laughing and grinning and jostling them. Metcalfe passed cigarettes among them, and one of the older women shouted to a young girl, who then brought a skin of sour goats' milk, the rich curdled milk which they drink in such prodigious quantities in those parts. Metcalfe told Mfupi to find out where Ras Guggla could be found, and they pointed ahead, further down the track, shouting: "Lakbar! Lakbar!"

They all took a long drink of the cool goats' milk, clambered back into the truck, and slowly went on their way. The crowd surged along beside them, shouting and waving, running lightly in their bare feet on the hard red earth. As they outdistanced them and the villagers dropped behind, Metcalfe said: "Astonishing how happy a man can be with nothing. Living in a place like this, it's a hard life, I suppose, but they seem to have all they want. The country is thick with fresh meat, and look at the richness of the soil. An occasional bit of excitement when there's a minor war on, but no complicated *mechanics* to their lives. No fuses to blow, so to speak. No trains to catch, no tailors to pay, no coal to buy, or income tax; nothing but the perfect serenity of loneliness. It's an ideal life."

"And not so lonely, either," said Pender. "Some of those young women were very attractive, even by European standards. Beautiful figures, anyway."

46

He went on: "You know, we've got ourselves far too complicated. There's a lot to be said for this sort of life. I remember an Englishman I met once up in the Nandi country, on the Kenya-Uganda border. He'd been there for donkey's years, living in a small mud bungalow, quite clean and tidy, home-made furniture, miles out in the bush where nobody ever went. Had two or three wives, a couple of cows and a good water-supply; that's all he had: no books, no music; he smoked cow-dung like the rest of them, hadn't been near a town—or even a village—for ten years or more. And he was as contented as any man I've ever seen. I asked him about music, theatre, that sort of thing. He had practically forgotten what a theatre was, and as for entertainment, well, all he wanted was to sit under the mango tree outside his hut and watch the sun go down. Absolutely contented. I'm not at all sure that he hadn't got the right idea. Nice to read a good book, but, quite honestly, the more a man knows the more he despairs. And this fellow was as happy as a man could be. Some prospectors turned up and found alluvial gold—just the usual five shillings' worth for every ten tons of earth they shifted, you know—and settled in about three miles away from this old fellow. So he kicked down his mud house, moved twenty miles deeper into the bush with his chattels and his wives, and built himself a new one. I never saw him again; but he'll still be there, and he'll still be just as happy."

The truck rumbled on toward the towering blue cone of the volcano, the dust hanging hot and dry in the dusty air, and two hours later they came to the town.

It was perched high on the side of the mountain, and round the entire village was a high stone wall, great blocks of grey stone carefully fitted together without cement. At the end of the track they were on, there was a high, wide gate; its wooden doors, thrown open, were studded with heavy brass spikes. Pender said: "Definite Arab influence. And it's easy to see how a man can hold out against the law in a place like this. First the dry moat and then a ten-foot-thick stone wall; rather like an English feudal castle. The defence, I suppose, was originally against the Arab and Portuguese slave-traders. Now it's against any undesirables who want to come in."

They drove slowly through the huge wooden gateway. The crowds were thicker here, with Ethiopians, Galla, a few Somalis and Arabs thronging busily about, with horses and donkeys and camels struggling to pass through the narrow streets. The houses, of brightly whitewashed clay brick, were huddled close together. The shops (and there were many of them) were open-fronted, and there were great piles of highly coloured fruits and vegetables, chillies and tomatoes, and melons and dates, and dried figs and lemons, and great hands of green bananas. Heavy, red beef carcases, fly-swarmed, were hanging in the shade, and the bustle and noise were incredible. They came to the market-place, where the throng was even thicker. Men and women and children and animals pressed close about them, unheeding, and the truck slowed to a halt. Pender scratched his head and said: "Can't move far in this mob. Where to?"

As if in answer, a soldier suddenly appeared, grinning broadly, and jumped on the running-board, shouting and gesticulating. Mfupi, calling from the back of the truck, translated: "This way, *effendi*," he shouted, "over here." He scrambled down from the truck and wedged himself between the cab and the body, chatting amicably with the soldier.

Another soldier appeared from nowhere and leaped

nimbly on the front bumper, bracing himself against the grill of the steaming radiator, gesticulating and yelling at the crowd in front. Slowly a way was opened and the lorry ambled forward. Pender said: "I suppose we just go where they tell us." They followed the road out of the main square till they came to a long, dusty driveway, bordered by tall eucalyptus trees, at the end of which was a long, narrow building, a low bungalow with a wide, open front and a verandah running down the entire length. It was surmounted at one end by a tower, some twenty feet high, atop which was a cross and the effigy of a lion. The lorry came to a halt and they climbed out to stretch their legs. The soldiers ordered the boys to stay in the back of the vehicle and escorted the two men into the building.

Once inside, it was cool and quiet and very pleasant. The room they were in was spacious and low, with narrow windows, covered in the French fashion with jalousies. The walls were washed in blue distemper, and there were small wooden seats, intricately carved, scattered about the place. On one of the walls was a painting, in charcoal and colour, depicting an Ethiopian victory over the Egyptians; headless and limbless bodies lay about the field of battle, a rather brownish blood pouring out at appropriate places. Metcalfe was standing in front of the picture, examining it carefully, when their host appeared at the far end of the room. He turned and waited.

He was a huge man. Metcalfe stood more than six foot three and was dwarfed in comparison. He had the chest of a bull on him and his neck was as thick as a man's thigh. He was dressed in white, the jodhpur trousers of the country and a white bush jacket. He wore a small black beard, imperial fashion, and his hair was cropped close to his head. He was barefoot.

He strode towards them from the end of the room, holding out his hand. Metcalfe was relieved thus to have solved the question of obeisance. In a booming, rasping voice their host said:

"I am Ras Guggla. Welcome to my palace. Please feel as you wish; I speak good English. Sit down and tell me what you want of me. I had news from Hargeisa that you wish to see me."

"From Hargeisa?" Metcalfe was astounded. "But that's a week's drive away."

"If my couriers travelled as slowly as your lorry, I would cut off their heads. You were held up once by some thief of a bandit, but you got away safely. You stopped at the border of my territory and you left there two men with six rifles. Am I right?"

Metcalfe had the grace to feel uncomfortable and hesitated. Pender said quickly: "We wanted to make sure that your men would not misunderstand our purpose in coming here. It seemed to us discourteous to come in here heavily armed. Your soldiers have the reputation of being, shall I say, alert at their jobs?"

Ras Guggla turned his cold, black eyes on Pender; he said: "You need not flatter me, my young friend. I spent a long time in your country. Long enough to understand something of your . . . diplomacy. You left your guns far away because you were afraid I would take them from you. You need not have worried; I have arms enough, and if I want yours, I shall take them."

Metcalfe said easily: "I brought my hunting rifle with me. I would like you to accept it with my compliments."

The Ras shouted an order to the guard at the door. He said, "You are most kind. I hope you will stay with

50

me some little time. I like to speak English when I can. We will soon have some food. First we have a little *tej*. We make good *tej* here; we have the best honey-bees in the country. Afterwards, you will tell me what you want from me. Tell me now only, are you from your Government?"

Metcalfe said carefully: "Well, in a way, I suppose we are; but not in the way that you would disapprove of our mission."

"Why do you come to me and not go to the Emperor?"

"What we have to say . . . our mission . . . well, it concerns only the people and the ruler of Lakbar. It is quite simple, really."

Ras Guggla was watching Metcalfe carefully. Pender, watching him in turn, was thinking, *We must not try and fool this man; he can be very dangerous.* The guard came running in with Metcalfe's Mannlicher rifle. He threw himself prostrate on the ground and waited. The Ras spoke to him, took the rifle, and the soldier retreated, bowing deeply. He held up the rifle and examined it. He said: "This is a very fine weapon, my friend." He loaded it, looked round the room, suddenly threw the gun to his shoulder and fired. The bullet shattered the water-jar on its stand in the corner of the room; he fired again rapidly, and again and again, and at each shot a smaller piece of broken pottery leaped into the air. He fired as rapidly and as smoothly as a gunnery instructor at his Bisley best.

Metcalfe was grinning with genuine pleasure. He said: "I like to see a man who knows how to fire a rifle."

The Ras said, shaking an enormous finger in his face: "I will shoot against any man in your British army; and with any weapon. Come, I show you."

He walked to the door and pointed towards the other end of the long avenue. He said: "Find me a target. Anything you like."

Metcalfe protested, "But there are people out there."

Ras Guggla smiled. "Of course. You see that Moslem? I do not like Moslems." An Arab, fully two hundred yards away, was sitting in the doorway of a shop. The Ras raised the rifle slowly to his shoulder, took slow and careful aim, and fired. The bright red fez of the Arab shot off his head. For a moment the man sat still; then he leaped to his feet and bolted from view, like a rabbit disappearing into his warren. Metcalfe breathed a sigh of relief. He said mildly: "That's a four-seventy, you know. I used to play tricks like that with an airgun."

Ras Guggla said: "It is a very fine rifle. Come, we drink some *tej*." He led them into an inner room and clapped his hands. As two women came in, they sat down on sheepskin-covered benches, and the women poured the fine golden drink from tall glass bottles into metal tankards and handed them to the men; first to the Ras, then to Metcalfe, then to Pender. They drank slowly, feeling the warm, smooth liquor spread its slow fire through their limbs. The Ras said: "If you came here to trade, you would have looked for the traders. Yet in Hargeisa they said it was the King you wanted to see. You are both soldiers, and yet you are dressed in civilian clothes. You come armed, with your own soldiers, and yet you hide your guns before you come to see me. Your Government has sent you, and yet you come as traders. I begin to feel that I do not like this. And I must tell you, before you leave here, you will have told me the truth. Forgive me if I ask you this before my duties as your host have finished: what is it you are looking for here? I begin to feel, how do you say, uneasy."

Metcalfe said: "Your Excellency, we have nothing to hide. We have come to buy one of your slaves. There is a man here, an Italian, and my Government wants him in connection with a police case; he is believed to have killed a British officer during the war. My Government is prepared to buy him from you, knowing that he is worth to them more than he is worth to you. That is our purpose here, and nothing more."

Ras Guggla said: "It seems a lot of trouble for one man. If he killed one of your officers so long ago . . . it seems a small thing for so much trouble. Are you telling me the truth?"

"Yes, your Excellency, I am telling you the truth."

"I see." There was a long pause. At last he said briefly: "We will discuss this matter after we have eaten. I ask you to forgive me that I talk of this before our food."

Metcalfe said lightly: "It is as easy to talk now as at any time. Your *tej* is strong. We may not be able to press so hard a bargain later on."

The two women lingered in the doorway. They kept their eyes fixed on the tankards, and as one was half emptied, it was as rapidly filled. The time passed slowly. Pender was thinking, *If we don't get some food inside us soon, to soak this lot up* . . . and at last a servant came, touching the ground with her forehead, craving permission to bring in the food. The dishes, great round steaming platters, were carried in by young girls, and with them came the officers of the Ras's Army; Ras Guggla solemnly introduced them, one after the other. Each bowed courteously, murmuring, " *Te'ena ysterling*," shaking hands and smiling, and the girls cast their eyes down and simpered. Ras Guggla said, with

53

great dignity: "For one year I was at your Sandhurst. I regret that my officers are not so formal as your own. But they are good soldiers; we have a very good army here. Colonel Tafaya here is my Chief of Staff. He was at St Cyr in Paris; also for one year. The Allies were very anxious to make good soldiers of us while we could help them. Then they tried to make my brother King here."

Metcalfe said apologetically: "A very unfortunate mistake."

"A mistake," said the Ras sharply, "that we were able to correct without your help."

One of the young girls, smiling, pulled a leg from a braised chicken, wrapped it in a flat pancake of bread, dipped it in rich red sauce, and held it out to Metcalfe. She giggled and shook her head as he tried to take it from her. Pender said: "Open your mouth, you fool!" And he obediently and affably held his mouth open while she placed it carefully between his teeth. It was as tender as butter and as pepper-hot as a charcoal fire; he felt the tears streaming to his eyes and the perspiration spotting his forehead, and Pender said conversationally: "You grow excellent peppers here, Your Excellency." There were hard-boiled eggs in oil and in more of the red-hot sauce, and spiced cheeses and rolled-up slivers of raw red beef, then more chicken, roast and fried and boiled and braised, and more beef and more cheeses, and *tej* and more *tej*, then honey and cakes and sweets and dates and more honey, then *tej* and yet more *tej*, till Metcalfe felt his head swimming. The Ethiopians were eating steadily, drinking and chewing, chewing and drinking, and still the food was brought in, food and more food out of all gargantuan porportion. Metcalfe said thickly: "I feel we shall not discuss much business today, Ex . . . Excellence . . .

Excellency." And Ras Guggla nodded and said: "First we eat and drink. Talk afterwards." Metcalfe tried to stop drinking, but the *tej* was forced upon him in so charming a manner that he feared to offend his hosts; and he knew, moreover, that a full appreciation of the hospitality would be better received than any polite refusal. With this thought comfortably in his mind, he reached his second wind, and was able to stand, unsteadily, when the meal at last came to an end. Ras Guggla, himself a little unsteady, roared out: "Sleep! Now we sleep. Ngatua show you where to sleep." He bellowed an order to the girls. Ngatua was the one who had been feeding Metcalfe. He felt her on his arm and let himself be led to a small dark room. He slumped heavily on the bed, a wooden couch covered with kapok mattresses. He felt the girl pulling his boots off ever so gently, and then his clothes. He fell asleep, and when at last he woke, his head throbbing and his stomach heaving, she was fast asleep beside him, her coffee-skin gleaming in the half-light, her body warm against his. *Never again*, he said to himself, *never again.* The room was turning round him, whirling madly, and he said to himself thickly, *But was I sober when I swore*, and the room went on turning round and he shuddered and closed his eyes and turned over on his back and put his arm on the girl's cool shoulder, and the room stopped its whirling and he fell at once into a deep and heavy sleep. He woke once to wonder what had happened to Harry Pender, and thought, *Well, what the hell?* And then he fell asleep again.

He woke at last to find the sunlight streaming into the room and he covered his eyes and grimaced. Pender, standing untidily above him, said: "Hey, Romeo, get up. It's gone midday."

Metcalfe struggled among the mattresses until he was

sitting up. He said: "Hell's bells, what a party that was! Oh, what a night! For God's sake shut those damned shutters. What the hell happened to you last night?"

Pender grinned. "Same as happened to you. Here, drink this." He held out a glass of *tej*.

Metcalfe said, shuddering: "Are you mad? I never want to see that damn stuff again."

"On the contrary, it's the one thing you do need if you feel as I did when I first got up. It's the prime virtue of *tej*—it kills its own hangover. Knock it back and you'll see."

Metcalfe took the glass with an unsteady hand. He said: "I wonder if it's really worth while. I have never felt so ill in all my life. I must admit, that was quite a party. Have you seen the big shot this morning?"

"He sent a servant to tell me that he would be at our service whenever we cared to see him. He seems a very affable sort of fellow. I only hope there's nothing . . . well, sinister in his rather exuberant reception of us."

"I don't think so; more like a natural goodwill. We'll go over as soon as we get cleaned up. Shaved? Yes, I see you have. What happened to the boys?"

"Ali and Yussuf are here, bedded down in the servants' quarters, and the others have been put in a barracks just across the road from here."

"Very naughty of us not to have seen to all that yesterday; but under the circumstances, I suppose, it doesn't really matter very much." Metcalfe climbed out of bed and reached for his trousers. "Have you located a bathroom of some sort?"

Pender said: "There's an excellent bathroom. A huge galvanised iron tub, and as soon as you go there, a dusky maid will pounce on you with buckets of hot water, bath salts, and olive oil."

"Oh no! Not again. Not at this hour of the morning?"

"Morning? It's nearly three o'clock in the afternoon."

"Good God!" Metcalfe was horrified. He slipped into his trousers. "See you in half an hour. Where the hell's this tub?"

He returned forty minutes later, bathed, shaved, refreshed, but smelling slightly of oil and perfume. They went together to the long verandah, spoke to the guard, and were escorted through the hall of the cool bungalow and into Ras Guggla's "state-room". The chief stood up as they entered and shook hands affably. He said: "Ah, my young friends. You sleep well? Comfortable? You need some food, perhaps?"

Metcalfe repressed a shudder. He said hastily: "Not at the moment, thank you, Excellency. Don't like to eat too early in the day. Are we disturbing you?"

"No, please sit down. Now you tell me about this Italian of yours." He sat down at a heavy table of crude ebony, elaborately carved and incised. He passed them a mahogany box of cigarettes, taking one himself. Immediately, one of the young soldiers standing guard at the door ran forward, pulling out a flint-and-touchwick lighter as he did so. He bowed deeply, then struck the wheel, blew on the tinder, and lit their cigarettes. He bowed again before running quickly back to his post. Metcalfe noted they were American cigarettes. He said, clearing his throat:

"This Italian, whose name is Franconi, is reputed to be in the town here. He is wanted by my Government in connection with the murder during the war of a British officer. We came to ask for his release. As he is no doubt being usefully employed here, we are quite prepared to pay compensation for him, if you will let him go."

3—R.G.   57

The chief said: "How much compensation do you think he is worth?"

Metcalfe said carefully: "Well, he cannot be worth very much here. On the open market, so to speak, he cannot be worth much more than a few hundred dollars."

Ras Guggla paused before replying. He said at last: "I remember that when I was in England one of your diplomats reminded me that we kept slaves here in Ethiopia; he was, how do you say, disgusted at the idea, and I think he believed that we were, shall I say, savages? He told me that the British were opposed, strongly opposed, to such primitive and uncivilised habits. Do I now understand that your Government is trying to buy a slave?"

"You have every reason to know, Excellency," Metcalfe said smoothly, "that we are a race of hypocrites. As far as I personally am concerned, we have come to buy this Italian. As a temporary diplomat, I feel obliged to ask instead for his release, and then offer to pay some sort of compensation to you."

The chief said: "I like your honesty, my friend. We could do much business together. You think he is worth only a few hundred dollars? After you have come so far for him?"

"Well, er . . . if you think he is worth more, I am at least prepared to listen to your suggestion."

The chief said promptly: "You are carrying five thousand dollars."

Metcalfe sighed. He said slowly: "I see. Of course, such a fact is not easy to hide, even if we wanted to hide it. Don't you think that's rather a high price to pay for one man?"

"In these days," said the chief, "we live on the trade we do here—skins, incense, livestock, cloth, coffee. We sell to traders and we buy from traders. We get as much as we can for what we have. In England you yourselves talk about the laws of supply and demand, I think. If you had brought with you only fifty dollars, I would be ready to talk business with you for fifty dollars. But you have five thousand. You are prepared to pay so much for this man?"

Metcalfe shrugged his shoulders. He said: "Excellency, I am not a trader. If I were, I should be happy to argue prices with you all day. As it is, my Government has seen fit to give me this money to pay out as compensation; I am quite sure they will not expect to see any of it returned. They are more interested in this man Franconi. As for myself, I shall be more than happy to exchange it for a lighter load on my truck." He smiled quickly. "I agree. Can we pick up this man right away?"

The chief waved a huge hand. "Wait, wait," he said. "You have made me very angry."

Pender looked up, startled. "Angry, Excellency?"

"Oh, not with you, my young friends. I am angry with myself because I see I am a fool." He pounded the table with his great black fist. "They cheat me!" he shouted. He stood up suddenly, kicking his chair out of the way. He roared: "I am a fool!"

Metcalfe and Pender stared at him. The chief calmed down just as suddenly as he had lost his temper. He smiled slowly. He said: "Forgive me, my young friends. I too am not a trader. I do not get the highest price for my goods. I am sorry that I cannot sell this man to you. If he is here, I sell him to you. But he is not here. He is gone."

"Gone? But how . . . gone where?" Metcalfe was flabbergasted. "I thought he was . . . unable to leave here. Where has he gone? And when?"

Ras Guggla said: "When? Two days ago. Where? I do not know. Everybody want this man, this Italian of yours. Two days ago I sell him to a good friend of mine. I sell him for one hundred dollars. If I wait two days, I get five thousand, that is why I am angry. Now, if I take your money, you will be angry too."

Metcalfe let this pass. He said urgently: "Can you tell me what happened, Excellency—who bought him?"

The chief said glumly: "Oh, I sell him to a trader. A good friend who brings me cigarettes from Djibouti. He came here two, three days ago on foot. He tell me lorry broken down a long way out. He tell me he know about this Italian; the Italian was mechanic in the Italian army, so he wants to borrow him to help fix his lorry. I say, All right, you take him. I give him donkey to carry the Italian because he can't walk very well." He added apologetically, "Something wrong with his leg, a little bit, how do you say, cripple. So then my friend is very pleased. He stay little while, we have food, drink a little *tej*, and the next day they go. Just before he go, he say to me, maybe I buy this man, keep him with me? And I say, All right, you pay me two hundred dollars and you take him." The chief sighed heavily. "This man say fifty dollars, and after little bit *tej* we agree one hundred. He pay me and go. Now maybe he is long way away. Too late to get him back. Too far away."

Metcalfe said stubbornly: "Well, we'll just have to find this trader. Do you know whereabouts his truck was broken down? They can't have got very far if they had repairs to make. We'll just have to find them."

Ras Guggla shook his head. "Other side of valley," he said. "Maybe they go north, maybe south. This man live in Berbera sometimes, sometimes in Djibouti, sometimes take leopard skins from Addis Ababa to

Mogadiscio. Very hard to find him now. My friend comes here not very often; maybe now he is already a hundred miles away."

Metcalfe said: "We'll find him. If he's in East Africa we'll find him. Let us have his name and his major trading centres, and if we can't find him in Ethiopia, we'll get him down on the coast. Will you tell us all about him—what goods he's carrying, where he's likely to go? And could you let us have a couple of trackers, just in case we can catch up with them? It won't be too difficult; they can't have got far in two days."

Pender said softly: "I have a feeling that all that is not going to be very important." He turned to the chief. "Would you tell us the name of your friend, Excellency? It is possible that we know him."

Ras Guggla said: "Yes, maybe you know him. Is an Englishman I think: maybe American. His name Dinesen. Dinesen buy for one hundred dollars." He said sadly: "If I wait two days, I get five thousand. Now what shall I do?"

Chapter Four

THEY covered the twenty miles from Lakbar town to the edge of the plateau in a little under an hour. Metcalfe was speechless with rage, and sat rigidly in his seat, staring ahead of him, ignoring the discomfort as the truck lumbered too fast over deep pot-holes and dusty sand-pits in the track. Pender sat silently, skilfully guiding the vehicle through the green scrub. It was nearly dusk and the sun was low on the horizon, pale yellow, its heat dwindled to a penetrating warmth. Far in the distance the plain spread out before them. When they reached the village at the tiny tree-trunk bridge, they pulled up and clambered out.

Metcalfe said to Ali: "Find out from the people here when a European last passed through here—a tall man on foot, with one of Ras Guggla's men. I want to know when they passed through, where they went, and if any further news of them has come in. Find out everything you can about them. And hurry up."

"*Ndio bwana.*" Mfupi and the Army were quiet and watchful, conscious of the anger in the air, fearful that it might be on their own account. Pender said: "Well, it's no good worrying. Either we find them or we don't. Actually, we have a good chance of catching up with them. There are only one or two ways they could possibly have gone, and if we come across any signs of their tracks, the two trackers will soon locate them for us. It's a good thing we have the chief's men with us."

"You don't suppose for one minute," Metcalfe said sulkily, "that their truck actually has broken down?"

"No, of course not. That was just a device to make sure he got hold of Franconi without any fuss and could get him clear of Lakbar plateau. But there's this to remember; Dinesen walked in. And knowing that we might be fairly close behind him, he would not dare take too long over it. It would take him a day to get from here to the town and a day to get back again. That's already a lot of time wasted if we were really so close behind him, and he wouldn't want to waste any more once he was clear of the plateau. If he left his truck on this side of the bridge, the information would soon reach Ras Guggla and spoil his story; and if he left it too far away on the other side, he would have to lose more time walking to it. *Ergo*, the truck was parked within reasonable distance of the bridge, on the other side. The people here might easily have heard it. That's another thing Mfupi can find out. Even if they made a quick getaway, they can only be a day or so ahead of us: in other words, a maximum of fifty or sixty miles in this sort of country. And as this is the only track leading from here, he must still be on it."

Metcalfe agreed. "Even so, when we have covered that fifty or sixty miles, he will still be that much ahead of us. Our only chance is that he might break his back axle in his hurry." He added grimly: "God help Dinesen when I catch up with him, that's all. Appendicitis! That's what makes me more angry than anything else; how the devil I fell for that tomfoolery I can't imagine. Hospital, indeed! He'll need a spell in hospital by the time I've finished with him."

Pender said thoughtfully: "There's another thing, you know. We mustn't forget that Dinesen will only be interested in the money; he's got to find it yet. Even if Franconi spills the beans at once, they've still got to find the loot; and that, we know from the reports,

63

is somewhere quite near here. Now, was there anything in the files we collected that gave some sort of clue as to where the hiding-place might be? Must we discount entirely the depositions of the Italians in jail? Isn't there some indication in their statements that might help us? Something that will tie up with what Franconi knows? Can't we make a short cut—stop trailing Dinesen and go direct to where he's going?"

"Well, if we knew where to look for the cash, that's where we should be sure of finding Dinesen; there, I agree with you. But we have no idea at all where to look, and if we have to take pot-luck over the whole of Africa, we might just as well go home now and done with it."

Pender said decisively: "No. It's not quite as bad as that. We don't know where the stuff is, but one thing we do know. Major Hewitt was killed near here —by all reports within, what, twenty miles of Lakbar? At a guess, or an intelligent semi-deduction?"

"Yes . . . yes . . . maybe. But that still leaves us a circle of forty miles across to search: it's not feasible."

"A further deduction. A lot of Hewitt's money was in gold sovereigns; and you remember what a bloody weight even twenty sovereigns is—remember how we used to hate carrying even that small amount with us during the war. Well, if Hewitt had a thousand of them, as we know he did, they could only have been moved by hand very laboriously, and although both Hewitt and the Italians had transport, their trucks were out of action. Furthermore, it was not very healthy moving about on foot in this part of the world at that time, with an irate Ethiop behind every bush. Must have hidden the stuff somewhere near the track on which the battle took place. A track. And how many tracks are there round here, for God's sake? There's only this one. So it's reasonable to suppose, at least, that the hiding-place is somewhere right on this very road."

Metcalfe said, frowning: "Yes . . . that's reasonable enough. So what have we got now? A narrow twenty-mile strip of territory to search for an unknown hiding-place; a hole in the ground, maybe, covered over with sand ten years ago."

Pender began to get exasperated. He said: "My dear fellow, must I spell it out for you? Where, in heaven's name, would you hide a quarter of a million pounds in a hurry? At least, not having too much time in which to get it safely stowed away? And remembering that the hiding-place must be easily recognisable again —which presupposes that you can't just bury the stuff in the desert?"

"In a cave?"

"In a cave, of course."

Metcalfe said hesitantly: "And as this track runs dead flat for a hundred miles or more, the nearest caves will be up near the top of the crater. I see what you mean."

"Wrong again." Patiently. "You can't get a truck up to the crater or anywhere near it; besides, we know that Ras Guggla, in Lakbar, was working for us during the war, so the Italians would have kept away from there, and they were on foot anyway. The reasoning is correct, but the deduction is quite wrong." He pointed down, tapping his index finger on an imaginary table. He said: "There's only one possible hiding-place."

Metcalfe yelped. "Of course! In the valley!"

"Precisely. This road runs over flat and therefore caveless territory, but down in the crevasse below the bridge there must be hundreds of caves; the valley turns in a circle like a dry moat, as we know. And down there, if my guess is right, is the hiding-place. As you say, a cave of some sort."

Metcalfe was thoroughly elated. His anger was gone; the excitement of the chase was in his blood. He said cheerfully: "And while we should never be able to find the loot unaided, we have our dear friend Dinesen to help us."

His companion said: "Exactly. We have Dinesen to help us. Franconi will lead Dinesen to the right spot in the valley. All we have to do is search the valley for signs of their presence. Does that sound too easy? I wonder if it's possible to get a truck down there?"

"Well, we can soon find that out." He called Ali over. "Find out," he said, "if there's a way down into the valley from here."

Ali said: "*Ndio, effendi*. People say here, one big man come through village walking before five days. Go to Lakbar, come back after two days, go over bridge, go that way." He pointed westward.

"Off the track?"

"*Ndio, effendi*. Go into bush. Say truck break down, take man from Lakbar to fix. No come back."

"Good. Excellent. Now listen, Ali. I want you to tell the villagers that I want to find this man. I think he is down in the valley here somewhere now. Understand?"

"*Ndio, effendi*."

"Find out what there is down there—find out all you can about it. And tell them that they can all help us look for this man. Tell them that I will pay one hundred silver dollars to the first man to find them. I don't care how many men help us; but there's a hundred silver dollars to the first man to find this European. Understand."

"*Ndio, effendi*." Ali went off to talk to the villagers.

Pender nodded his approval. Metcalfe said grimly: "I'll teach that bastard to plays tricks like that on me. I might have known something like this would happen."

Pender said mildly: "A pity, you know. He's a rattling good fellow, Dinesen."

"A rattling good fellow? He's a bastard, an absolute stinker."

"Well, isn't that the same thing? When you come to think of it?"

Metcalfe grunted. "I suppose you do have an argument there. But he's overstepped the mark this time. I'll have his guts for a necktie when I catch up with him."

"*If* we catch up with him. He's got several days' start on us, remember."

"We'll catch up with him." He called for Ali again. He said: "Listen, Ali. We'll take the truck over the other side and pick up Tadessa and Dastar with the rifles. You and the others stay here and get all this information. We'll be back in about an hour. Don't let any of the men get drunk while we're away. Mfupi!"

Mfupi came running up. To impress the villagers, he saluted smartly. Metcalfe said: "We're going over to pick up the others. Come back soon. Stay here with Ali and the boys."

Mfupi saluted again. He said: "*Ndio*, captain." Metcalfe grinned and returned his salute. He said: "That chap would make a good sergeant-major. I wonder where they found him?"

Pender said: "Well, according to Withers in Aden, he's a professional cut-throat they've never been able to pin anything on. Makes his living by theft and murder. Good type. Let's get weaving."

They drove off in the truck, moving slowly through

the dusty street of the village, then speeded up as they left the mud huts behind them. They crossed over the log bridge and drew into the bush at the side of the track. As they climbed down from their seats, their two men came running up, clumsily carrying the six rifles. One of them said something rapidly in Amharic.

Metcalfe said: "What's he trying to say?"

Pender said: "I don't know." He said to the man: "*Kalimu Swahili? Arabi?*"

The man shook his head. He said hesitantly: "*Kule, effendi,*" pointing to the hills to the west. "*Garri, effendi.*"

Metcalfe said excitedly: "What's that, a lorry over there?"

The man shook his head and held out his hands. "*Hapana . . . hapana . . .*"

Pender said: "It'll have to wait. We'll have to camp in the village for the night, anyway. Shall we get back?"

Metcalfe said: "He's seen something, obviously. We should have brought Ali with us. We'll get back to the village."

The men clambered on the truck. Tadessa, grinning through his bandages, pulled a half-eaten young boar from the bushes and threw it in the back. Metcalfe said: "Well, they haven't been asleep all the time, anyway. Let's go."

They drove quickly back to the village. The Army was surrounded by a crowd of villagers, waving and shouting as they drove up. Metcalfe jumped down and called Ali over. He said: "Well?"

Ali was full of self-importance. He said, "Plenty men help *effendi*, all village look for the *bwana*. Say you sleep here tonight, sleep in house of chief." (Pender said: "Ah well, here we go again.") "Tomorrow, early, everybody go down to valley and look. Plenty lions down there, *effendi*, nobody live there. Say no way for truck. There is small path one mile *huku* . . ." he pointed west. "Say maybe truck not go down. Tomorrow we take one hundred men maybe. But chief say one hundred dollars not enough; want three hundred."

Metcalfe said: "Tell them we will pay one hundred to the first man to see this European, fifty to the chief, and fifty to the village. No more."

Ali nodded his head, approving. He said: "Is enough, *effendi*. Want too much money. I tell them."

"Wait. Tadessa and Dastar said they saw a truck, I think. Find out what it was." Ali beckoned to the two men and stood talking to them for a while. At last he said: "They say, *effendi*, somebody in hills over that way. Yesterday see something shine, maybe glass from lorry. Stay there all morning."

Pender said: "Ask them if it could have been binoculars. Did it move or was it in the same place all the time?"

Ali translated, then said: "Same place, *effendi*. See for little while, then go away, after see again. See many times, same place. Afternoon, sun go there . . . no see any more."

Metcalfe said: "Binoculars, all right. That raises a problem. Do we shoot over there in the truck and try and locate them or do we search the valley first?"

"Search the valley," Pender said promptly. "First of all, we may not be able to get through the bush very easily, and we can't afford to get stuck now; secondly, that reflection may have been something else altogether; and thirdly, we might never find their tracks over there. Best plan is to go down into the valley at crack of dawn. My guess is the place we want is west of here—that should make it that much easier."

"Right. Nothing much we can do tonight except sleep. We'll start very early in the morning, as soon as it gets light. Ali!"

"*Ndio, effendi?*"

"Tell the men to bed down here for the night. We'll start very early tomorrow. Who's the head man in the village?"

Ali pulled a wizened old man out of the crowd. He said: "This man, *effendi*. He say one hundred men come tomorrow. Tonight you sleep his house, over there. He bring you food, *tej*, women . . . In the morning, all go down in valley, take guns, plenty lion. He say best you pay him fifty dollars first."

The sun had not yet risen when the party set out. It was cold on the plateau, but the air was still and fresh. Partridge and bustard and guinea-fowl scuttled into the bush as the truck lumbered heavily through the bush along the lip of the chasm, pushing the light scrub over as it went. Twenty or thirty men ran easily ahead of it, hacking at the thicker saplings with their broad, sharp knives. A wild pig ran out of a thicket, and one of the Ethiopians threw his rifle up, fired, shot the beast, flung it across his broad shoulders, and went on with his hacking. The others had gone on ahead, and some had already climbed down the steep slope into the ravine. The tense excitement of the chase could be seen on every face.

They reached the narrow goat-track winding down from the plateau and stopped; one of the Ethiops, his hand pointing down at the earth, was waiting for them. As Metcalfe jumped down from the truck, he stood silent, feet apart, his rifle held loosely across his shoulder, his double bandolier crossing his smooth brown chest.

His sharp, alert eyes looked up. Metcalfe said: "That was a good guess of yours. Here they are."

Pender walked over to them and stood looking down at the tracks on the ground. He said: "That's a jeep. So that's it. A jeep could get down there without too much difficulty. Don't know whether it could get back again, though." He called to Ali. "Tell the two trackers to stay with us," he said.

Metcalfe said: "We'll have to leave the lorry here, and follow these on foot. Have two of the men stay behind to look after the truck. Tell them to keep their eyes and ears open."

They followed the jeep-tracks down the rough, steep slope. The worn footpath ran neatly in the middle of the tyre-marks. Ali called out from behind them: "*Garri mbele, effendi.*" Pender looked down at the tracks carefully. He said: "I don't know, perhaps he's right. I believe there are two sets of tracks."

Metcalfe stopped. "Two sets? Or the same set twice? Have they been up and down here? That would mean they've found the stuff and have brought it up again. We must be careful about this. There are too many tracks—I don't like it."

"Well, he can't have brought an army with him on a job like this. This is just the sort of thing that requires more secrecy than you'd get with a whole crowd of people."

Metcalfe called Ali and the trackers over. He said: "Let them examine these tracks carefully and tell me if they're made by the same car." As soon as he had translated, both trackers said together, not deigning to look more carefully: "Two vehicles. One heavy, one light; both same size." Then one of them added: "Two go down, only one come up."

Metcalfe said triumphantly: "Ah. Now we've got

71

them. This is going to be easier than I thought. Come on, let's catch up with them. It looks like sand all the way; it's going to be very easy to find them." They hurried on down the slope.

As they reached the valley floor, Pender asked: "What is the drill when, and if, we catch up? You don't think he's likely to make a fight for it, do you?"

Metcalfe stopped dead. He looked worried. "I hope not. Not very nice to drink beers in the Crown with a man one week and shoot him down the next." He shook his head. "No, he won't. After all, we've been friends . . . at least, acquaintances . . . a long time. I don't believe it will come to a show-down like that."

"With all that money involved?"

"I don't think even Dinesen would risk open warfare. Good God, the idea's preposterous; this is a Government mission. No, no. If he could have got away with it, well . . . cleanly, he would have done so, that's certain. But now that the game's up, he surely won't try and shoot his way out. No, no, no; it's not possible. After all, we were knocking back your drinks together only a week or so ago."

"Quite. But London is a long, long way away. This is Ethiopia, not Knightsbridge. I'm inclined to agree with you, I think. But we shall have to be careful, all the same. Dinesen is a very determined man and he won't give up the idea of all that money quite so easily."

Metcalfe said thoughtfully: "When, and if, we find him, I think we shall have to look for trickery rather than force of arms. I just can't believe that he'd be such a fool." He was not very happy about it.

They walked on slowly through the valley. The bush was thick here, and the tyres of the jeeps, clearly visible in the soft sand, had followed a devious and difficult route. Ahead of them and on both sides they could hear the chanting of the men as they hacked their way through the bushes. Pender said:

"A pity we can't do this silently, just in case we come across them here. But with so many lions reputedly about, the only way the men can safely work is noisily enough to scare them away. It will also scare Dinesen away if he's here, but at least we shall catch up with him. Even a jeep can't move as fast as we're moving on foot through this sort of bush."

Just as he spoke a shot rang out. They stopped short and looked up, startled. For a moment there was silence, save for the sudden screeching of birds. Then two more shots rang out in rapid succession. Ali came running up, shouting: "*Kule, effendi, kule,*" and pointing to one side. They ran quickly into the bush. Pender shouted: "They may be firing at us—be careful."

Ali answered him, grinning: "*Hapana, bwana*; they find something."

Metcalfe said, panting: "How the hell does he know?"

They slowed down. Pender said: "Probably arranged a signal among themselves. We'll soon see."

They ran on into the bush, pushing aside the sharp thorn scrub, ducking under the branches. The yellow dust above their footprints hung still and poised in the stifling air.

Chapter Five

THEY came to a small clearing in the scrub, close beside the northern slope of the valley, the cliff rising almost sheer above them. One of the soldiers, loosely holding his rifle, smoking a cigarette, was standing on top of an overturned jeep, watching for them. He started shouting at Ali as soon as he saw them. The two white men stood looking down at the vehicle. It was lying on one side, its wheels twisted, a great hole in the radiator, its sides dented here and there, the metal torn in one place as though ripped open with an axe; the cushions were flung about and two or three wooden boxes were broken savagely open. In the solid metal floor of the body was a sharp circular hole, nearly six inches across, and the soft sand bed of the valley clearly showed where the jeep had been bodily dragged for nearly fifty feet. Metcalfe said: "What the hell . . .?" They all stood round the vehicle, staring at it. The Ethiopian said something, and Ali nodded his head in agreement. He said:

"*Jusu effendi*. Rhino." He looked round about him anxiously. Pender said to him: "Don't worry, Ali, that rhino will be a long way away by now." He felt the radiator of the jeep. "Cold," he said.

Metcalfe said to Ali: "Get the story from the trackers. See if they can tell when this happened."

Ali and the trackers walked slowly over the scene, piecing the evidence together bit by bit. There were deep marks in the red sand, the heavy prints of the rhino clearly visible, and the marks of bare feet, an

74

outline of a boot, and a series of long scratches. Over them all were the tyre marks of the second jeep. They sat down in the shade of a tree and watched the trackers at work. They worked slowly and surely, walking upright, but with their eyes on the ground, heads bent forward, resting their hands on the extremities of their guns, which were slung like staves across the backs of their shoulders parallel with the ground. They covered the whole area systematically, walking up and down slowly, occasionally pointing at the sand and speaking quietly to each other; once they stopped for a while and argued. Metcalfe and Pender sat smoking and chatting. The others came and stared at the jeep for a few moments, discussed and wondered at it among themselves, and then went off again into the bush in search of their own rewards. At last the story was complete. The trackers came over and joined them, accepted cigarettes, and sat down on the sand, now warming in the heat of the sun, while Ali told what had happened. From time to time the trackers joined in to stress a point.

"Like this, *effendi*," Ali said. "Jeep come this way, rhino come from salt-lick over there. This animal track is for lion, leopard, pig, all go this way to salt-lick. Rhino see jeep, jeep see rhino. Jeep no go back, because no room to turn, but try to move this way. Rhino charge, hit jeep in front, here . . ." He patted the broken radiator. "Jeep stop. Three men jump out, run this way, one man and woman climb this tree, two men climb that tree. Rhino charge again, push jeep in bush, break jeep up, very angry, lose part of horn in lorry, see?" He pointed to a piece of broken horn one of the trackers was holding out.

Metcalfe held out his hand for it; it was a piece of coagulated hair from the base of the horn, scored sharply down one side by the hard metal of the truck. Ali went on: "After rhino break jeep, he go into bush, wait maybe one hour. Men stay in trees, so rhino go away. Men come down from trees, another jeep come along, load boxes from first jeep, then go. But first, one man break branch off tree, here . . ." he pointed at the white scar of a broken limb on the tree they were sitting under, "and wipe out tracks of feet."

Pender said, puzzled: "What on earth would he do that for?"

Ali went on: "Wipe out marks near jeep. Tracker say, only one man wear boots, others go no shoes."

"One white man, the rest Africans?"

Ali said stolidly: "No, *bwana*. *Hapana*. One white man wear boots. Two white men and woman no shoes. Two Africans only. Altogether, five men, one woman. Only one white man wear boots."

The trackers, seeing their puzzled looks, started arguing among themselves. Pender said: "Are they sure about that?"

"*Ndio, bwana*. They sure. I say, white man always wear shoes. They say, these white men take off shoes."

Metcalfe said: "Well, what the hell's the idea of that? And who, for Heaven's sake, is the woman?"

Pender said slowly: "I think I know what they are trying to do; there's a picture of some sort forming in my mind, but it's not very clear. Is he perhaps trying to make us believe that he has a party of Africans only with him? He might have wiped out the marks they made jumping out of the jeep—that would account for his use of the branch—and then told the other Europeans, whoever they are, to take off their shoes to give the impression that they were natives. He ought really to have realised that a good tracker would spot the difference at once by the shape of the foot; but if he was trying to fool only us, not expecting us to have trackers with us . . . Is that possible?"

"It's possible, I suppose, but why, for heaven's sake? He's obviously expected us to follow him down here, and he's tried to persuade us that he is alone except for a few Africans, whereas actually he has two others with him. And who the devil can they be, anyway?"

"That, my friend," said Pender, "we are obviously fated to find out. I suggest this. If he wants to fool us about the strength of his party, then he obviously expects us to catch up with him, for some reason or other. And it looks as if he realises that he is overloaded and may not make very good speed. He seems to have six people and all his stores on one jeep, plus, if he has found it, the money. He's very well loaded, and our chances of catching up with him are very good indeed. And, what is more," he said, with a certain admiration in his voice, "if this is so, we have also accounted for the flashing binoculars in the hills yesterday."

"Huh? How come?"

"Knowing that we could more easily catch up with him now that he's down to one overloaded jeep, he's got off the track, where it will be that much harder for an ordinary truck to follow, and he has stopped at a strategic point in the hills from which he can watch our arrival and departure with his glasses. I am beginning to have a high regard for friend Dinesen."

Metcalfe said: "I must admit that I have never found anything wrong with his sense of strategy. I don't like this nonsense about the other Europeans. If they are all in on the deal, it's just going to make it harder to reason with him."

"And he's got some other trick up his sleeve. He's trying to hide the fact that he's got some other Europeans with him. Does that mean he expects us to catch up with him and wants us to believe that he's alone?"

"We'll find that out when we catch him."

"*If* we catch him."

"We'll catch him," Metcalfe said grimly. "He's had a bad bit of luck with that rhino; just what we needed to make it possible for us to get him."

"And you see," Pender said, "he even came prepared for that, in a way—two vehicles. If we'd run into a rhino or even a major breakdown, that would be the end of our party."

"All right, don't sound quite so pleased about it." Metcalfe was still a little angry. He said: "We'd better get on with the job. Ali! Tell the men to keep on following the tracks. We'll see where they lead."

It was nearly a mile further on that they found the cave. Deep under the shadows of an overhanging creeper, some of the Ethiopians were standing, chattering excitedly together. Close up against the wall of the red sandstone cliff, two huge boulders marked the entrance to a narrow, dark and dismal cavern. It was no more than a deep slit in the face of the cliff, some twelve feet high, and only a couple of feet wide, and the sun struck sharply into it for a depth of about five feet. There was already a fire burning in there, fed by two of the men, who were busy throwing on dry twigs to make a bright illumination. As Metcalfe squeezed his bulk with difficulty through the ragged aperture, they called to him and pointed excitedly to one side of the cave. A shallow trench had been scooped out of the floor, close under an overhanging shelf. Small stones had been freshly piled to one side, and a forgotten spade lay in the shadows. Metcalfe said:

78

"Well, there we are. A better hiding-place than that would be hard to find. Off the beaten track, yet easy to locate. With a couple of shovelfuls of sand on top of the stuff, it could have lain there undiscovered till the end of the world. So now we know. He didn't waste much time."

Pender said: "We've done all right so far. The next step is to catch up with them. That won't be so easy."

"If we don't get them soon," Metcalfe said gloomily, "we never shall. We can have him stopped at any decent-sized port, in theory, if we can get to a town of some sort with a cable office before he reaches the coast. But with his knowledge of the country he's not likely to try and ship out of Berbera or Djibouti. He'll leave by any one of a hundred of these wretched little Somali coastal villages, if he leaves at all."

Pender pondered awhile. "He'll probably fly out," he said at last. "To get here so far ahead of us, he must have flown straight here—to Hargeisa or Dire-Dawa, perhaps. And then he could easily arrange for a charter plane to take him practically anywhere in Africa. The only answer is to find him before he gets much further. If we lose him now, we've lost him for good."

"You're probably right," Metcalfe said. "At least we can follow these tracks out again, and take it from there."

He called to Ali again. "Some more work for you, Ali. Find out if we can get up on to the plateau again further west. Get hold of Tadessa and Dastar, get them to tell the villagers where they saw the sun on the binoculars yesterday or the day before, and find out how we can get over in that direction. Find out if there are any villages over there that might have some news."

Ali said: "*Ndio, nkwenda sasa hivi,*" and trotted off to

find the others. Metcalfe said: "We'd better camp here till we can round up the men. It's no good looking here any more. We'll follow the jeep as fast as we can and see what happens."

They waited a while, smoking incessantly, until Ali returned with some of the villagers. Patiently he began to explain. He swept his arm out to embrace the area to the south-west of them.

"Out there," he said, "only bush. Nothing. All bush, *effendi*. Lorry no go there. Over there"—he pointed to the south—"track go back to Harrar, same track we come. In middle, no village. Up in hill, only sheep and cows and goats. . . ."

"And a village?" Pender asked quickly.

"No village, *effendi*. Women stay with cattle, come from village *kule*." He drew the word *kule* out long and high, a falsetto *ku-u-u-u-le*, meaning a very long way indeed. Pender interrupted him again. "How do they get there, these women?"

Ali said: "Go to hills from village every day. Maybe truck get there too, from village. From this side, truck not get there."

Pender said: "Let's get this straight; we can get up into the hills from the village which is *south* of them, is that it?" Ali nodded agreement.

"And from that village is there a way back to Harrar? Another track?" Ali nodded again.

Pender turned to Metcalfe. "Well, that's it. He's got up into the hills with his jeep—feasible enough, even if our truck can't get there; we can try it, anyway. Then he'll go south to the village, on to Harrar, and from there he can take either the road up to Gondar, which is unlikely, because he can't get anywhere from there except deeper into Ethiopia, or else the road down to Dire-Dawa and the airport, or back the way we came to the coast. If you ask me, it's either at Dire-Dawa or on the main road through Jig-Jigga that we'll find him, and Harrar is our first bet. I don't think that even with a jeep he can afford to go too far into the bush; he's tied now with a big load, so he can't have much fuel aboard. That means he'll have to refuel in Harrar—there simply isn't anywhere else. What do you think?"

Metcalfe said: "You're right, by God! It all hinges on fuel. He'll have to get fresh supplies soon, unless he's got some cached by the wayside." He added glumly: "He might easily have thought of that."

"I don't think so." Pender sounded quite excited. "I expect that's what the second jeep was for. He couldn't foresee so violent a breakdown as he had, and if he made a cache by the road he would have tied himself down to a pre-arranged escape route which he might not have been able to keep to. Harrar is the place—I'm certain of it."

"All right then. We'll head for Harrar, and we'll stop on the way at the village over in the hills. It may be a little further, but we might get news of him there."

"There's a question of payment," Pender pointed out. "Let's not take too long over it."

Metcalfe grinned. "That's easily settled." He gave instructions to Ali. "Tell the villagers," he said, "I'm leaving five hundred dollars at the village for them. They can share it out just as they like. We're going to Harrar now, so tell Mfupi to get the Army together quickly and meet us at the top of the escarpment, near the truck. Understand?"

Ali said happily: "*Ndio bwana.* I tell them." He ran off.

Metcalfe and Pender stood for a while looking at the long slit in the cliff which was the hiding-place. The fire inside was leaping up now, casting its eerie light and shadows about the darkness.

Metcalfe said: "I wonder what they felt, those Italians. They couldn't all have been bad. And yet they murdered a man here for the sake of his money." He said sombrely: "I wonder what qualms they had as they shovelled the sand over it all. Most soldiers loot, I suppose; it's part of the perks of warfare; but murder . . . This was just cold-blooded murder, just for the sake of money." He said savagely; "That isn't warfare; murder isn't warfare."

Pender said sadly: "It's a fine distinction. The man with a bullet in his head has precious little time to reflect on the gain he's dying for. I'm a professional soldier, but if I stopped to think about it . . . I don't know. I'd as lief kill for money as for somebody else's political aspirations. There can be no possible argument for war, if you allow anybody any morals at all. And if you don't, then it doesn't matter what you kill for. The whole thing is a dressed-up hypocrisy, and only the fool is taken in by it. It's easier to respect the man who kills to better himself than it is to condone mass killing at someone else's orders."

"That depends," said Metcalfe, "on your interpretation of the term 'to better himself.'"

"And there," said Pender, "is the rub. Let's go. This place sickens me."

They climbed slowly, panting, back to the top of the escarpment. The sun was getting hot now, and the heat down in the valley was stifling; it was a clean refreshment to reach the top and suddenly to feel the wind, fresh and cool across the plateau. The Army was waiting for them, standing round chatting with the villagers, smoking and laughing with the day's excitements. Some young girls were among them, giggling and casting their eyes down coquettishly, looking up at the men through half-closed eyes; Metcalfe thought, *There's not much difference, really; put some clothes on them and imagine they're white—you might as well be in London.* He winked at one of the girls; she clasped her hands together with a little screech, then ran off laughing. She stopped a few yards away and turned to watch him soberly. He said:

"All right, let's get this over with." He pulled one of the heavy boxes off the floor of the truck and placed it on the ground in front of the villagers.

"There you are," he said, patting the box. "Five hundred dollars. Ali! Tell them we are very pleased with their work and we hope to see them all again."

Ali was as pleased as the rest of them. His face lit up as he told them about the money. Metcalfe caught fragments of Amharic here and there. "Don't fight," Ali was saying, "don't fight over it." Metcalfe shook his finger at them. "That's the idea," he said in English, "no fighting. Share it out among you." The older men among the villagers, not understanding, nodded their grizzled old heads wisely, grunting agreement. Nobody touched the box until the truck moved off. Pender said: "That's as good a way as any; the chief will see that it's shared out properly. The primitives have a hell of a lot better idea of communal discipline than we have. Hell for leather for Harrar?"

"Hell for leather. Watch out for a track leading into the bush to the right somewhere—we want to get into that village by the shortest way. Should turn off about twenty miles further on."

Pender said, looking at his watch: "It's only two o'clock. We've had a good day. Do you want to drive all night, taking turns? We don't want to waste time sleeping."

"All right. I'll have a kip now and take over at six. Four-hour spells right through the night."

Metcalfe wedged himself comfortably back in the corner of the cab. He said: "We shall probably reach the village during the night, which is a bit of a nuisance. We shall have to stay over till daylight—I want to find out if they've been through there."

"Oh, I don't think that's necessary. They'll all wake up and turn out when they hear us coming, anyway. We can probably find out all we want to know just as well in the dark."

"We'll see. Not likely to be there before six. But if we are, wake me up, won't you? I'm going to sleep now."

"Pleasant dreams," Pender said with a grin. "You can dream about the Lakbar lovelies."

The truck droned on, the engine humming sweetly, bumping heavily over the hard sand track.

They went steadily on their way, a busy insect at the head of its own dust-trail, winding its slow and persistent way through the bushes, twisting and turning, buzzing monotonously onward through the sleepy heat. Presently the soft, deep purring of the motor merged with the scattered noises of the bush. Metcalfe nodded once or twice; then all was silence.

Chapter Six

THEY reached the village at ten o'clock. The night was dark and the lights of the Ford cut a wide bright swathe ahead of them as they forced their way through the thick vegetation and crawled painfully in among the mud houses, with their tumble-down, broken walls and rickety grass roofs. It was quite deserted. Metcalfe was driving. He reached out and shook Pender.

"Wake up," he said. "We're here. Nobody about by the look of it." He called out to Ali in the back of the truck: "Ali! Everybody to stay near the truck. We shall only be here a few minutes."

Pender shook the sleep out of his eyes, and together they clambered down from the cab. Rifles in hand, they started to explore the narrow, dusty road which comprised the village. With a flashlight they examined the soil for tyre marks; there were none. All was silent save for the subdued murmuring of the boys in the truck. In the near distance the embers of a fire flickered, and they heard voices whispering softly.

Metcalfe said quietly: "Let's see."

They went to the end of the tiny village. Half-a-dozen men were sitting round a small thornwood fire, the scented blue smoke curling lazily upwards and filling the cool air with an overpowering smell of incense. The natives rose silently as they approached; they were all heavily armed, and stood sullenly staring at the intruders. One of them suddenly barked out a question roughly.

Metcalfe said: " *Te'ena ysterling. Te'enanu?*"

Some of the men answered gruffly, shortly: "*Te'ena.*" The speaker stared at them angrily, and shouted a question again. Metcalfe signalled him to wait, using the universal signal with his upturned fingers and thumb puckered together in a slow up and down movement. He called loudly: "*Ali, Njoo!*" Ali came running up, looked uneasily at the men, and said: "*Effendi?*"

Pender said: "Tell these men that we only stop here to ask if any other parties have been through here lately. Tell them they have nothing to fear from us."

Ali spoke to the men and there was a short and angry argument. At last he said, swallowing hard: "They say not afraid, better you be afraid."

Metcalfe smiled easily and nodded his head at the men. He said: "Tell them that neither of us has anything to fear; we are all friends." He took out his case of cigarettes and offered it to the natives; they took them greedily. None were returned, some of the men taking two or three each. The last man found only one left; he took it and slipped the case under his belt. Metcalfe shook his head and held out his hand; the native laughed at him and spat, pulling his rifle towards him. Metcalfe said: "Ali, tell that man to give me back my case." Ali, trembling visibly, said: "Better call Mfupi, *effendi.*" Metcalfe said sharply: "Do as I tell you." Ali obeyed hesitantly. The native tucked the case more firmly under his belt and stood up, drawing his long dagger. Metcalfe raised his rifle; the others stood up, drawing together.

Pender moved forward and said quietly: "*Ngoja.* Wait!" He was idly tossing a small round object up and down to catch their attention; as soon as he saw they had recognised it for a Mills bomb, he tossed it

86

lightly into the glowing embers of the fire. The natives sprang sharply back with an exclamation; two of them ran well back into the shadows. Metcalfe and Pender stood still. The Africans started shouting to each other, and Pender leant forward, took the bomb calmly from the fire, and began idly tossing it up and down again. The villagers, muttering among themselves, drew back. Metcalfe said gently: "Tell him I'm waiting, Ali." Ali, plucking up courage, spoke sharply. The Ethiop took the case out, angrily tossed it on the ground and stalked off. Pender said quietly: "There's somebody behind us," and Ali said cheerfully: "*Hiku Mfupi, effendi*," and Mfupi stepped into the dim glow of the firelight. In the half-light of the shadows, with the red gleam of the embers on his huge bare chest, he looked enormous. A rifle was hanging loosely in one hand, his *panga*, the long, sharp African bush knife, was in the other. On the other side of the narrow, dirty street a match glowed, then a cigarette; Metcalfe glanced across and saw three of his Army silently spreading out. He grinned and said: "Well done, Mfupi. I'll make you a sergeant-major yet." Mfupi sprang to an exaggerated attention. He said: "*Ndio*, Captain. I hear men talking trouble. I come. Maybe I kill them?"

Metcalfe said: "Just ask them if anyone else has been through here lately."

Mfupi grabbed one of the villagers in a huge, beefy hand and spoke to him sharply. The man answered, a sullen, angry look on his sallow, yellow face. Mfupi pushed the man away and said: "Nobody come, *effendi*."

The other natives, sullenly watching, shook their heads, their lined, Mongoloid features reflecting their hatred. Metcalfe said: "Let's get back to the truck and get the hell out of this place. And for God's sake, Harry, don't ever throw a Mills on the fire again when I'm within a mile of you. You scared the guts out of me."

"Scared the guts out of them, too," Pender answered, "Safe enough, actually, as long as it doesn't stay there too long. Seemed the only thing to do; if they'd started anything, we'd never have got out of here alive. And these gentlemen can be very unpleasant if they want to." He grinned quickly. "No sign of friend Dinesen here. That could easily mean that we've overtaken him and he's still on the way here."

"I was wondering about that. He ought to be ahead of us somewhere; can't think he'd take three days over a trip we've done in eight hours. And our route was much longer."

"Don't forget that there is no track along the way we think he's coming. He may have to cut his way through if the bush is too thick. Even a jeep can only make ten or twenty miles a day sometimes. He might easily be behind us still; he's no way of guessing that we'd come into this village at all, and he may be assuming that we would take the normal route along the main track—and if that is so, he will go from here back to the road quite slowly, keeping behind us rather than ahead of us."

"Yes . . . that would enable him to keep an eye on us, and would account for his watching us from the hills back there; in which case our pawn attack is going to collapse the moment he comes into this village and learns that we have been here. He'll realise right away that we must have seen him up in the hills—the only thing that would explain our presence so far west."

Pender said tentatively: 'We could wait for him here."

Metcalfe shook his head. "I'm afraid the village doesn't like us very much; wouldn't be safe to stay here.

And, moreover, if we have guessed wrong, it will simply give him a chance to get further away. The question now is, do we go back the way we came or take the short route to Harrar?"

They stood around the truck, discussing the situation carefully, thrashing it out. Pender said: "If he's still north of us, in the direction of the hills, he's only got a footpath to follow in the jeep to get back here—the one the women take when they go up there with their livestock. He might easily still be on the way here. But I agree, this would not be a good place to confront him."

Ali was talking earnestly to an elderly man who had appeared from one of the houses. He came up to Metcalfe and said: "Maybe, *effendi*, you want to buy petrol?" Metcalfe said: "We've enough, haven't we?"

"Plenty," said Pender. "Enough to get us down to Somaliland whichever route we take. They'll charge us the earth for it in a place like this. No; our answer is to decide what Dinesen will do now that he's short on transport, with an overloaded truck, two or three Europeans to dump, and heading presumably for an airport small enough not to bother him with Customs formalities—he won't want to declare a quarter of a million pounds in ready cash. He will also need to get petrol supplies fairly——" He broke off and looked at Metcalfe. "So we were right after all?"

Metcalfe shouted: "Of course! What the hell would petrol supplies be doing in a dump like this? Ali! Ask this man where he got the petrol from."

Ali spoke to the old man again. They talked a long time together. At last Ali said: "He say he buy it long time ago, buy it from trader. Maybe he not tell truth, *effendi*. I think maybe he steal it."

"Tell him we will buy it from him pay him a good

price, if he will tell us where it came from." He said urgently: "Listen, Ali, I think he got it from the man we were looking for in the valley, the man with the two jeeps. Try and find out for me, understand?"

"*Ndio, effendi.*" Ali took the old man by the arm and walked him off a little way. When he came back he was grinning broadly. He explained. "This man say, *effendi*, other man leave petrol here ten days ago. Other man have two small trucks, with five men, one woman. Go north from here, say come back after ten days to get petrol. Man say he think you same man first, when he hear truck. Now he want to sell for you."

Metcalfe said delightedly: "It couldn't be better! We were right on every count. So he's on his way here after all."

"It's a good thing the old man is dishonest," Pender said. "He saw the opportunity to cash in on Dinesen's petrol and tried to take it. Otherwise, we should have believed the story the others told—that they hadn't been here." He added gravely: "There's only one thing I don't like about this. We are not so very far across country from the point on the main track where we were held up. It could easily be that the bandits came from here. If that is so, are we justified in assuming that Dinesen set them on to us to hold us up? He knew the route we were taking. And he might have needed a lot longer to find his precious loot—wouldn't do at all if we had been close behind him. Doesn't look very pretty, does it?"

"It doesn't," Metcalfe agreed grimly. "If he wants the gloves off, that's all right with me. The bastard!" he said. "This is where he gets paid off." He said to Ali: "Tell the old man we will buy the petrol from him, all of it."

Pender nodded. He said: "Harrar?"

"Exactly. With no supplies here, there's only one place he dare make for—Harrar. We'll go up there and wait for him."

"The old man will disappear, of course, so that he won't have to explain to Dinesen," Pender said, "but none the less, Dinesen will soon find out that we took his supplies. He will also deduce that we are waiting for him in Harrar as a result. What then?"

"Well, we have to assume that he's nearly out of fuel—hence the cache here. Harrar is the only possible place he can get fresh supplies, and there aren't more than four or five places there where he can buy. He'll probably send his two Africans in from the bush, a few miles out, to carry it to him, so as to avoid bringing the jeep into town. We'll put a man at each petrol point to watch for supplies being carried out of the town by hand—and another man on each road leading out; he can't possibly refuel without our knowledge. The rest is easy."

Pender said: "Check. Let's pick up this petrol and go."

They haggled with the old man over the price for a while, and finally bought it at ten dollars a tin. There were ten four-gallon cans, boxed in pairs. They piled in on to the truck, threw out their own empties, and moved on in the darkness. They found the rough and narrow track leading to Harrar, and gently eased the vehicle into the darkness. Pender said: "You know, I feel rather sorry about all this. Dinesen's a good fellow, and I have a sneaking regard for the work he's put in on this deal. Only thing that doesn't make sense is that he didn't ask his friend Ras Guggla not to disclose his identity. If the chief had not told us that it was Dinesen, the whole thing could have been kept secret."

"Yes." Metcalfe was silent for a moment. He said at

last: "There's a reason for that too, if we could only puzzle it out. He couldn't very well make a secret of it at Lakbar, or the chief, who's nobody's fool, would have realised that there was some monkey-business going on; he might then have refused to part with his pet prisoner. He knew we must have been fairly close behind him and couldn't afford to wait and argue. Remember, he obviously tried to make the deal appear like a last-minute idea; he got Franconi out ostensibly to repair a truck, and only suggested as he was leaving that it might be a good thing if he stayed with the party. That would also prevent trouble if, later on, the Ras were to find out about their digging up his territory; it wasn't until later that he knew where the stuff was hidden—it might just as easily have been cached right there under Ras Guggla's nose, so he had to establish some sort of title to Franconi before he went to work on him."

"So far," Pender said pessimistically, "we've had a tremendous amount of luck. It's going to break if he decides to make a fight for it; that is going to be very unpleasant indeed. And who the hell are the other Europeans? And the woman? Who, for God's sake, is the woman?"

Metcalfe said: "I think we can discount the woman. She is probably his current love-light; though it seems a bit hard on her to bring her out to this sort of country. Ah, well."

"With any luck we shall be in Harrar sometime tomorrow. We shall find out then."

But the road was bad. The truck bounced slowly over the hard earth, labouring in the deep gullies cut by last season's rain. There were two dry river-beds to cross and in one of them the truck was stuck fast, bedded down to the axles, while the Army sweated and laboured with poles and branches to lever it out. At the second river there was a steep far bank, and they toiled with their shovels for nearly four hours to cut a broad ramp gentle enough for the vehicle to climb. They stopped once in the midday heat to rest under a tree while the boiling engine cooled down, and they found water, cloudy and gypsum-sour, in a forty-foot well, cut deep into the earth and reinforced with rough-hewn logs. It was on the morning of the second day that they arrived at the ancient, walled and historic city of Harrar, where the tarmac road began, and the gracious white houses, built for the most part by the Italians during the occupation, were of smooth and solid stone, with colourful gardens and bright green lawns, with scarlet and purple bougainvillea hanging down from the walls and scented jasmine creeping over the verandahs. They placed a man at each of the three petrol-stores, another on the main road to the coast, and, as an added precaution, a fifth at the top of the steep mountain road that led down to Dire-Dawa.

Metcalfe said: "There's one place he won't go to, and that's Dire-Dawa; if he gets in there we shall have him bottled up—there's no other road out again. But we'll have a man there, just in case. Let's go and get a bath at the hotel."

Dirty, dusty, unshaved, their khaki bush-jackets soiled and their shorts rumpled and stained, they went to the Europa Hotel and wallowed in the luxury of soap and hot water. Within an hour they were on the main street again. "Ready for the fray," said Pender.

They sat in the shade of a bright umbrella on the quiet terrace of the hotel and sipped Dubonnet. The town was quiet and peaceful and the hours went slowly by. The Greek waiter brought them *meze* from time to time; small plates of spiced cheeses, pickled cucumbers, salted herring, prawns in rich gold mayonnaise, gherkins dipped in sour cream, small squares of pork wrapped in crisp bacon, and cashew nuts, pecan nuts, walnuts, groundnuts. They sipped and munched slowly, watching the idle town at leisure, enjoying the laziness and the warmth and the soft overall blanket of sloth.

It was towards the cool dusk of the evening that news of Dinesen came. Ali and Tadessa came running up, panting. The Greek waiter eyed them cautiously as they stopped at the terrace. Ali said: "*Hiku jeep, bwana!*" Metcalfe, leaning back with his chair at a sharp angle, crashed forward noisily and got to his feet. He said: "Good! Now we shall see. Where are they?"

Ali said excitedly: "*Tariku Dire-Dawa, effendi.*"

Pender said: "So that's it. They're on their way to the airport." He flung a note on to the table, and they ran quickly to the truck. Ali completed the story. The jeep, he said, had come from a side-street and turned on to the main road leading down the escarpment. There were three white men, a white woman, and two Africans aboard; one of the Africans was a Somali and the other—"*Sijui, bwana,*" he said, "maybe Arab, maybe *nusso-nusso*, a half-caste." Pender said: "That's Franconi, without a doubt. He'll look like a native after ten barefoot years in Lakbar." Ali told them that they had tried to stop the jeep to ask if they were the people the *bwana* was looking for, his friends from Lakbar, but the driver had accelerated and shot past them. It was very heavily loaded, he said, the passengers piled high one on top of the other, "Like a Mombasa bus," he said. This was maybe ten minutes ago.

Metcalfe said hurriedly: "Go and get all the others. Tell them to follow us down to Dire-Dawa on foot, on

94

the bus, any way they can; here's some money. Tell them to hurry, and you can look for the truck when you get there." He said to Pender: "We can catch them. Do you know the escarpment road?"

"Well enough. It's in a sorry state of repair."

"Well, get weaving. Bats out of hell. We've got to catch them before they reach the airport. Thank God it will soon be dark; there's no night flying at Dire-Dawa, no facilities for take-off, so they can't get out till morning unless they go now."

Pender had already started the engine and the truck was moving off as Metcalfe spoke; he leaped aboard and slammed the door; the truck gathered speed and a moment later they were hurtling down the main street at fifty, the horn blowing and the tyres screeching. A policeman ran out from the shade of a doorway to stop them, and as they shot past him shouted an oath, then stood and watched them disappear in a cloud of dust and finally went back to his piece of shade, under a tall blue jacaranda tree, to get on with his day-dreaming. The long stretch of road to the top of the escarpment was badly corrugated, and they hit fifty-five to keep the rhythmic bouncing of the wheels on the tops of the ridges; they sped along smoothly, hugging the curves between the tall and stately eucalyptus trees to their left and the rich black soil by the lake on their right. Pender was hanging grimly on to the wheel, leaning into the sharp curves, forcing the heavy truck faster and faster, his foot hard down on the floor-boards. The needle went up to sixty, sixty-five, lingered on seventy and passed it. Metcalfe said admiringly: "Not a bad truck. They can't do more than fifty in their jeep. Keep her going."

"Cross your fingers," Pender said. "The tyres won't stand this for long."

The road turned sharply to the right and they swung round the curve at sixty. Metcalfe suddenly sat bolt stiff in his seat and yelled: "Look out!" Pender braked hard as the road dropped away before them, and the truck skidded to the side of the road, swung back to centre, half turned, went broadside on for a yard or two, bounced once against the bank on their left, shuddered a moment and then shot smoothly forward again. To their right the broken tarmac stopped short and the mountain fell steeply away from them, down, far down into the valley below. Metcalfe saw the steep red slope, dotted with round white *tukuls*, the thatched little one-roomed houses of the farmers, and the long, fast-dropping stretch of black soil, richly covered with corn and vegetables and pasture, then closed his eyes. After a moment he said: "Just for my peace of mind; were we out of control then or not?"

Pender grinned. "Well, just a little bit perhaps. Not a very good road for speeding."

The truck swung round another bend fast, grazing the left-hand bank then swinging on to the centre again. It careened violently from side to side as the potted road twisted and turned; the needle stayed at fifty. Metcalfe said: "For God's sake, take it easy." The precipice on their right was steeper now, dropping down straight and sheer to the hard rock valley below. They took a hairpin bend at thirty, ran dead level for half a mile, gathering speed, then swung into the bends again at fifty. Miraculously, the ravine was now on the left, a sheer drop of a thousand feet; the sharp grey rocks cut their angles down to the wide dry river-bed below, interspersed with patches of red soil and green moss, and twisted roots clinging drunkenly along the face of the cliff; on their right, the precipice rose high above their heads, a solid wall of hard, grey granite, jutting

96

viciously out at them as they tore along. As the road twisted and writhed, they caught glimpses of the rest of the mountain range, green and blue and turning to grey in the distance where it met the slate of the evening sky, with the sun setting fast and red, now behind them, now in front. Faster and faster they drove, hurtling dangerously down into the infernal depths of the canyon, hauling the truck savagely round the bends. Pender said: "I wonder if it's worth it?" and they tore relentlessly on, forcing the road behind them with ever greater fury, spitting it out from under the rear wheels in a delirium of speed.

Metcalfe said: "He'll know for sure that we're close behind. He won't be wasting any time either. I wonder how the hell he got through Harrar without our seeing him?"

"Oh, one of the side-streets somewhere. We'd better make straight for the airport when we get there. We know he hasn't been able to refuel since Lakbar—and probably a long way before that—so he can't be going much further by truck."

"He can get all the petrol he wants in Dire-Dawa."

"But the only way out again is back through Harrar; he's in a cul-de-sac as far as road transport is concerned."

"That's true. The airport it is. I had a sneaking feeling all along that he'd use an aircraft on a job like this."

Suddenly Pender shouted "Hold tight!" and swung the truck in a violent tight curve, into the side of the road and out again to the middle. Metcalfe gripped the edges of his seat as the sheer drop of the cliff seemed to shoot suddenly in towards them, then swing violently back again. He caught a glimpse of something white

4* 97

and glistening on the road. He said: "What the hell was that?'

Pender said, a note of grimness creeping into his voice: "A broken bottle in the road; two or three of them by the looks of it. They're trying to hold us up." He slowed down to forty. "A burst front tyre on this road won't be much fun. He's beginning to play rough." Metcalfe looked across at the deep ravine below them and shuddered.

He said: "Take it easy till we hit the straight. I'll have that man's guts for a necktie."

They slowed down a little. The speedometer needle held steadily on forty as they twisted and turned with the road. They switched the headlights on. "Doesn't help much, but it will show up any more broken bottles."

The sun had dropped and dusk was falling as they came to the last long level stretch of road, patched and repaired now, leading into the town. Pender looked at his watch. It was six twenty-five. He said: "We made that in forty minutes. I used to take more than an hour over it last time I was in these parts. Straight to the airport?"

"Straight to the airport. I believe they're going to be just too late for a take-off. If that's their intention, that is."

They drove steadily through the pretty little town with its wide, clean streets and its Europe-in-Africa shops. Down the main street to the railway station, where the crowds were already gathering for the night train to Addis Ababa, then along the dusty road, tree-lined, which led out to the tiny aerodrome, they kept a sharp watch for any sign of the jeep. There were few cars or lorries here: an occasional taxi and one or two huge ten-ton Diesels up from Mogadiscio with loads of fruit and trade goods from the port, looking for return loads of skins or coffee. There were tables set on the terraces above the pavement where waiters lounged, serving the chattering French and Greek and Armenians, with white-robed *commis*, Nubians mostly, standing discreetly in the background. The glasses on the tables shone brightly with their wines: Moselle and Vermouth and Marsala and Anisette and cloudy Pernod. Pender said: "Be nice if we have to hang out here for a week or two. I have very pleasant memories of Dire-Dawa."

Metcalfe grinned. "This looks like the end of the chase. Couldn't be a better place. I've been thinking about this. We can't afford to ask the police for help if there's any difficulty, you know."

"Of course not. Too many complications if we get involved with authority. We can handle it. After all, Dinesen will be in just the same boat. He'll have a lot of explaining to do if it comes to a show-down. There's the airport."

The road came to a full stop half a mile ahead of them. A painted red-and-white barrier was across the road, a uniformed guard beside it. Pender shouted: "There they are!" and swung the truck off the road. A light plane, a Bonanza Cub, it looked like, was completing a turn at the end of the runway. Pender shouted: "Hang on!" and the truck fairly leaped across the shallow ditch, struggling up the other side, while the guard ran towards them, shouting. It bounced and lumbered over the grass verge, then shot rapidly on to the runway. Pender pressed his foot hard down as they hit the smooth grass surface of the landing-field. Some men came running out of the small white building that doubled for office and control tower as they gathered speed, shouting and waving their arms. Pender ignored them and drove furiously at the aircraft, now running fast across their bows five hundred yards ahead of them. Suddenly it began to climb, and as the truck swung into its path it rose steeply, banked into the wind, and roared away. Pender slowed the truck down to a halt and took out his cigarettes. Nobody spoke for a moment. Then Metcalfe said, savagely: "The bastard! The bloody bastard!" He climbed out of the truck and slammed the door behind him. Pender climbed out slowly, and they stood looking up at the aircraft, now disappearing into the horizon. Pender said placidly: "Well, that's that. What's the next move? I think a bottle of Scotch at the hotel would do us a lot of good."

Metcalfe said: "Let's get over to the office and see what we can find out."

Two airport police came running up, shouting angrily at them. Behind them, a plump and self-important little Englishman was indignantly calling to them. He said: "What the devil do you think you're doing? You can't do that sort of thing here. There might have been an accident."

Metcalfe turned to him. "I'm sorry," he said. "It seemed important to stop that plane. We wanted to speak to the pilot; he's a friend of ours."

The man said, not in the least mollified by Metcalfe's placatory tone; "I don't care what you wanted to do. You can't drive trucks all over my airport. I won't have it."

Metcalfe said again: "I'm sorry. It was really quite unforgivable. Do you know where they're going?"

The man said fussily: "I shall have to report this. Of course I know where they're going. I'm the Superintendent here. They're going to Addis Ababa."

"How many passengers?" said Pender, patiently.

"Only two. Contessa Mancini and her servant, that's

all. And now you really must get that truck off the runway; it constitutes an obstruction."

Metcalfe said urgently: "Are there any more aircraft leaving tonight? Or first thing in the morning?"

The little man said: "No, of course not, we have no night-landing facilities here. Shouldn't have let that aircraft go really—they're fifteen minutes over the limit as it is. In the morning there's Y 82 for Addis and the Army transport plane at midday. There's nothing else till Wednesday. Where do you want to go?"

Metcalfe said happily: "Nowhere at the moment. That was the wrong plane. We're trying to find a man called Dinesen; do you know him?"

"Never heard of him. And you'll have to get this truck out of the way. At once. I can't stand arguing here any longer."

They climbed back into the truck. Metcalfe said pleasantly: "Sorry to have been a nuisance. Come into the hotel for a drink later on if you've nothing better to do."

An hour later they were sitting comfortably in the dimly lit lounge of the Eden Hotel on the other side of the town at the bottom of the escarpment road. The barrier across the road was closed. They were bottled-up for the night.

Dire-Dawa is a cul-de-sac. It lies, a tight and pretty little town, deep in the hollow formed by the rocky foot-hills below the Harrar escarpment. There is only one road in or out, and as dusk falls each evening a barrier is placed across the road, a knife-rest of timber and tangle barbed wire—a left-over from the old days of the Italian occupation and now a safeguard against the intrusion by night of the thieves and robbers who still infest the mountains. The verandah of the big hotel, with its yellow-washed walls and bright hanging creeper, with hibiscus and poinsettia and frangi-pani coolly colouring the garden, faces across the dusty main road just at the barrier post.

Metcalfe said, putting down his pewter tankard, the frosted condensation streaking the dull grey metal at his touch: "I wish we'd waited to bring the boys down; we could have had them out scouring the town for him; we dare not go to the police on a matter like this."

Pender said: "Well, I rather enjoy the pleasant expectancy. He's in the town somewhere and he can't get out. We'll find him. It's not easy to hide a jeep in a small place like this. I'm a bit worried, though, that there were no other charter planes on the airstrip, but it's a reasonable deduction that one will soon be coming to fetch him. If our reckoning is as correct as we think, then he only came this way at all in order to fly out."

"Or to get petrol. And if he does that, he's got to pass this barrier to get out again. One of us will have to sleep by the truck tonight; better still, we can both sleep in it and take turns at watch. Can't afford to give him a head start this time, as we did in Harrar."

"All the same, I can't believe it's going to be quite as easy as all that. The idea of Dinesen allowing himself to be trapped like this . . . well . . . seems strange, to say the least of it." He sounded worried.

Metcalfe got up and walked across to the bar. He said: "Two beers, please." While the barman filled the tankards, he asked:

"You didn't see a jeep come into town this evening, did you? The road's in full view of the bar. Came in from Harrar some time about six."

The waiter said: "Yes, sir. A party came in from

Somalia. A gentleman named Dinesen. He came in a few minutes ago. A friend of yours, sir?"

Metcalfe was conscious that his mouth was hanging open. He stammered: "Dinesen . . . here . . . in the hotel?"

"Yes, sir. Shall I get his room number for you?"

"Good God! Good God!" He stood staring at the barman for a moment. He said again: "Here, at the hotel? Are you sure?"

"Yes, sir. He's staying here." The waiter turned and gave an order to one of the boys; the *commi* nodded and ran across to the reception desk. The waiter said, smiling: "The boy will bring you the room number. One dollar and a half, sir, please."

Metcalfe paid and took the drinks back to the table. He said: "In Heaven's name . . . I can't believe it."

Pender was sitting bolt upright in his chair. He said: "Did I hear aright? He's here, in the hotel?"

"That's what he said. But it's impossible; it doesn't make sense."

Pender said philosophically: "Well, let's go and see. Let's look at the back of the hotel first."

"What for?"

"The jeep."

The native *commi* came running up, handed them a slip of paper, smiling, bowing. Metcalfe read: "Room twenty-seven." He said: "Let's go."

Chapter Seven

THEY went out into the garden, where the honeysuckle hung and the bright hibiscus was a vivid pattern in red against the sombre greens of the shrubbery, and round to the parking space at the back of the hotel.

The jeep was there, dusty, grimy, an oil stain marring one of the tyres, down on its springs with the weight of its heavy load. Everything was covered with the fine red dust of the Lakbar plateau. They stood and stared at it for a moment.

"I don't like it," said Pender. "It's too damn easy. I don't like it."

"Well," Metcalfe said grimly, "Room twenty-seven. Come along."

They walked quickly back into the hotel, climbed the wide, carpeted stairs and stood looking down the corridor. Pender read out the numbers, "twenty-three . . . twenty-four . . . twenty-five—it's the first room round the corner."

They almost ran to the door, hesitated, then knocked. They stood staring at each other. A voice said: "Come in."

Pender whispered: "That's him." Then, irritably: "What the hell am I whispering for?" They flung open the door.

Dinesen, neat and lean and bathed and looking extremely elegant, was sitting in a rattan chair over by the window, an open book on his knee, a glass of whisky in his hand. He stood up and walked towards them, beaming, holding out his hand. He said:

"Come on in. Hullo Ian, Harry. Nice to see you. Won't say it's a surprise, but it's delightful to see you both looking so well. Did you have a good trip? Have a whisky. Or would you rather have beer?"

Metcalfe said angrily: "Well, of all the damned effrontery!"

Dinesen interrupted him. "Yes, I know. I suppose I owe you an apology . . ."

"Apology! Of all the damned impertinence . . ."

Dinesen said sympathetically: "Yes, I know. But do come in and sit down. It won't do you any good at all to stand there looking furious. Have a whisky; it'll cheer you up. Takes the edge off the point of defeat, don't you think? And you must be tired after your journey."

"Defeat! I'd have you know . . ."

"Sit down." Dinesen was smoothly insistent. "First recover your habitual good temper and then we can have a nice little chat." He pushed a chair forward.

Pender, smiling quietly to himself, sat on the edge of the bed. He said mildly: "You must admit, it's . . . surprising to find you here. You're supposed to be having your appendix out. Again."

Dinesen grinned quickly. "A necessary subterfuge. I must confess I'd forgotten you knew about the first time. Unpardonable. Whisky or beer?"

Pender said: "We may as well be comfortable. I'll have Scotch, thank you."

"Ian?"

Metcalfe said sullenly: "All right. But you've a lot of explaining to do."

Dinesen said: "That's better. So much easier to discuss these things in comfort." He took two glasses from the tray on the cane table. "You see, I was expecting you"—and poured out the drinks. He handed them round.

Metcalfe said: "Well, where is he?"

"Franconi? He's in town. Waiting for you two, as a matter of fact."

"And the money?"

Dinesen smiled. "That was a clever move on your part. How did you know it was down in the valley? I left no tracks near the road."

Pender said: "We saw the sun on your binoculars. That showed us you had gone westward; we went the same way. Once we came across your tracks, the rest was easy."

A shadow of irritation crossed Dinesen's deeply lined features. He said: "A pity. Much tidier if you hadn't seen me, and I'd have been in Somalia by now. I'd have been there anyway if you hadn't found my petrol supplies; that made things very awkward for a moment. I realised, of course, that you were forcing me to go to Harrar; would have been tricky if we'd met there. Sound strategy on your part. Very sound."

Metcalfe asked again: "Franconi?"

"I told you. Right here in town, waiting to be picked up. He's yours whenever you want him. Probably getting drunk as fast as he can. Poor fellow's delighted to be free again—he'll be overjoyed to see you."

"And the money?"

"Oh, that." Dinesen drew on his cigarette for a moment. He went on: "As I recall our conversation in London, the prime interest in this affair was Franconi. The money was only of secondary importance?"

"And I still want it. If you don't mind."

Dinesen said thoughtfully: "Of course. And since you know that I found it, there is no point in my denying it. You do not, however, know how much there was. It is perfectly feasible to suppose that Hewitt had already used up—shall we say *half* the money?—before

106

he was murdered. Or, if we stretch a point, we could suppose that he had already cached the whole lot some-where—that I found only his stores and his records: the papers, remember that Sir John was so anxious to have?"

Metcalfe said heavily: "So that's it. That's the game."

"That's the game. Precisely."

Pender said quickly: "You're still a British subject. Apart from the moral implications, which, of course, are not of great moment to you, there is the question of the law."

Dinesen looked at him coldly. He said: "Perhaps my morals do not run in such smooth grooves as your own. I will not say that they are irreproachable . . . how-ever, that is all beside the point. Legally, in England, you can do nothing. Do you understand that— *nothing*? If I choose to hand you an empty tin trunk and say to you, 'This is what I found at Lakbar. Isn't it a pity there's nothing in it?' what could you do about it? I tell you—*nothing*. You wouldn't believe me, of course: but could you find proof that I had . . . stolen?" He poured out a fresh drink and said lightly: "I hold all the cards; *all* of them. I have Franconi, I have the papers, and I have . . . whatever money there was."

Metcalfe said stubbornly: "A quarter of a million pounds."

Dinesen raised a delicate brown hand. "A quarter of a million? Surely not. Shall we say . . . ten or fifteen thousand? That's quite a lot of money."

Pender said: "In exchange for the remainder of the money, just what do we get? Assuming, of course, that you expect us to go back and tell Sir John that we only found fifteen thousand of his quarter million. A likely story."

"You get Franconi; you get the papers; and, if you want a face-saver, a few thousand pounds in cash."

Metcalfe said: "And if we refuse?"

Dinesen said: "Then you get nothing. You can go and tell them in London that I hi-jacked Franconi from under your noses; that I will deliver him, in exchange of course for a consideration, when I am ready; and that the Italian Government will no doubt put them in the picture when, and if, they feel so inclined."

"You realise you won't be safe in England if you do that?"

"Safe?" He repeated scornfully. "Safe? You cannot touch me there. Besides," he added lightly, "my villa at Rapallo is a far more pleasant place to live, anyway."

Pender said: "Where is the money now? Purely as a point of academic interest, of course."

"It's safe. Perfectly safe. Resign yourself to the idea that you have not the slightest hope of seeing it. Ever."

Pender thought, *he's very sure of that*. The germ of an idea was slowly forming in the back of his mind. He said casually: "You've been very lucky. Who was the woman in your party?"

Dinesen said easily: "A friend. You know how dull a safari like this can be; just a friend. I dropped her off in Harrar."

Pender noticed that Dinesen's eyes were very alert. He said: "In short, you are offering us Franconi and the papers—in exchange for what?"

"As a gift. I've finished with Franconi, and the papers are of no interest to me. After all, you have nothing to offer in exchange, have you? You can't hold me here by force, and you won't attempt to . . . shall I say, clear me? . . . in London. I wouldn't ask you to. I will tell you where Franconi is, and here are the

108

papers." He walked across the room and took a mildewed leather briefcase from the cupboard. He threw it casually on the bed. He said: "I've looked through them, of course. Nothing there to interest me, but I can well understand Sir John's anxiety that they should not fall into unauthorised hands; they're political dynamite. But unfortunately," he sighed, "I cannot bring myself to sell them to you. So accept them as a gesture of good will."

"And Franconi?"

"He's in the Café Olympus, getting drunk. He can't move from there because he has neither papers nor money." He smiled apologetically. "I said you'd pay his bar bill when you came to fetch him. He won't give you any trouble: he's quite an inoffensive little man."

Metcalfe said: "What's all this about the Italian Government?"

"If you take Franconi, then they have no interest in the affair. They know nothing of it."

"And the two Europeans who were with you?"

Dinesen smiled. "Yes, of course, one of your boys spotted them in Harrar." He poured himself a drink. He said: "Forgive me if I boast a little. I wasn't sure that I'd get Franconi. I brought two other guides along just in case."

Metcalfe frowned. He said: "But that's impossible, no one else knows about it except the two Italians in jail and the two in America."

Dinesen said, turning away: "More things in heaven and earth, my dear fellow. Finish your whisky and have another."

It seemed to Metcalfe that there was nothing more to be said, that there was nothing much he could do. He took the briefcase and moved towards the door. He said stuffily, conscious of the insufficiency of the remark: "This is not the last of this affair, by any means."

Dinesen said: "Won't you finish your drink first?"

Metcalfe walked back to the table. He took his whisky and drank it slowly. He said: "One of these days, Dinesen, I shall pay you back for this. I don't like being made a fool of. You'll hear more of this, I promise you."

Dinesen smiled. He said: "I am not alarmed. I've been ahead of you on every single move. Don't take it so much to heart, my dear fellow. After all, you've got what you came for. You really can't object to my being, perhaps, a little overpaid for my services to you. Resign yourself; it'll make our future meetings so much more pleasant.

They left the room in silence. Metcalfe suppressed a desire to slam the door behind him, and they walked slowly down the stairway into the lounge and out into the moonlight. They stood for a moment looking up at the stars.

Metcalfe said, at last: "He's right. He holds all the cards. There's nothing we can do." The palsy of his emotion still gripped him. He repeated angrily: "There's nothing we can do."

"It's not too bad, actually," Pender said, consoling him. "We have the papers and we shall shortly have Franconi. As he said, the money is of secondary importance."

"That may be so. I still don't like being made a fool of. We've done what we came to do . . . and yet . . . I feel as though we've failed absolutely. It's a let-down. It's exasperating."

"Exactly. Exasperating, but no more. Anyway, I have an idea. I am anxious to see this Franconi."

"What's on your mind?"

"He was too sure that the money was safe, far too sure. It made me think of something. May be a wild-goose chase, but I'd like to see our fussy little friend at the airport again."

They walked into the town and found the Café Olympus without difficulty. The street was full now of dinner-time strollers enjoying the coolness of the night. On the dull grey verandah of the café with its bright green trellis, a bent old man, brown as an African but bearded and long-haired, dressed in new and crumpled khaki, was pouring *rezina* into his glass with an unsteady hand. As they climbed the steps of the café, he put down his bottle and watched them anxiously, his wild, frightened eyes staring and his fingers playing nervously with the edge of his jacket. The waiter was eyeing him with distaste. Metcalfe went straight to him. He said:

"Franconi?"

"Si, signori." The little man stumbled to his feet and spoke to them rapidly in Italian.

"I didn't kill the officer," he said, almost in tears.

"Signori, I swear it was not me. . . . I could do nothing . . . the soldiers . . . they were deserters, I had no control over them. The man Ricci, the sergeant, he was the one . . . you must believe me, signori . . ." He glanced apprehensively over his shoulder. He was stammering with anxiety. Metcalfe thought, *This was once an officer in the Blackshirt Battalions.* He said brusquely, in carefully correct Italian:

"I am not interested. You can tell your story in London. My job is to get you there, nothing more." He added: "Are you hungry? Have you eaten?"

Franconi said apologetically, trying hesitantly to risk a smile, only his lips moving, his eyes worried and frightened: "No, signore, I take only a little to drink. Signor Dinesen told me to wait here. . . . I have no money. . . . I did not want to eat, in case . . ." He stammered apologetically: "Please believe me, signori, I am not an assassin. I am just an Italian, a simple man. . . . I am not even a good soldier. . . . I swear to you that I did not kill the officer. Signor Dinesen did not believe me, but he told me . . . he said that perhaps *you* would."

Pender could not restrain a smile. He said gently, his Italian not quite up to the effort: "You have nothing to fear from us if your own conscience is . . . clear. It is up to you to . . . Anyway, sit down and have some food." He called for the menu. He said: "You speak English?"

"No, signori."

Pender caught Metcalfe's eye. He said in English: "He's not likely to, I suppose. I want to find out about Dinesen's girl friend. I have a hunch she may be useful to us."

They ordered a meal: a salad of langouste, followed by veal cutlets covered in breadcrumbs and fried in butter, with sauté potatoes and asparagus and a litre of a light red wine. Franconi watched the arrival of the food hungrily. He was a nervous little man, the strain of his ten years' sojourn in Lakbar showing plainly on his wrinkled face. He looked like a biblical prophet. Pender said in English: "I wonder if he knows anything about our trouble with Dinesen?"

Metcalfe pondered a moment. He said, at last: "No, I don't imagine so. Why?"

Pender did not answer. He said instead, in Italian, speaking as casually as possible, making conversation:

"A very attractive woman, that. The one with our friend Dinesen."

Franconi grinned nervously. "Si, signori." He nodded his head vigorously. "A very beautiful woman.

We did not have such as that one in Lakbar." He looked at them anxiously, gulping his food hurriedly.

Pender refilled his empty glass. He said carefully: "You must realise, Franconi, that we are merely your . . . escort. We have to take you back to London, where your case can be heard. Meanwhile, we may as well be friends."

Franconi nodded eagerly. He was pathetically grateful. Pender went on: "A very beautiful woman. I don't remember her name."

Franconi said: "Her name? Contessa Mancini. Lala Mancini. A very beautiful woman."

Metcalfe looked up sharply. "So?" he said. "The woman on the charter plane?"

"Precisely. For once, two and two actually do make four." Pender spoke in Italian again. "Do you know what part of Italy she comes from?"

Franconi said: "Yes, of course. She talked a lot to me; she is very gracious. She comes from Trieste."

"Are you sure?"

Franconi shrugged. "You know, signori, how the women of Trieste talk; their accent is unmistakable." He hesitated. "I heard her talk about Rome, but she is not from that place; she is a *Triestina.*" He spread his hands apologetically. "I do not wish you to think that I listen too much to the conversation of others, but . . . it is so long since I heard my own language . . . the beautiful accents of my own country . . ." He said quickly: "The Italian language in the mouth of a beautiful woman . . . it is so very long . . ."

Pender said: "What did she say about Rome?"

Franconi lifted his shoulders. "I do not remember, signori. But sometimes, at night . . ." he stopped, embarrassed. Then he said: "At night we slept on the ground by the jeep. Signor Dinesen and the signora slept a little to one side. Sometimes, I could not sleep . . . after all those years . . ." He hesitated again. "Can you understand, signori, just to hear them talking? Sometimes I went over and listened to them . . . so long since I heard my language . . . and such a truly beautiful woman. . . ." He watched their faces for any sign of reproach. He said: "I do not like to listen to the conversation of others, but . . . can you understand? I did not wish to do wrong."

Metcalfe said gravely: "I understand. A beautiful woman . . . so far from your home. Try and remember what they were talking about when they spoke of Rome. Did they mention money?"

Franconi looked at them thoughfully for a moment; he frowned slightly. He said: "I think perhaps she spoke of taking some money there. I do not know, signori."

Metcalfe hesitated before making up his mind. Then he said: "You may as well know this; the money which was recovered belongs to the British Government. Dinesen has stolen it."

Franconi said: "Ah. . . ." He stared at them for a minute. It was as though he were horrified to find himself once more among thieves. He said slowly: "I see. Forgive me, signori, but it is good to know that so much money is a temptation also to others. . . . I am not really a thief, signori. Perhaps now you can understand how strong that temptation is?"

Metcalfe nodded grimly. He said: "It is my intention to return that money to London. If you overheard anything that will help me to recover it . . . I ask you to tell me." He added quickly: "I can make you no promises, understand, none at all. But I can say, I think, that your behaviour at this time will prove or disprove your good faith."

Franconi thought for a while, playing with his wine-glass. Pender fancied he could see the spirit slowly returning into the pathetic creature who sat drinking his wine so nervously before them, as though the fear of his past and future were always with him. At last he said:

"There are many things, signori, that I heard; at the time they meant nothing, but if it is true that Signor Dinesen wished to steal the money also. . . ." Pender noticed an almost unconscious accent on the "also"; was it a subconscious effort to excuse, if not condone, the original theft? "If he wished to steal it . . . one night I heard them say that it would be safe in Rome . . . the signora said she would be there the night before the feast of St Christopher but that she would stop at her own home for a day or two first. Then . . . then they began . . . to make love, and I went away and slept."

Pender held his glass up to the light and watched the smooth red translucence. He fancied that he could see the picture clearly; Dinesen and the beautiful Triestina lying side by side in the cool night, with the black shadow of the giant thorn-tree above them against the purple sky and the saffron stars, and the smoke from their cigarettes curling up silently above them. They would be lying on their backs, or perhaps Dinesen would be propped up on one elbow, the better to admire the soft blond hair and the blue pale eyes of his companion, while in subdued tones they coolly disposed of a quarter of a million pounds together. The woman's soft hair would be a bewitching carpet under her head, and her pale Triestina eyes, with all the history of Hun and Tartar and Slav and Latin in their wide steadiness, would wear that distant, calculating look, but still be responsive, instantly responsive, to the light touch of Dinesen's delicate hands on her slim white body under the coarse grey blanket where every sliding contact with the rough woven wool would be a caress, its coarseness exciting her, stirring her deepest animal emotions, feline with masochism, working its secret fires deep inside her, stirring her loins. They would talk softly about the money, until at last the woman would throw away her cigarette and say urgently: "Love me, Petar, love me . . ." and Dinesen would smile and flick his cigarette away into the darkness where Franconi was standing in the shadows of a bush, watching, listening, dreaming of "*paese mio*" and trembling with fear and emotion. After a little while he would steal, like a native, in accustomed barefoot silence, back to his blanket and tremble, blinking up at the stars.

Franconi said hesitantly, embarrassed: "I did not pay too much attention. But if they were planning to steal the money, I think the Signora will take it to Rome."

Chapter Eight

As Sir John walked into his office in St. James's Street at ten o'clock on a fine sunny morning, Claire met him at the doorway, a telegram in her hand. She said: "A telegram in from Dire-Dawa. Ian Metcalfe wants some help. Something seems to have gone wrong." She handed the wire to her boss. Sir John frowned as he read:

"*Have Franc friend and papers. Dinesen and group of presumed Italians have removed secondary effects. Am following up. Meet me Eden Hotel Rome earliest with all repeat all local information on Dinesen. Urgent.*

"*Metcalfe.*"

He handed back the paper and said: "Come inside."

They went into the long, blue-carpeted office. The Colonel sat down and asked: "Have you any idea just what this is all about?"

Claire said: "Yes, I think I have. At least . . . you remember that Dinesen dropped out at the last moment because of an operation for appendicitis? Well, Ian told me at the time that he was . . . well, half glad, in a way, because he didn't quite trust him with all that money involved. Now it looks as though he was right. It looks as if Dinesen has managed to join them and has got his hands on the money. If that is so, and he made off to Europe with it, it's logical to suppose that Ian would want to chase him and recover it. That means they are probably going to Dinesen's Rome address, which we know, of course. The problem is, does 'presumed Italians' mean an official body or not?"

Sir John said: "Yes . . . quite. Yes, that would certainly account for his wanting this information." He paused for a moment, staring down at his desk. He said: "Do you feel happy about going there yourself?"

Claire smiled. She said diffidently: "As a matter of fact I'm due for leave in a few days, and I'd intended to go to Italy anyway." She hesitated. "We rather thought it might coincide with Ian's return; he was going to stop off and meet me in Rome so that we could have a few days together." She said apologetically: "You know how it is."

The Colonel stood up and walked over to the big window. He said:

"I see. In that case you'd better get all the information you can and fly out there right away. I think he's worrying unnecessarily about the money, if he already has Franconi and the papers. After all, those are the things we really want. However, he won't want to come back and tell us that Dinesen has made off with it—if it's only a matter of personal pride. He can be very pig-headed at times. He's right, of course." He said sharply: "You'll want all the background stuff you can find about Dinesen: his address, the clubs he belongs to, his favourite haunts—all that sort of thing. Send a cable to our office in Rome before you go and find out if the Italian Government knows anything about this; if they do, tell Ian to drop it at once and come straight back. Otherwise . . ." The Colonel broke off. He went on abruptly:

"Get in touch with a man called Mendels in Rome. An American. He's not attached to us or anything, but he's interested on behalf of the State Department in the Major Hewitt side of the case—the extradition business. His address is in the files somewhere. He did some work for us during the war. I must confess I don't like the phrase about the Italians. Pity Metcalfe wasn't more explicit . . . Anyway, if they're not officially involved, see Mendels; put him in the picture."

Claire was making notes in shorthand. The Colonel said:

"Yes . . . see Mendels. Might be able to help quite a bit. Keep in touch with us here through our Rome office."

Claire said: "If I hand over right away, I should be able to get away tomorrow. Can you spare me?"

"Yes, I suppose so. Make a report to Major Reynolds before you go, and we'll get Scotland Yard working on it just in case he turns up here—wouldn't put it past him."

He lit a cigarette. He said slowly: "Give my regards to Mendels, and drop the whole thing at once if the Italian Government is involved. And get back here as soon as you reasonably can."

He smiled. He said: "After all, I need you too, you know."

The following afternoon as the aircraft droned persistently over the mountains, the snow-topped scars of the Dolomites thrusting awkwardly through the smooth white mist of the clouds, Claire sat back comfortably in her lounge chair reading through the mass of papers which she had collected. The clouds were like cotton-wool. The engines whined incessantly till at last they bumped down and lumbered heavily over the bright green Roman grass at Ciampino airport.

Metcalfe was there to meet her. He threw his arms

around her, grinning delightedly, the sun shining warmly on them.

He said: "This makes everything all right again. Come and have a glass of Frascati and I'll tell you all about it."

He took her bag, and arm in arm they walked over to the restaurant. They sat down in a corner and ordered drinks. He said:

"You have never looked more lovely."

"That," Claire said, "can wait till later. Tell me all about Dinesen."

Metcalfe frowned. He said: "Have a cigarette. First of all, this appendicitis story was a lot of eye-wash. As far as I can see, he'd already made plans, once he had the details of our own party, to go out there and get this stuff for himself. He wanted only the money, of course, just as I feared. By flying out as soon as we were on the way, he got there ahead of us, walked into Lakbar as large as life, picked up Franconi, dug up the loot, and if by the merest chance we hadn't seen the sun on his binoculars a few miles away while he was watching us, we should never have seen him again. Anyway . . . we chased him, and finally caught up with him in Dire-Dawa. He had the effrontery to admit that he'd stolen the money—couldn't very well deny it, come to think of it—and told us quite brazenly that it was hidden safely away."

The waiter brought them a bottle of wine, hovering, fussing about them.

He went on: "But this is the point: as we tore hell for leather into Dire-Dawa, a Bonanza aircraft took off with a woman named Lala Mancini on board. Dinesen doesn't know . . . Did you say something?"

Claire shook her head. "It'll wait."

Metcalfe thought for a moment, *Italy is full of beauti-*

ful women. None is as beautiful as my Claire. He looked around him at the other women in the restaurant, as though to justify his claim. He thought, *She's the most beautiful woman in the room.* He felt a little smug about it. Claire said: "Well, go on with your story."

He said: "Well, Dinesen doesn't know that we know this, but Lala Mancini is apparently his latest *amore*, and Franconi overheard them planning to bring the money to Rome. I think the assumption is a fair one that she was bringing it here ahead of him; he was so damned sure that we should never see it again, that no other explanation will do. The money had already left the country when we met him; that's why he could be so complacent about it. Obviously, he will follow her here, and what we have to do now is to get hold of her before he arrives. I don't know," he said, "if we dare approach the police about this Mancini woman. There may be fifty Lala Mancinis in Rome."

Claire shook her head decisively. She said: "Not necessary. We know all about her. The reports I have brought for you to read are full of her name—part of the Dinesen background."

"Do you have her address?"

"Of course. And you know what? It's the same as the address we have in Rome for Dinesen himself. She lives most of the time in Trieste, but her Rome residence is in Via Nerone—a parental palazzo of some sort. The family is old and highly respected, but completely impoverished. Except, that is, for Lala Mancini. It seems she has provided the funds for some of Dinesen's latest exploits—black market, mostly. The Rome office told us about it; the Colonel nearly had a fit when he saw their cable."

Metcalfe nodded grimly. He said: "I could have told him. He seemed to think——"

"Well, actually, there's nothing, should we say . . . vicious about him. It's just that by our standards he's probably a bit, well, amoral. He did some very fine work for us during the war. And you must admit he's a very nice man in many ways."

Metcalfe said nothing.

Claire said: "Well, there's a whole lot of stuff for you to look through. The Italian Government knows nothing about this, according to the Rome office report—I'll show you a copy soon; but we have to go and see a man called Mendels, an American——"

"Joe Mendels?"

"You know him?"

"Well, bless my soul. Yes, of course I know him. He was with OSS during the war, pulled off some very fancy jobs with the Yugoslav Partisans up around Trieste. Well, bless my soul," he said, "Joe Mendels in Rome. Ha! Damn fine fellow. Knows all the answers. Always got everything at his fingertips. You know where to find him?"

"Of course I do. He lives in Via San Basilico, just near Via Veneto." She said thoughtfully: "You know, this is going to be very tricky if the police find out what we're up to; they're more anxious to get Franconi than we are. I hope there's not going to be any trouble getting him out of the country now that he's here. Incidentally, how on earth did you manage to get him in without any papers?"

Metcalfe grinned easily. He said: "Simple. I just got into uniform, dressed him up as my batman, and wrote myself a Movement Order on War Office paper. Said we were with the Military Attaché's Office. Easy. Everybody was most co-operative when I arrived."

Claire smiled. "As long as the Attaché doesn't get to hear about it."

Metcalfe said briefly: "He won't. Let's go and see Harry Pender."

They took a taxi over to the hotel. Pender was in his room studying a map of the city. He smiled happily at Claire as they came in.

He said: "Nice to see you again. Good trip?"

Claire nodded. She said: "So our friend Dinesen made a fool of you after all. What are our chances of paying him back?"

Pender rubbed his hands together. He said: "Pretty good, I think, pretty good. Have a glass of wine and we'll have a council of war."

Metcalfe kicked off his shoes and stretched out lazily on the bed. Claire sat beside him. He said:

"My idea is this. We go over to Dinesen's house, or Lala Mancini's house, whichever you like to call it. . . ." Pender raised an eyebrow.

Metcalfe continued: "Same house, apparently. We'll go through the files as soon as we've had a drink, but it looks as though both live in the same place. Well, we look at the house and see if this woman has arrived yet. She probably hasn't. We know from Franconi that she was going to spend one day in Trieste and then come straight here with the money. In theory, at least, that means she ought to be here tomorrow, though we don't know how long she had to wait for a main-line plane after she left her charter aircraft in Africa. If she hasn't arrived yet, we break in, hide ourselves away like any professional thugs, and then wait for her to get installed before we disclose ourselves; go through her baggage, pick up the cash, and beat it. It's as simple as that. If she has arrived . . . well, we shall find her there, that's all. Lock her up or something while we search the house, I suppose. We shall have this advantage: she doesn't know us from

Adam, but we have a pretty good description of her. Once we are inside the house the rest ought to be easy. Ought to be. Any comments?"

Pender said: "No help at all from the local authorities. What we have to do must be done quickly and quietly; then out of the country at top speed before she pulls any strings to have us stopped. She may have friends in the police."

Claire nodded gravely. She said: "Exactly. She has friends in all the high places. Getting clear is going to be the hardest part of it."

"All right, Claire. You take care of a quick way out of the country. Think up something which doesn't involve Customs inspections and all that nonsense. That's your pigeon."

"What happens if the house is full when you and Harry break in?"

"That's a problem that will resolve itself when we've taken a look at the place."

"And supposing that she hasn't arrived when you get there. She turns up the next day accompanied by several others—what then? And don't forget you may find yourselves confronted with half a dozen Neapolitan thugs when you do get in."

Metcalfe shrugged. "A problem we shall have to face if and when it arises. Surprise is supposed to count for something in these matters."

Pender said: "Remember Dinesen's somewhat cryptic remarks about the friends who were with him in Ethiopia? I wasn't very happy about it at the time."

"Well?"

"Could be the whole mob is there."

Metcalfe said grimly: "We're going to get that money—that's all there is to it. Now. Let's see where the house is."

Claire took the map from Pender and spread it on the bed. Her silver pencil traced delicate lines across it for a moment. She said: "Here . . . here, somewhere, Via Nerone . . . number 217a, must be about there." She drew a small circle on the map. She said: "A museum right beside it, here somewhere . . . it's apparently one of those big old mansions, half fallen down, stands back from the road a bit . . . must be just here, opposite this hotel."

Metcalfe said. "Hm. I think I know the area. There's a row of shops and a small *pensione* just nearby. We can stay in the hotel to watch the place. Better get over there and have a look."

Pender said: "I went out and hired a car while you were meeting Claire."

"Good."

"What about Franconi?"

Metcalfe said: "We'll leave him in the hotel here. He's quite safe in his room—he won't dare move in case the local police nab him. He's desperately anxious to make an honest woman of himself, so he's very much on our side."

Claire said: "What about Mendels?"

"Ah, yes. Harry, you go and make a recce of the house; Claire and I will go and see Joe. He's an American friend of ours. Going to help out if necessary. Take the car, and watch for us there in about an hour."

Harry finished off his drink. He grinned at Claire and left.

As soon as he had gone, Metcalfe put his arms around Claire. He said: "Nice to see you here, my love."

She touched his cheek with the tips of her long fingers. She said: "We mustn't waste time, you know."

"I know."

She kissed him quickly and disengaged herself. He said: "All right, let's go and see Joe Mendels. You'll like him."

They finished their drinks and went out into the bright yellow glare of the Roman evening. The sun shone back at them off the white stone walls of the buildings. They walked round to the Via Basilica, arm in arm, like lovers, enjoying the sunlight and the music and the rapid swish of the shiny sports cars as they swept down the Via Veneto, and the brightly-covered tables on the pavement, and the green shade of the big chestnut trees, and the strident shouting of the newsboy at the kiosk on the corner; enjoying most of all the feeling of closeness. Metcalfe thought, *This is how it ought to be, always, close beside her*, and the longing for her was sharp and pressing within him.

Claire squeezed his arm. She said: "We're here."

Metcalfe pushed the button over the card on the big grey portal that said, simply: "*Joseph Mendels, Export.*"

He grinned at Claire and said: "Export, indeed."

The door opened with a buzz and they climbed the dark stairway to the second landing. Mendels met them at the door. He said: "Hi there, come on in. Long time no see, Ian."

Metcalfe said: "Joe Mendels. Claire Stone. Nice to see you again."

They shook hands. Mendel's eyes lingered on Claire. He said: "Hullo. What'll it be? I got rye, bourbon, scotch, gin, rum . . . the works. Or you want some of this domestic wine?"

They walked into the spacious and gracious living-room. Mendels said: "Make yourselves at home, fellas. Your cable was very discreet, but I gathered you've got some new angle on the Hewitt case. Things have been moving pretty fast these last few days. What did you want to know?" He was putting glasses and bottles from the darkly polished walnut commode on to a big silver tray.

Metcalfe said: "The boss said, 'Put him in the picture.' It was like this. . . ."

They sat and drank, and Metcalfe outlined the story of their chase in Ethiopia. Mendels said nothing. From time to time Claire made a point or two, and he watched her with a sharp, calculating stare. She thought, *This man has a good brain.* He was a man of middle age, slight, wiry, nearly bald, elegant in the Roman fashion. His forehead gave the impression that he ought to be wearing shell-rimmed spectacles. He said at last:

"Well, there's the heck of a lot I can add to what you've told me. First of all . . . Lala Mancini."

He walked over to a cabinet, intricately carved and polished to a soft and mellow lucidity; his fingers lingered on it for a moment, lovingly. He took out a file and extracted a couple of photographs. Tossing them on the desk, he said:

"There she is. As you see, a pretty nice-looking gal. But don't let those big blue eyes fool you. She was the wife of a Fascist big-wig in Mussolini's time, when she made a heap of money out of her husband's ministerial position. Then when Marshal Badoglio took over, she worked first for the Germans and then for us. During this time her husband disappeared, and popular rumour is that she killed him." He shrugged his shoulders indifferently. "That may or may not be true. Later on she was tried on charges of collaboration with the Germans, but the principal witness against her, who was in jail, was found one morning dead in his cell." He shrugged again. "Possibly she had nothing to do with it. Then there were some smuggled diamonds, quite recently; they arrested a man—a Greek skipper —for safe-keeping, and he was to testify that he had handed them over to her for disposal on the local black market. He escaped from prison a few days later and hasn't been seen since; just a messenger, of course, but one who could easily have put *la bella Mancini* behind bars for a long time. She's currently living with your friend Dinesen, but he's been out in East Africa for the last six months or so, and there is at least a suspicion that he sent the diamonds in the first place from the mines in Shinyanga—stolen, of course. And when they took the Greek, they also took a load of stones. That might account for your friend's anxiety to get his hands on the Hewitt money. To recapitalise."

Metcalfe picked up the photographs and studied them. They showed a fair, pale-eyed woman of thirty or so. Her lips were full and sensual, the nose straight and delicate, her eyes wide and heavily-lidded. There was a certain arrogance in her look, a cold aloofness of spirit. Her long blond hair hung down to her shoulders and she was very, very beautiful.

Mendels said: "Now hold on to your hat. Just under a month ago, two men named Buitoni and Elletti escaped from the main prison in Naples. Elletti was recaptured at once, but Buitoni got away and disappeared. The names mean anything to you?"

Metcalfe shook his head. Claire, leaning forward in her chair, was watching Mendels' face intently.

He said: "Buitoni and Elletti were two of the men concerned with Ricci, in Major Hewitt's death. How does that add up to you?"

Metcalfe stared at him. He said: "But . . . good God . . . why the devil haven't we heard about this?"

Mendels spread his hands delicately. He said:

"I'm working on this case for the State Department. Even I haven't heard about it—officially. But it's just common sense. Take a look at it. The Italian Government is trying to extradite this guy Ricci and his friend from the States, and just as it begins to look as if the States might finally accede to their request, their prize witness disappears. Of course they hush it up. Common sense."

Metcalfe said: "A month ago. . . . That means . . . Dinesen said he'd come to Ethiopia with other guides just in case he couldn't find Franconi."

"Precisely. Begins to make sense, doesn't it?"

"But there were two Italians with him; the other man was recaptured? Elletti?"

Mendels got up and refilled their glasses. He paced up and down the room for a moment. He said, slowly: "Two and two don't always make four, but I'll give you the final digit, for what it's worth. Ricci, the man who did the actual shooting . . ." he said, with a gesture, "allegedly . . . nothing's been proved yet, has it? Ricci has been under surveillance in the States ever since this extradition request came up. A few weeks ago he dropped out of sight. Took a powder. Disappeared."

"You think . . . ?"

"I don't think anything. When a guy disappears in New York, he could be in San Francisco, Chicago, New Orleans, or in Little Rock, Arkansas. Or," he added, "in Africa."

Metcalfe was silent. Claire said: "What's the chain: Foreign Office to Dinesen, Dinesen to Mancini . . . ?"

Mendels nodded. "Mancini to Ricci. It's at least *possible* that when Dinesen put the scheme up to his lady friend, she got in touch with Ricci in the States

—the extradition case has made the headlines here and she'd certainly know all about Ricci."

Metcalfe said: "All I know about Ricci was contained in the note Hewitt left behind when he was killed—have you seen it? Not very much to go on."

Mendels nodded. He said: "It's a bit misleading, too. You remember, Hewitt was dying when he wrote that note, and he didn't have all the facts to go on either. He was with Ricci for less than twenty-four hours: first as a captor, then as a prisoner. He was right about two things, at that. First, he spotted the accent correctly—Ricci is a Sicilian; second, he was also right about his good English—of a sort. Perhaps fluent would have been a happier word. Ricci is an Italian American, more or less. One of the bad boys from way back— Chicago at its worst. He was one of the lesser hoodlums who flourished in the lush old days of Prohibition."

"Then what the hell was he doing in the Italian army?"

"That was something even friend Ricci couldn't get out of. He was visiting his family in . . . Palermo, I think it was, in nineteen thirty-nine. He was drafted; as simple as that. I don't doubt he made a relatively good thing even out of the army; he was the type. You know . . . shoot first and argue afterwards. A professional gunman. A gorilla. A hood. In the old days, he'd been arrested more than a dozen times— and never once indicted. He had a lot of influential friends and a smart lawyer. It was a pretty familiar pattern in those days."

"Any particular . . . rackets?" Metcalfe thought the word sounded strange. He said: "I'm supposed to be working for the Foreign Office. Ever since I left the army I've worn a black Homburg hat and carried an umbrella; when I do manage to get out into the field, it's khaki shorts and sandals. I'm afraid you're opening up a world for me that I'm not too well acquainted with—paper-back novels and Hollywood movies. The racketeers are a bit off my beat."

Mendels said thoughtfully: "It all ties up. Make no mistake about Ricci. If he's here—and it's a mighty big if—if he's here, you can forget the old-boy angle with friend Dinesen. He's playing for keeps. Ricci is a professional killer."

Metcalfe said: "It doesn't make sense. Dinesen's not the kind of man to get involved with people like that. Some of his operations are, well, not entirely legal, but he's never been tied up with murder."

Mendels raised one finger. He said didactically: "That, my friend, is the weak point in all your planning. If you decide beforehand that you can't get hurt because your opponent isn't the type of man to hurt you . . . brother, are you in trouble! You'll find yourself looking down the barrel of a pistol, and you'll just have time to reflect on the words of the Dauphin."

Metcalfe said startled: "The Dauphin? When did he get in this argument?"

Mendels said:

"'. . . 'tis best to weigh
The enemy more mighty than he seems. . . .'

Henry the Fifth, Act Two. Shakespeare. Guess you may have heard of him." He went on. "In any case, look at your . . . connecting link, so to speak: the Countess Mancini. She's not as bad as Ricci, and not as—for want of a better word—good as Dinesen. C is blacker than B and B is blacker than A. Super-ego, Ego and Id."

Metcalfe said: "Back to Ricci for a moment. How did he get back to America after the war?"

Mendels shrugged. He said: "You name it. He turned up in Detroit in 1948, then moved over to New York after some trouble or other—drugs, I think it was." He opened the cabinet again and pulled a sheet of yellow paper from a file. He said: "In brief—1948, dope peddling. 1949, armed robbery, dope peddling, armed robbery. 1950, armed robbery, armed robbery, murder. 1951, smuggling, armed robbery again . . . shall I go on?" He said disgustedly: "Fourteen arrests; indictments, nil. The kind of man who always carries a gun and doesn't care who knows it. A gun in one pocket and a judge in the other. The only real question is *why?* Why should they have bothered to get Ricci *and* Buitoni *and* Franconi. Answer that, and you might begin to see just how his mind is working."

Metcalfe said: "Assuming that all this hypothesis is fact, then it's not hard to find reasons. He needed Franconi so that we wouldn't get him and find the hiding-place first. He needed Ricci in case Buitoni got himself recaptured as—Elletti, was his name?—as Elletti did, or if the jail-break didn't come off. And he needed Buitoni just in case Ricci turned sour on him, wouldn't play ball, or tried it on his own. In other words, he's doubling up on everything. He's making damn sure that no emergencies can upset the apple-cart."

Mendels nodded. He was smiling. He said: "Precisely. His emergency precautions include Ricci. Velvet gloves if all goes well. But if anything goes wrong . . . then he's got a killer up his sleeve. See what I mean?"

Metcalfe said stubbornly: "I still don't believe it. I say he wanted Ricci as a guide—nothing more. In case Franconi and Buitoni failed. He's taken care of every possibility so far, all the way down the line. If

132

anything went wrong and he couldn't get Franconi, then he had Buitoni. And if the Buitoni escape didn't succeed, then he had Ricci."

Mendels walked over to the window and adjusted the Venetian blinds. He stood staring down at the street below. He said: "Well, maybe you're right. Just so that you realise you may be wrong. 'Weigh the enemy more mighty . . .'"

"And in any case, all this is pure supposition."

"Uh-huh. But if it turns out to be fact, then be pretty careful how you go. Watch that guy Ricci. He's trigger-happy."

Glancing up at Claire, Metcalfe said: "He seems to have surrounded himself with thieves and murderers."

"Well, as you say, it's all conjecture. But this way, he'd have half the original mob together, and his chances of finding the stuff would be pretty good, with or without Franconi. It's all conjecture, of course."

Claire said, brusquely: "It's easy enough to find out. Franconi. Franconi must know."

"Then why the devil," said Metcalfe angrily, "why the devil didn't he tell us if Ricci and this other man were with Dinesen? They spent several days together; he must have known about them. Why the bloody hell?"

Claire said calmly: "No reason why he should, is there?"

Metcalfe glowered. Mendels said: "Have another rye. What are you going to do now?"

"We're going to break into the Mancini house and get the money back. It's simple enough." He outlined their plan. He said: "Any reason why it shouldn't work?"

"Only this. You're up against an extremely clever and dangerous woman, regardless of whether Ricci is

133

in on this. Watch your step, Ian. Take it easy." He added, cheerfully: "Without prejudice to your admitted capabilities, I can tell you this: if you tangle with Lala Mancini, you're very liable to come out of it second best—a very poor second best too. But it might work, at that. It has the saving grace of simplicity. You realise that you'll have to watch out for the local police; if they find out what you've been up to, the Colonel's going to get pretty mad."

Metcalfe nodded. He got up to leave. Mendels said wistfully: "If you run into any trouble, let me know. A long time since I had any excitement—if you know what I mean."

They shook hands. As they left, Mendels said to Claire, smiling: "Don't let him get into any trouble. . . . Come and see me again when you can."

They took a *carrozza* over to Via Nerone, sitting close together on the quilted leather bench, the slow clop-clop of the horse adding a counterpoint to the music of the evening overture. Crowds were thronging the streets after the lunch-time siesta, freshly groomed and shining with that suppressed excitement which is so particularly Roman.

As they entered the Via Nerone, the yellow sun began to settle over the tops of the houses, casting its shadows sharp and clear on the pavement. Somewhere down the street a delivery-boy on a bicycle was singing. His high-pitched, immature tenor was sweet and clear as he slowly pedalled past them. Metcalfe leaned back, smiling, his eyes closed, listening to the catch of melody:

> "*. . . mansuete e pure,*
> *O mani elette a bell' opre pietose,*
> *A carrezzar' fanciulli, a coglier' rose. . . .*"

The cyclist swung round the corner at the end of the street and the music faded with him. The *carrozza* clopped to a stop.

Standing below them on the café terrace, Harry Pender said: "You're looking impossibly smug. Come on down."

Chapter Nine

NUMBER 217a was a big square building in grey stone,
set back from the road in an iron-fenced enclosure. It
was solidly built, in the heavy and comfortable style
of the seventeenth century, of square-cut, carefully
dressed stones, with windows that came nearly down to
the floor-line, and a porch that was supported on slender
pillars. The black paint-work on the supports of the
iron gates, half obliterated with age and with neglect,
read "Miratevere 1629," and Metcalfe looked at the
modern buildings all about the old house and wondered
if the Tiber could still be seen from its windows. It lay
a hundred yards or more back from the roadway,
holding itself coldly aloof from the bustle of the street,
the twentieth century held firmly and distastefully at
arm's length.

The garden was unkempt and neglected, but the
fence itself was covered with bougainvillea and morning
glory, red and purple and blue and green. The house
was silent, the air about it deserted. The café was almost
directly opposite.

Pender said: "I've had a good look round, but I'm
not sure whether it's empty or not; I *almost* saw a
movement of some sort across one of the windows.
Couldn't be at all sure."

They sat at one of the tiny, cloth-covered tables on
the pavement and ordered coffee.

Pender said: "Just as it shows on the map, the two
buildings at the sides are apartment blocks, but the
museum at the back isn't a museum at all—it's just the

museum warehouse and it's quite deserted. I want to have another look at it after dark. It looks to me as though there ought to be a passage running along the side which will lead very close to the back of the house itself, which is the obvious point of entry—one of the ground-floor windows."

Metcalfe said: "That movement across the windows —male or female?"

"No idea at all. I may have imagined the whole thing. Just had the idea that something moved. Couldn't be sure and I didn't want to attract attention by looking too long or too hard. Sort of . . . well, caught a movement out of the corner of my eye. But that's quite logical; there's almost certain to be a caretaker there, even if the place is technically unoccupied."

Claire said: "And that raises a complication. When she arrives and rings the doorbell, she'll expect to be met by some Boris Karloff type; what happens if she finds instead a couple of charming delegates from the Foreign Office? She'll probably yell for help."

Metcalfe said: "We'll manage. Yank her into the house and silence her."

Claire said: "Don't be dramatic. How do you silence a screaming woman?"

Metcalfe grimaced. He said: "There are bound to be . . . well, some unpleasant aspects to all this. I've not much experience of this sort of thuggery, but I imagine you simply clap a hand over her mouth or wallop her smartly on the point of the chin; it happens every day in the cinema. It's one of those things that require . . . instinctive action."

"Like a non-swimmer thrown in at the deep end?"

"Precisely. We'll worry about individual problems as they arise."

"That," Pender said, "is where intelligence and sound training pay off. Any fool can make a plan; it takes a well-equipped man to carry out a plan that doesn't exist. Instinctive reaction. Quick decisions. Cross your bridge when you get to it." He sighed. "Only sometimes the bridge isn't there."

Metcalfe said cheerfully: "Well, we bash on regardless. Now. Harry can wait here till it gets a bit darker, then make another reconnaissance of the passageway at the back. Claire and I will go up to the pension next door and get rooms and start a watch on the house. When you've finished, come on up and we'll go to work."

"Good." Pender called for another coffee.

Metcalfe drained his cup. He said: "Is that the car?"

Pender nodded. "A bit rough, but she goes like a bomb."

Metcalfe stood looking down at the little Fiat roadster. It was several years old, the bodywork shabby and neglected, the leather seats covered with faded green cloth. He kicked at the wheel idly. He said:

"See you at the pension soon after dark. Let's go."

Arm in arm with Claire, conscious as always of the gentle articulation of her warm and lovely body close beside him, Metcalfe walked up to the little hotel. The clerk in the dim foyer looked up as he spoke. He said:

"A double room and a single, please. A friend will be along later. In the front of the building, and about the third or fourth floor if you can." He spoke very careful and precise Italian.

The clerk nodded. "*Si signori*. Your baggage, please?"

"They will send it from the station."

"*Va bene, signori.*" He range a bell with a quick and delicate motion, peering down into the darkness of the hallway over the top of his spectacles. He said to the porter: "*Camere 47 e 49.*"

"*Prego, signori.*" The porter took them up in a ramshackle lift, slowly groping its tumbling way up to the fourth floor. He stepped aside as they entered their room.

Metcalfe said: "You might send up a bottle of Chianti and three glasses, will you? In a little while?"

The porter nodded, his bright black eyes gleaming with hotel understanding.

When he had closed the door and gone away, his soft shoes padding gently along the worn carpet, Metcalfe put his hands on Claire's shoulders and held her at arms' length. He stroked the soft sheen of her hair, feeling the electric vitality in its smooth loveliness. He said:

"I missed you, you know."

Claire straightened his tie, standing close in front of him. She said: "I should hope so. Was it a good trip?"

"Uh-huh. Held up by bandits once, nothing serious. Got very drunk with Ras Guggla."

"What's he like? As bad as he's painted?"

"Very fine fellow. Do you love me?"

"You know I do." She looked at him steadily with her pale, thoughtful eyes. The wide, symmetrical curve of her eyebrows gave her a faintly madonna-like air. Only her eyes were smiling, quietly quizzical.

He sat on the edge of the bed and put his hands on her hips. He drew her close to him and felt the smooth delicacy of her skin under the cashmere of her skirt. He said:

"It was a long time. Too long."

His hand rested gently on the pointed bone of her hip, rubbing it softly, then moved up to her breast. He said again: "Too long. Too damn long." He raised his face and saw her smiling gently down at him. He was suddenly aware, more than ever before, how deeply she loved him, and the thought was a sudden pain inside him, his love for her almost hurting him with its insistent tightening across his chest. He thought, *I must never leave her, never.* Holding her urgently, he said: "I must feel you close beside me. . . . I must."

She said: "The waiter will be here in a minute."

"To hell with the waiter."

"And Harry will be along soon."

"The hell with Harry too."

"And there's work to be done."

Metcalfe straightened up and put his arms around her, holding her tightly, pressing his loins close against hers. He said: "I love you, I love you, I love you."

Claire said again: "The waiter will be here very soon." She raised her face to his, her lips parted. He kissed her softly.

He said: "Just a cold-blooded fish. Cold-blooded English fish." He kissed her again, urgently.

After a moment, she said lightly: "When their breath starts getting heavy, that's the time to leave them."

Metcalfe grinned happily. He said: "All right, all right. You win. Let's get to work."

He went to the window and stood staring at the house across the way, grey and sombre in its untidy grounds, aloof and cold behind its high iron fence, remote in the darkening light of the evening. The lights on the street came on, yellow in the unfinished

140

daylight, the great glass spheres high above the road suddenly flaring with a weak, insipid brilliance, hastening the night, casting their premature shadows impatiently. He was frowning a little. He said:

"I don't know . . . it appears to be deserted. I hope to God we're on the right track."

Claire was tucking her blouse into her skirt. She said: "Is it really going to be so easy? Just a question of smash and grab?"

Metcalfe said moodily: "I don't know. All we can do is try. This is the only lead we have—it's the only possible path we can follow. Even if we have to wait a month, we simply must wait for her to turn up."

"And if she doesn't?"

Metcalfe paused. At last he said heavily: "Then we've failed." He said doggedly: "She's got to come soon, she *must*. . . . And there's Franconi." He said angrily: "We've got to find out from Franconi if Ricci was one of Dinesen's friends. Can't imagine why we didn't think to question him about the others in the party in the first place. Didn't occur to me. Too rushed, I suppose . . . and too pleased with our discoveries about Lala Mancini. Too eager to catch up with Dinesen. Not that it makes any difference." He was talking to himself.

Claire was close beside him. She said: "Did it occur to you that she might not come at all?"

Metcalfe frowned. "You mean . . . ?"

"That she might simply take the money herself and disappear?"

"It did occur to me." He said: "I don't think it's likely. He would never have given her the money in the first place unless he was absolutely sure of her. He must be certain that he can trust her. Can't imagine

Dinesen, of all people, handing over a quarter of a million pounds unless he was pretty damn sure he'd get it back again. Probably got something on her . . . enforced honour among thieves."

"Unless he's in love with her."

"Dinesen? In love? She's a very attractive woman indeed by all accounts. Dinesen will be in love with her looks and nothing else. He's wise enough not to let his emotions interfere with his mind."

Claire raised her eyebrows: "Wise enough?" she said. "*Wise* enough?"

Metcalfe grinned broadly. "I beg your pardon," he said. "I should, of course, have said *foolish* enough." He added: "In any case, if she should double-cross him and hide the stuff safely away in Trieste somewhere, I'd almost be happy to let her keep it—the whole damn lot. The prospect of Dinesen's discomfiture would be ample recompense under the circumstances. But knowing Dinesen pretty well, I don't doubt for one moment that he will trust his lovely *amore* just about as far as he can lightly toss her, and no further. . . . No, the only risk is that she may not be alone. And it's a small risk at that. We shall have the advantage of surprise."

"Are you armed?"

"Of course." Metcalfe slipped his revolver out of his shoulder holster and showed it to her. It was a long-barrelled Bayard .32. He said: "Nice little gun. A bit small, but easy to carry and it has a good long range. But we shan't use it, except for show, possibly."

Claire said nothing. She rested her hand lightly on his arm. There was a worried look in her eyes.

He said: "Don't worry; there won't be any trouble."

He put his arm round her again and kissed her, his

arm right round her back and under her armpit to feel the contour of her breast trembling under his touch, holding her tight. She was slim and soft and incredibly supple, her body yielding, unresisting, a liquefaction of limbs close against his, unbelievably soft and light and infinitely desirable. Enjoying, not the possession, but the contemplation of it, feeling more and more the extent of his love for her, a tangled delirium of pride that left his thoughts unbalanced and incoherent, knowing only that this was the woman he wanted, this was the body above all things that he wanted to feel beside him, no other but this for all time. She said, close beside him: "Not now, Ian . . . not now . . ." and he said:

"'For God's sake hold your tongue and let me love,
Or chide my palsy or my gout,
My five grey hairs . . .'"

and he took her to the window and sat on the hard wicker chair, holding her close against him, his head against her body, enjoying the feeling of his love for her, and he sat for a long while saying nothing.

There was a knock at the door. It was Pender. He called out: "Are you decent? Can I come in?"

Metcalfe said: "Damnation!"

Claire went across and opened the door. The colour in her cheeks was high.

Pender was carrying a bottle of wine and tray of glasses. He said cheerfully: "I ran into the waiter and relieved him of this. I hope it was ours?"

Claire nodded. She took the wine and filled the glasses. Raising her own, looking across at Ian and smiling with her eyes, she said:

"Here's to a hi-jacked fortune."

They drank slowly.

Harry Pender said: "Wasn't really dark enough, but I've found a way in."

"Yes? Good show."

"There's a door at the side of the museum warehouse that leads to a passage—sort of delivery alley, I suppose—and this passage runs to within a few feet of the ground-floor windows at the back of the house. So if we move in that way tonight, before the moon gets up——"

Claire said: "Moonrise eleven fifty-two."

"Bright girl . . . we can get to the kitchen windows, which we can easily force, under cover the whole way." He started fumbling in his pocket. He said: "While you were with Mendels, I did some shopping. Bought all the kit we need." Laying them on the bed, he announced: "Glass-cutter, suction-cup, cord for tying up obstreperous bodies . . . and this."

This was a short length of lead piping. He said: "Used to read lots of whodunits, once. I can assure you that a short length of lead piping is absolutely indispensable. Only wish I knew how hard you're supposed to hit, but I suppose we shall find that out." He said: "You know, I'm beginning to enjoy this."

Metcalfe said: "We ought to start out at about ten o'clock. Give us an hour and fifty minutes before moonrise and there'll still be enough noise on the streets to cover any sounds we might stir up getting hidden away. Best, perhaps, if we both get in together; then one of us tackles the caretaker, or whoever's there, alone. The other can wait below somewhere as an emergency reserve. Sort of Support Group. If anything goes wrong . . . I think that perhaps I'd better do the donkey work, Harry; you keep out of sight once we're inside, and cover me. I'll explore the house, and if I'm not back in a reasonable time, you can come and get me out of the trouble I've got myself into. We'll both carry pistols, and hope to hell we don't have to use them. Quite apart from other considerations—the police and the Carabinieri, and all that sort of thing —let's keep this thing on as gentlemanly a plane as possible. No rough stuff. Let us not forget our manners. Homburg hats. If the place turns out to be empty and we have to stay all night, then one of us can sneak out and let Claire know. There'll be the question of Franconi to worry about. As his confidence returns, he may start thinking he'd rather not stay with us any more."

Pender said emphatically: "Not a bit of it. He knows he couldn't last long in Italy without any documents, and he knows damn well that it will be far easier for him in England. He'll stick with us like a limpet. He'll never leave that hotel bedroom without us."

"Perhaps you're right."

Claire said: "Assuming you get the stuff out tonight, where do we put it? Any plans?"

"Back at the Hotel? Should be safe enough there."

Pender said: "What about your friend Mendels' place?"

"I rather thought," Claire said, "that the obvious place would be the Embassy. Probably fix it with one of the Secretaries there. After all, it's Government property."

Metcalfe said: "Better still, we'll take it round in the car to our own office. Let them fight it out with the Embassy people. If we try it on our own we'll have a fussy little Third or Fourth Secretary raising horrified hands at us. Let the Rome office handle it."

Claire said: "I'd better see about some air reservations out of the country just in case she tries to pull any strings to have us stopped. Where to? Paris? Straight to London? London via Paris? And am I coming on this house-breaking junket?"

"You are most certainly not!"

"Then I'll phone for some reservations tonight. Did you say Paris?"

Metcalfe grinned. "Want to do some shopping? All right, Paris. We can always cancel if we're stuck here for a week, which God forbid."

Claire said: "There's a small thing you can do to make me happy. When you get safely inside, can you signal to me in some way—just so that I'll know you're all right? Am I being foolish?"

Metcalfe put his arm round her waist. He said: "Not to worry. It's a cup of tea."

Pender said: "Tell you what. As soon as we're inside, I'll flash a light from one of the front windows upstairs, then signal again every hour on the hour. Check your watch with mine. Will that do?"

Claire smiled. She said: "I always did believe you had the brains in this outfit. Good. And I'll stay at the window all the time. If you need me, flash your light and I'll come on over. Are you all ready to go?"

Metcalfe nodded. "I think so. There's one thing. We've three hours to wait. Harry can nip over to the Eden Hotel and see that Franconi's all right. And find out about Ricci from him. We'll watch the house from here. We'll wait dinner for you."

Claire said: "Best if we have them send some food up here later on—won't interfere with our bird-watching."

"Good idea." Harry Pender got up to go.

Metcalfe said blandly: "Don't be too long, Harry, will you, there's a good fellow?"

146

Harry was twisting his glass between his fingers. He said: "It'll take me about an hour, I should think. Be back at about eight. Soon after, anyway." He left the room and closed the door softly.

Claire looked across at Ian and smiled.

At eight-fifteen, in defiance of the Italian law forbidding the sound of motor-horns after dusk, Harry Pender tooted his horn outside the *pensione* and a few minutes later knocked on their door.

Claire let him in. Her colour was high, her hair carefully combed, her clothing neat and precise. Pender was carrying a paper bag. He said: "I wasn't too long, was I?"

Claire said: "All right, Harry, don't overdo it."

He laughed. He said to Metcalfe: "I went to your room and brought your crêpe-soled shoes—noticed you were wearing leather. We'll have to be pretty quiet tonight. We may also have some fancy running to do."

Metcalfe said: "Franconi?"

"He's all right. And it was Ricci. And Buitoni."

Metcalfe swore. He said: "Then why the hell didn't he tell us before?"

Pender sat down in the arm-chair and lit his pipe. He put his hands behind his head and stretched his legs. He said slowly: "Not too sure myself, really. I tackled him about it, of course. He said that, well . . . apparently he thought at first that Dinesen was a policeman and that the others were, well, sort of under arrest. He said Dinesen kept a very sharp eye on them. Both he and Lala Mancini carried pistols; the others were unarmed. Then when he learned in Dire-Dawa that Dinesen had stolen the money, he was too frightened, too confused to say anything about it. He didn't realise, of course, that we didn't know who the others were. So he just left things as they stood. Didn't want to get any more involved than he already was. I think I can understand that. He says he never spoke to them at all; says they were very . . . well, the word he used was '*beffatore*.' Says they all kept their distance, except, strangely enough, Lala Mancini. He seems to think a great deal of her. What does '*beffatore*' mean—to sneer, or something like that, isn't it?"

"More or less. I suppose it's understandable. The question now is, whether Ricci will dare come to Italy or will go back to America and wait for his cut there. Doesn't seem likely. Probably doesn't even matter."

"That's a thing we can't possibly even guess at. Franconi is obviously scared stiff of Ricci, but he says Buitoni is just a nonentity. And he's pretty sure that Lala Mancini is due here tonight. She definitely said *the night before the Feast of St Christopher*, and that begins tomorrow morning."

They were just above the street-lights, round and bold and yellow. Beyond them, beyond the darkness of the unkept garden and the high iron fence, the old stone house was dark and silent. On both sides open windows gleamed brightly in the apartment blocks: behind were the thousand illuminations of the town; below them, on the street, the cars were moving and the people chatting, the café a bustle and clamour of wildly gesticulating bodies. Only in the centre was there darkness; a tenebrous silence, a dark menace hung over the house.

Metcalfe was staring out of the window again. He said: "Well, we know a lot more, but we're no wiser. Our plans remain the same. Thanks for the shoes."

Claire said: "Nearly two hours to go."

Metcalfe said: "You know, I feel pretty good. Let's have another bottle of Chianti."

Claire looked at him and said nothing. She was smiling quietly to herself. She rang for the waiter

Chapter Ten

THE clock in the elegant tower of the renaissance church, poised high and slim and graceful above the cobbled street with its grubby gutters and broken paving-stones, was striking ten-fifteen as they crouched in the darkness under the window. On the upper floor of the old stone house, a single light was burning.

Pender took the glass-cutter and the small suction-cup from the pocket of his coat. Moving with infinite care, he stuck the cup in the centre of the lower pane, traced a triangle of sharp, straight lines around it, tapped once, and pulled the segment clear. He reached through the hole, slowly and carefully, flexed his elbow and un-fastened the catch. Then inch by inch, cursing sound-lessly at the almost imperceptible noise, he eased up the sash. When the window was fully opened, he signalled Metcalfe to wait, then slipped silently into the room.

It was darker inside and silent. Standing still in the darkness against the wall, quite motionless, hearing his own soft breathing, ears strained to catch the slightest sound, he waited for his eyes to become accustomed to the deeper blackness. Outside, on the road, a lorry rumbled by. At last, after a long pause of silent still-ness, he took out his flashlight and shone it round the room.

He was in a kitchen, old-fashioned, neat, severe. Against the opposite wall was a black iron coal range, its highly polished steel furnishings gleaming brightly. To his right there was a high wooden dresser, its pottery dishes neatly displayed. On the left was a heavy oak cupboard, and a plank table and chairs occupied the centre of the room. In the corner was a door. He walked quietly across to it, opened it gently and listened. There was no sound. He closed it again and went back to the window, padding gently in his rubber shoes. He whispered to Metcalfe:

"All quiet. Come on in."

Without speaking, Metcalfe eased his clumsy body over the sill and dropped inside, quietly, on the balls of his feet. He pulled the window down softly behind him. They were alone in the silent darkness.

Pender whispered: "This way."

Silently they tip-toed across the kitchen and through the door into the hall. They waited a moment longer. The soft yellow beam of the flashlight slewed round and up the stairway to the landing, then switched suddenly off, leaving a pounding, silent darkness again. Metcalfe could feel the deep, unaccustomed thumping deep inside him, throbbing, the darkness pressing about him, and a wondering *What am I doing here?* pulsing in his loins; and for a moment another moment tumbled into the forgotten net of memory—a similar dark and silent moment, standing in the stillness outside a young girl's door, scratching in nervous fear at the woodwork, feeling his way in stockinged feet, a boyish, adolescent agitation vibrating from his loins to his hairless hands; he turned the brass knob slowly and near-fainted at the broken silence, and crept across the floor to hear the frightening creak of bed-springs. . . . "Did anyone see you?" she whispered. "Are you sure?" And the pulsing in his body was stronger, and then Pender touched his arm and the net fell suddenly away and only the silence and the stillness and the pulsing fear were there, and he shook them off brusquely and said softly: "What the hell?"

Pender said: "Up the stairs and to the right. There must be a passage at the top of the stairs," breathing the words into his ear.

Metcalfe nodded. They eased up the wide stairway, touching the wall with their finger-tips, keeping close to the side, away from the creaking centres, creeping silently, conspirators in the darkness. They turned the corner at the landing and stood watching the thin edge of yellow light that seeped under the door ahead of them. Metcalfe took out his gun. Outside a bird screeched suddenly, and a car on the road sped by with a scream of tortured rubber on asphalt.

Metcalfe said softly: "The caretaker—I'll take care of him. Go back and wait at the window till I give the signal. Give me half an hour. If you don't hear from me by then, come and look for me."

Pender nodded. Then, conscious of the darkness, he whispered: "Easy does it." He touched Metcalfe's arm and was gone.

Metcalfe mentally rolled up his sleeves and moved forward. He reached the door and delicately, ever so lightly, searched for the door-knob with groping, lightly poised fingers. He found it and turned it slowly, counting the seconds, with infinite patience forcing himself to slowness. He could hear the ticking of his watch in the silence. Behind the door there was a rustle of paper and the creak of springs, and then a rustle again, and he said to himself, *He's reading in bed—so much the better.* His left hand felt that the handle had turned to its limit. His right hand was holding the revolver at the ready, close in to his hip, his hand drawn back, the barrel close against his side.

The colonel—what was his name?—said: Hold it close against your hip if you want to live, keep it part of you, close to your hip. He said: Stick your arm out in front and you're a dead man. Look, I'll show you. And he felt again the bruises as he went flying along the floor, nursing a twisted arm and looking up at the colonel's grinning face as his weapon cluttered heavily against the wall. See what I mean?

Holding the gun properly, his lesson well learned, he tested the door. It was unlocked, With a sudden, brusque movement, a short two-footed leap, he was inside the room, legs apart, the door slammed tight behind him, taking in every corner of the room at a single glance, all his old training painting the picture clearly on his mind, pulling his reflexes into action almost before the picture was clearly there.

Then he was staring at the bed, suddenly conscious that he must have looked a little foolish, chasing a mosquito with an elephant gun. He knew his mouth was open, and closing it, said:

"Well, I'll be damned. I'll be damned . . ."

Lying among silk sheets, propped up on enormous pillows, a fashionable magazine on her knees, was a woman.

He said again: "Well, I'll be damned."

There was a sudden look of fright on the woman's face before she recovered her composure. She dropped her paper and sat bolt upright among the pillows, staring at him, wide-eyed. With an almost subconscious movement, she brushed her fair hair back from her eyes.

She said angrily, no fear on her face, speaking Italian: "What does this mean? What do you want? How dare you . . ."

She was staring at Metcalfe's gun. He noted the wariness in her eyes, a sharpness only carelessly masked by indignation. He said smoothly, consciously covering his confusion and surprise:

"I must apologise. We didn't expect you back from Ethiopia quite so soon."

"Ethiopia?" The woman hesitated. Then: "I see. I see. And what do you expect to find here?"

Metcalfe said: "Allow me to introduce myself . . ."

The woman interrupted him. She said brusquely, in English, speaking the English of the international Italian, of the cosmopolite, fluent and free and accurate, slightly accented:

"I know who you are. Petar described you well. Ian . . . Ian Metcalfe, isn't it? A big English oaf, Petar said."

Metcalfe inclined his head. He said: "And you, of course, are the Contessa Mancini. Your photographs do you small justice. The police photographs, don't you know?"

She stared at him coldly. She said: "Don't you feel you could put your gun away? I find it a little offensive. Or did the police say I was so dangerous?"

She eased herself back into the pillows restfully, quite calm, a woman in bed chatting with her lover. She said: "There is no one else here."

Metcalfe slipped the gun into his holster. He said: "But please don't reach for that bell-rope. I should hate our tête-à-tête to be disturbed."

She eased her shoulders into the cushions, moving her body sensually, writhing, a serpent in silk. Her long fair hair hung loose against the peach-coloured silk of the bed-clothes. Her skin was smooth and tanned and alive, her eyes pale and widely spaced under her pencilled eyebrows, her mouth full and red and mobile. She was wearing a nightgown of black satin, edged with lace and cut low about her shoulders. The skin between her firm, high breasts, was smooth and pale, whiter than her shoulders, fading imperceptibly from olive to ivory. She made no attempt to cover herself.

Metcalfe said, brusquely: "May I at least sit down?"

154

She nodded gravely. "Of course. Would it . . . discomfort you to sit on the bed beside me?"

Metcalfe pulled up a quilted satin chair. He said: "When did you arrive?"

"This morning."

"You couldn't have stayed long in Trieste?"

"Trieste?"

"Your home, isn't it? I thought the arrangement was that you should go there first and then bring the money here."

A shadow of puzzlement crossed her face. She said: "You seem to be very well informed. No one knew except Petar and myself." It was a question. He said to himself, *She thinks we've seen him.*

He said, shrugging: "I'm not boasting. I merely want you to know that we are well informed. Just in case you should deny that the money is here . . ."

"We?"

"My friends are in the hotel across the street."

There was a long silence. Metcalfe was conscious that she was watching him carefully, apparently relaxed, deep among her cushions, impressing him that she was at home, that he was the stranger; using her body on him.

She had that alabaster quality of flesh, that soft and placid tension in the skin, a pure unblemished depth of loveliness . . . but more—a vital, alive, compelling texture.

He said aloud: "Where is the money?"

She raised a supple arm and pointed. He noted the delicacy of her fingers and the gentle movement of her breast. As he saw the mockery in her eyes he coloured. He said: "Where is it?"

"Over there. In the box." She said casually: "Mostly in dollars. Some pounds, some francs, some lire. I changed the gold in Trieste; that's what I went there for. Or did you know that? It was too heavy to carry, of course, but in any case the present rate for gold sovereigns . . . Very nearly a quarter of a million pounds' worth, all told." She said softly: "That's a great deal of money."

She spoke carelessly accurate English, just the hint of an accent, a flexibility of intonation.

Metcalfe walked over to the tin trunk in the corner. He saw that the hasp was unlocked, and with a quick movement of his foot he flipped it open. The tin trunk, its once-green paint worn and scarred, was packed to the top, packed tight with bundles of notes. He stared at it for a moment, staring at the large denominations. He saw Franconi and Ricci and a ragged group of hungry, weary deserters, gaping at more money than their combined efforts could conjure up in a lifetime, standing around in an untidy group, the hot sun beating down on the rocks about them, the vast emptiness of Africa all around them, and a fortune at their feet, and he felt for a moment a sense of bewilderment. . . . He looked up quickly towards the bed. She was smiling at him gently, almost affectionately; she might have been a lover, smiling gently at him and inviting an embrace. He felt the vivid presence of her, close across the room, and the old familiar pain came back to his loins, the rising, throbbing pain of her animal beauty, and he was angry with his longing, but could not subdue it. The urge to touch her flesh was almost irresistible. He said irrelevantly:

"You are a very beautiful woman. . . . I wish . . ."

She said: "I know." And added calmly: "I know my attraction for men."

"It will do you no good now."

"I know that too. Petar told me. Devotion to duty.

156

Flags of Empire. The perfect Civil Servant. The English gentleman. The oaf, Petar said."

Metcalfe blushed angrily. He felt Dinesen's contempt in her suave and measured voice. He said, his voice level, dispassionate: "Under other circumstances I should be happy to correct that impression. . . ." With heavy sarcasm he said: "You won't mind if I take this away?"

"Please do."

Metcalfe hesitated. He glanced round the room. He said: "All right. What's the catch?"

"The catch?"

"Do you imagine you will be able to retrieve it later? Within an hour this will be safely lodged at the Embassy."

She said, almost casually: "I don't think so." She threw back the bedclothes and stood up beside the bed. She was tall and full-breasted and lovely. Metcalfe was conscious of the power of her body.

She said: "If I ring for my servants . . .? There are several of them in the house. Will you shoot me if I try to ring? Or what . . . will you merely man-handle me, perhaps?"

Metcalfe took a pace towards her. He said heavily: "I know there are no servants here, but I shall use force if I have to. Don't delude yourself on that account."

She said coolly: "Perhaps you will. I know that you are conscious of me . . . sexually. It would please you to lay your coarse red hands on me, wouldn't it?" Mocking him, she said: "You'd like that, to use your strength against mine?"

He said again stubbornly: "I shall use force if I have to. I hope it won't be necessary."

For a moment she looked squarely at him. Then she deliberately stretched out her hand for the bell-rope, deliberately inciting him to touch her. Before she could reach it, Metcalfe moved.

He sprang across the room at her, seized her arm, and spun her round. He put his arm round her waist from behind, holding her close, astonished at her fragile suppleness; his other hand moved lightly, gently, up her body to her throat, then touched her mouth.

He felt a sudden uneasiness, a consciousness that he could not easily do battle with a woman, particularly not with this woman, feeling a little foolish and out of his depth, knowing with distaste that there were circles in which men fought with their hands over money, but not in his; feeling that he was entering into another sphere, an underworld; not very much liking it.

He said stubbornly: "I hoped this would not be necessary. I told you . . . if you scream, I shall choke you—don't make me do it." The pressure of his arm around her unresisting flesh was acute; he felt her go limp and eased his arm. With a sudden, twisting motion like the strike of an animal, she swung round in the circle of his arm and struck at his face. He caught her wrist, then lost it, and felt the sharp, hot sting of her nails and stepped backward against the bed. He sat down heavily, brushing at the blood on his face and looked up to see her holding a heavy ceramic lamp above his head. He thought for a moment, almost conscious of the humour of it all, *Hell, this won't do,* and threw himself sideways, catching at her wrist. His hand fastened on her elbow, and the heavy ornament smashed into his head. He said aloud, *God damnit,* and fell sideways, feeling her on top of him. He said angrily: "Damn you, keep still," and struggled to hold her twisting flailing arms, then threw her free and stood

158

above her. With his open hand he struck her full on the side of the head, conscious of the ungallantry of it, worrying about it, and as she caught her breath he took her two arms and held them close together, forcing her down on the bed, bending her over backwards, putting his weight on top of her body. He pushed her arms above her head and took them both in his left hand, holding tight, firm, a cruel pressure on her wrists, his right hand free. She stopped struggling. She lay still, panting.

He eased his shoulders back and stared at her, still holding her hands. She was limp beneath him, her eyes closed, her lips slightly parted, breathing heavily, her breast rising and falling.

He said: "That was a damn fool thing to do. Did you really think you could fight me?"

She opened her eyes and stared at him coldly. She said calmly: "This is not the end, oaf."

He said: "I know. What's the next step? If I let you go . . ."

She said: "You're hurting my wrists, oaf."

"I know that too." He ran his hand through his hair, brushing it back from his face, then laid it on her breast, feeling the ripeness of her under his finger-tips. He said sombrely: "There's a quality in your flesh only one woman in a thousand has . . . do you know that? It's something in the skin itself—in the surface of the flesh . . . it's . . . I don't know what it is. I suppose this isn't really the time to discuss it."

She said: "Of course I know. Many Italian women have it. And Petronius wrote about it with better eloquence." She said: "May I get up now?"

Metcalfe turned his head and looked at her. He did not move his hand away, feeling the soft roundness of her.

159

He said at last heavily, his voice troubled: "I don't know. I don't know."

She looked him full in the face for a moment, not speaking, her eyes untroubled, almost sympathetic. She said at last: "Petar would kill you."

He said slowly: "There are a good many reasons why I shouldn't follow my natural impulse . . . but that . . . that is the least of them." He said: "I find myself in a new environment, a place where people murder for money, a place where all the things I was brought up to believe good, are false. . . . I don't know. . . . I just don't know."

She said: "Well? Am I to suffer this . . . this discomfort, while you make up your mind? While you search for some way to justify yourself? It should be easy for you. A race of hypocrites."

Metcalfe felt a sense of detachment creeping over him. He said: "Hypocrites? In this respect at least we can be truthful. The only right involved is a stupid convention made by society to control the only common function it can never possibly oversee. There's precious little hypocrisy involved in this."

"I don't doubt that you can reason with yourself . . . argue a way out——"

"Reason? What have reason and argument to do with an activity which is only emotional and . . . instinctive?"

"Emotional? I see no emotion. I feel you pawing me with a kind of animal excitement while you try to find the courage to make love to me. Is this your English emotion? An Italian would be more direct."

He said angrily: "I don't doubt it." He said: "There's a philosophy which separates mind from matter in these things. My interest in you is physical and temporary, nothing more. If that is wrong, I will still not deny it. I do not subscribe to the belief that a cold shower will ease these pangs."

"And your little English miss? Is she so cold, then, that you must love the purity of her mind while you satisfy yourself on my body?"

Metcalfe stood up angrily, releasing her. He said savagely: "That, of course, is your only argument. But it would not be a satisfaction." Wanting to hurt her, wanting to avenge his dignity, conscious of the pain in him, he said: "That would have been a contamination."

She was struggling to her knees on the bed, her hand pushing at the pillows behind her. He saw for a moment the venom in her eyes, almost before he saw the revolver in her hand. He touched his holster and felt that it was empty, and wondered briefly when his gun had fallen out. Then there was a red flash and a roar, and a blackness of nothing but the savagery in her eyes, and he felt a dull and heavy blow on the back of his head, not painful, and saw that the bed was above him and felt the soft carpet under him, and it was swinging round him, swaying, throbbing, swinging from side to side, and he looked up and saw her standing above him, and he felt the gun drop to the ground beside him and saw her fall to her knees, and then the pain in his chest hit him a savage, sudden blow, a sharp, searing burn that shot right through to his backbone and raced up to his head and blinded him, and he felt his own warm blood pulsing viciously out of his side into the cup of his hand that a moment before had been on her breast, and with a vague sensation that the telephone bell was shrilling somewhere, seeming part of his hurt, he felt the blackness and the stillness suddenly sweep down upon him. . . .

He had no way of knowing how long he had been unconscious. When he came to, he was stretched out on the floor, and she was beside him. He felt that his chest was bare, and in the brief moment before he blacked out again he saw a bloody towel and his shirt piled on the carpet beside him, and he felt her, heard her turning him over on to his side. He felt the stinging in his side, burning acutely now and throbbing, and sensed the smooth touch of her fingers at the plaster, and he groaned and tried to say something, anything, and then the blackness came again. When he awoke, he heard the sound of water running. He turned his head painfully and saw the black satin, loosely thrown across the bed, its paler lace torn and bloody. The door to the bathroom was open; she was taking a shower. His head was throbbing and he closed his eyes. When he opened them she was standing above him, wrapped in a white bath towel. She stood looking down at him for a moment, then crossed on bare wet feet to the table by the bedside. She took two cigarettes from an ormolu box and lit them. Crossing back to Metcalfe, she crouched down on the floor beside him and put one between his lips. She waited till she saw that he was drawing on it, then stood up. He touched the plaster on his side and back. She said:

"You've lost a lost of blood. I tried to kill you."

Metcalfe said nothing. She unwrapped the towel and began drying herself. He watched her as she moved, turning his head painfully to watch her, follow each movement of her long and slender body. She stood above him with her feet apart, like a man, moving the towel across her back with a vigorous rhythm, shaking the moisture out of her long hair. He stretched out a hand along the floor and touched her ankle.

He said: "How did you get my gun?"

"It fell out on to the bed while we were . . .
fighting. Then, I was lying on top of it." She said:
"If you had . . . what did you call it? . . . followed
your natural impulses, you would have found it. As it
was . . ." She shrugged. "I wanted to kill you. You
should not have said what you did."

Metcalfe tried to move. The effort was too much and
he lay back exhausted. He said: "I know. I was angry.
You caught me on a raw spot. I didn't mean it, of
course. But . . ."

She said: "Lie still now. You're not badly hurt, it
passed right through you. Let me make you a *zaba-glione*."

"I'd rather have a Scotch and soda."

She grimaced. "All right."

She walked slowly to the long white and gold
cupboard and took out a négligé; she stood for a brief
moment looking at him before she slipped it on,
standing there motionless for a moment, with all the
smooth and sculptured perfection of a statue. She said:

"Why didn't you make love to me? You were going
to."

"I almost did. I don't know. . . . What about that
drink?"

He moved himself painfully to a sitting position, and
groped for the chair. She came across the room and
helped him on to it. She said quietly:

"You're too weak to fight me again, and the money's
gone. And I still have your revolver. When you feel
better, you must go. Don't try to fight me again."

He saw that the tin trunk had been removed. He
thought, the pain in his side worrying him, but the
strength coming back already, *Where the devil is Harry
Pender?* He said:

"What have you done with the money?"

163

"It's in a safe place. You'll never find it. Not alone."

He said: "What do you mean, 'Not alone'"?

For a moment, she stood looking at him with that thoughtful expression in her eyes that he had seen when she stood over by the cupboard, solemnly staring at him, wide-eyed, like a child. Then she dropped quickly to the floor beside him and said impetuously:

"There's plenty there for both of us. Let's go away together, now, this minute, quickly, before it's too late. Let's go now, with the money."

He said, flabbergasted: "But good God . . . good God in Heaven . . . but what about . . . what about Dinesen, for God's sake? What about—— Are you out of your mind?"

She said urgently: "You said yourself there was a philosophy about these things. I would go back to him . . . after. It would not last for long . . . a few months, perhaps." She said: "I'd get tired of you when the money was gone."

He said: "But for Heaven's sake! Where should we go?"

She looked up quickly. She said soberly: "No, I suppose not. I should never be able to trust you with it. You would want to return it to your Foreign Office. That's the trouble with honest men; you can never trust them." She said the word *honest* as though it were an insult. She said: "Anyway, there isn't time now. Not any more."

Metcalfe stared at her. He said: "You are a remarkable woman. I wish I could feel as you do."

She put an arm round his knees. She said: "Are you so rigidly bound by your principles? Can you feel nothing more than your obligations? Isn't there more in your life than the things which are . . . right; the

164

things which you *must* do. Is your whole life so very restricted?"

"No, no. Not restricted." He said coldly: "I'm in a position of trust. I don't want to abuse it, that's all." He said wrathfully, the strength creeping back into him: "You make me feel terribly smug. It's not that at all; just say we don't see eye to eye and leave it at that."

"But for all that money? There's so much of it, so very much. Can't you feel the . . . temptation, just a little bit? Do you really want to cart it off and hand it over to your stuffy Government? What difference will it make to them?"

Metcalfe said: "You promised me a drink."

She laughed suddenly. She was genuinely amused. All the old venom had gone from her eyes and she was laughing. She said: "When two conflicting philosophies meet like this, we could solve a lot of problems if we could only try to understand one another. Isn't that so?"

She went to the door and paused. She said: "I'm going to get the drinks. Can I trust you?" She added: "You won't find the money or the gun, even if you feel strong enough to look for them." She turned and was gone.

Metcalfe struggled to his feet and stood swaying by the chair for a moment. The pain in his side was severe and his head was throbbing. He wondered if there was much damage done. He stumbled across to the window, pushed the casement open, and leaned out, feeling the cool night air on his forehead and on his chest. Down below him all was in darkness. He steadied himself at the sill, and stood there till she returned.

She came in holding a tray of glasses, a siphon, a bottle of whisky. She said:

165

"Better get away from the window; you'll get pneumonia. Let me find you a shirt."

She went to the closet and found a white silk shirt. She said: "It may be a little tight on you, but your own is not fit to wear. Are you feeling better?"

He nodded. He said, grimacing: "Did you get the bullet out?"

"It wasn't necessary. It went right through you. It may have cracked a rib; I don't think so."

He felt his side gently. The wound was high under his shoulder, close to the side. He said sullenly, feeling it: "How the hell did that miss my shoulder blade?"

She was busy pouring the drinks. He noticed there were three glasses on the tray. He said: "Company?"

"Yes."

Metcalfe took his drink and sipped it, feeling the slow warm fire of it coursing into him. He said: "I thought I heard the telephone ring."

"That was what saved your life." She said coldly, as though discussing a bird shoot: "My attention was distracted. I had no intention at the time of merely wounding you."

He slipped into the shirt; the label on it said "Charvet, Paris." He picked up his tie from the floor and put it on. She was staring at him again, watching.

He said: "In repose, your face is truly beautiful. You're a lovely woman."

She said softly: "Tell me about your English girl. Is she beautiful? Is she as beautiful as I?"

"No." Metcalfe shook his head. "She's not as lovely as you. She has . . . a sort of . . . Madonna-like quality about her. She's . . . restful. We get on very well together, like the same things, have the same tastes——"

"Is that what you call love in English? That you get

166

on well together? I get on well with my servants. Is she a virgin?"

Metcalfe said irritably: "No, of course not. She's . . . I'm very much in love with her. She's sweet and kind and she's everything I've ever wanted. Does that satisfy you?"

"The question is, does it satisfy you? You wanted me just now. Do we get a diplomatic apology for that?"

He smiled. "No, not that. The cure for love-sickness is gratification. I will not apologise for wanting to be cured."

She said: "You're very candid. And not very flattering."

Metcalfe shrugged. He said: "I'm not being unflattering. Physical desire is common to all the animals, but only man suffers from it." He slipped his whisky, "Inhibitions, I suppose. If you release the sexual urge from the limiting factor of the mating season, which is common to all the other animals, and if you add the complications caused by a higher nervous system and the power of speech, the result is a completely divided purpose. One of those purposes at least, can be satisfied by immediate gratification. The hell with the conventions."

He stood in front of the mirror, knotting his tie. He said slowly: "You told me a while ago that this was not the end. It's my turn to say the same thing now. You must know that I won't give up so easily."

He saw her reflected in the mirror, raising her delicate shoulders. He knew that some of the feeling in him was a strong desire to see her again. He touched his side gingerly.

She said: "I offered you a share. You refused. As far as I am concerned, that's the end of it."

He said, staring at his face in the mirror:

"My God! I look ghastly! A ghastly sight. Next time we meet I will endeavour to put up a better show. It's not easy to swallow an indignity like this. It isn't always——"

He broke off and swung round in amazement.

Reflected in the mirror, framed in the open doorway, gun in hand, silent and scowling, stood Dinesen. He said, stammering his surprise: "Dinesen! But . . . I didn't expect—— Where the devil did you come from?"

Dinesen's sharp, alert eyes moved slowly, unsmiling, from Metcalfe to the woman, glanced briefly but adequately to the rumpled bedding and the torn night-dress, then at the blood-stained shirt on the floor. He looked again at Metcalfe, and his eyes were hard. He said coldly: "Isn't that my shirt you have on?"

Metcalfe swallowed hard. He said angrily: "You know damn well why I'm here."

Dinesen said: "I know you have an ostensible reason for being here. Who've you been fighting?"

Lala Mancini said mildly: "I had to stop him taking the money, Petar."

For a brief moment, a thin smile crossed Dinesen's face. He said: "Has he harmed you . . . in any way? In any way at all?"

"No. Not in any way at all."

Dinesen said lightly: "I'm so glad. I should hate to have to avenge your honour, or anything maudlin like that. Is he armed?"

"No. He was. I took his gun away from him."

Dinesen smiled faintly. "I see. I hope he didn't give you too much trouble."

Metcalfe said irritably: "For God's sake stop discussing me in the third person. And put that damned revolver away. I've had a bellyful of this damn nonsense tonight. Even if I had a gun, you know bloody well I wouldn't use it on either of you."

Dinesen slipped the gun into his pocket. He said casually: "No, I don't believe you would. But make no mistake, my dear Ian, I would. This time the stakes are too high. Far too high. I'd like you to understand that. If I have to kill for this money, I will. There's too damn much of it to fool around with."

There was a hard look on his lined, bitter, prematurely old features. He crossed the room and put his arm round the woman, kissing her lightly on the mouth, then holding her close to him. Over his shoulder she stared at Metcalfe; there was a sort of silent pleading in her eyes. He felt as though he were sharing a guilty secret and turned away heavily.

Dinesen said: "Where's the money, *carissima?*"

"In the safe."

Dinesen went to the bedside table, opened the drawer and took out a small key. He crossed to the closet, pulled aside the long array of clothes and disclosed a wall safe. He unlocked it and pulled out the battered tin trunk. He said carelessly: "Is it all here?"

She nodded. She said: "Yes. I changed the gold sovereigns in Trieste. It's all there."

Dinesen said suddenly: "Where's Harry Pender?"

Metcalfe said easily: "At the hotel across the street."

Dinesen stood staring at him for a moment. Then he strode to the door, shut it, and turned the key in the lock. He went quickly to the open window, leaned out and called softly:

"Giovanni?"

There was an answering call from below.

Dinesen picked up the trunk, examined the lock on it briefly, snapped the padlock, and dropped it out into the darkness. He turned and said:

169

"You always were a bad liar. Is he in the house here?"

The Countess looked up quickly. She said: "No, Petar, I don't think he is. He would have come to help earlier . . . when our friend here was in difficulty."

Dinesen went to the window again. He called out: *"Portatelo alla machina!"*

He turned round and said: "Just to be on the safe side." He picked up a glass of whisky and drained it, pouring himself another.

Metcalfe said: "Giovanni? That must be Giovanni Ricci, then."

Dinesen put his glass down carefully. He said: "I had rather hoped you wouldn't know that. Yes, it's Ricci. The man who actually killed Major Hewitt. I don't really like working with people like that, but . . . well, as I said before, the stakes are high. I've no particular obligation to explain my actions to you, but . . . I've dabbled in the black market quite a bit, smuggled a little, a fast one here and there; I've never done anything . . . well, anything I could really reproach myself with. As you know, my morals are sufficiently elastic. But this time—this time the gloves are off. This isn't a cargo of American cigarettes smuggled in from Tangier. It isn't even a thousand-dollar diamond from Tanganyika. It's quarter of a million pounds—in cash. I'm going to keep it. If that means playing rough . . ." He shrugged his shoulders eloquently.

He said: "Keep out of it, Ian; keep out of it. I don't want to cause you trouble. Stakes like these are too high for . . . for nice people. That's why I've brought Ricci along."

"And you think you can trust him?"

Dinesen grinned quickly. He said affably: "Have another drink, my dear Ian. No. Of course I don't

170

trust him. But he came into the country on a false passport and the police would dearly like to know that he's here." He patted his breast pocket. "I have his passport here. The rest is easy. He's very anxious to get back to the States with his share."

Metcalfe said shrewdly: "He'll get a share?"

"Well . . ." Dinesen shrugged. "Something for his trouble." He added: "You must admit we were well organised."

Metcalfe said: "I never doubted your executive ability."

"Then tell me one thing. How did you get on to this house?"

Metcalfe said: "You made one mistake. The Contessa used her own name at the Dire-Dawa airport. The rest was deduction."

"You were very lucky." He poured another drink. He stood holding it, idly kicking at the bloody shirt on the floor. He said: "Are you badly hurt? I suppose I ought to check and see."

"No. A little shaky, that's all. I'll pass."

"And what are your plans, now? This time, surely, you must realise you're beaten?"

Metcalfe said crossly: "So you told me before. I'd like another drink, and then I'll go back to my hotel and clean up."

Dinesen grinned. He said apologetically: "Of course. Am I forgetting my duties as a host?"

He handed Metcalfe a glass. He said solicitously: "Are you sure you feel strong enough to get back under your own steam? Can I give you a hand?"

Metcalfe drained his glass. He said briefly: "I'll manage." He walked across to the door; he was feeling a little dizzy. He stopped and looked at the Countess, standing there calm, aloof, silent. He said slowly:

"Good night, Contessa. I hope next time we meet . . ."

Her face was expressionless. "Next time?" she said. "Next time? There will be no next time, signore."

Dinesen said affably: "Good night, Ian. You may keep the shirt; it fits you quite nicely. A memento. A booby prize."

Metcalfe stepped out into the dark hall and closed the door behind him. He thought, *The bastard. The bloody bastard.* He pulled himself up suddenly. He said to himself savagely, *Harry Pender. I'll have that bastard's guts for a necktie.*

Chapter Eleven

THERE was a violence raging in him as he stepped out of the heavy oak front-door into the garden, an unreasoning, inexpressible hatred of everything and everybody. The battered tin trunk with its tight-packed thousands, in its tangible form the complete and successful fulfilment of his assignment, was a weight on his shoulders as vivid as if it were physical. He had touched it and the touch still burned.

The lights were on in the house now, a chandelier in the hall casting its oblique shadows through the doorway and on to the grass verge in front of the building, across the trim privet hedges and into the dark-leaved shrubbery. A man was standing by the stone pillars of the porch, loafing, leaning, arms akimbo. He was thin, close-cropped, under-nourished. His wizened face was sunburned, but not with the deep and healthy tan of the white African; there were raw patches of red flesh on his nose and about his temples the skin had peeled off. He was smoking an American cigarette, just the last half-inch or so drooping out of the corner of his mouth. His clothes were new but cheap. His grey jacket was open, and the falling light struck sharply across the Luger stuck ostentatiously in his belt, his clothing held open on purpose to show it. He was grinning, his expression seeming to say: "*Vede la pistola, caro?*"

He chuckled offensively as Metcalfe moved past him. Metcalfe said: "*Ciao*, Buitoni," stressing the name. He added: "Be careful, Buitoni," accenting the name again.

His guess was right. There was some compensation, a useless one perhaps, but none the less satisfying, in the man's sudden start, as he dropped his arms, a sudden pathetic fear clearly visible on his emaciated, grotesquely burned face. Metcalfe smiled and stepped out of the light into the heavily wooded garden.

The lights on the road were clear and bright three hundred feet or more ahead, through the trees and beyond the dense foliage about the fence, the buildings across the way towering high above the garden, but below in the shrubbery all was in darkness. He picked his way carefully on the paving-stones of the pathway, conscious with a sort of bitterness that somebody was following him out, close behind him. Buitoni? He half turned. Buitoni was still visible in the lighted doorway; he saw him light a fresh cigarette, and the splutter of the match was clearly audible in the silence. He shrugged and moved on towards the gate.

He saw the car now, long and sleek and powerful—Dinesen's Maserati, squat and low and gleaming, a car of astonishing power and speed, scintillating brightly at every reflected light, its top down, its windshield folded flat. Another guard was sitting up on the bodywork, his feet on the seat. He was staring at Metcalfe as he went by, his gun, a Beretta machine-pistol, casually carried across his knees, in impudent disregard of the consequences. He thought: *This is Rome, the middle of the city, in the twentieth century, would he dare to fire if I attacked him?* Then he was conscious of the presence close beside him of another man who detached himself from the trees at his left. *Three of them*, he thought; *which one is Ricci?* He stopped for a brief moment and felt with a sudden surge of indignity the pressure of a gun in his back. He heard a low voice, "*Avanti*, friend, keep moving," and he shrugged again and moved towards the big iron gates set in the creeper-covered fence. He swung one of them open and stepped out on to the pavement, and all the anger welled up inside him again. He stood in the roadway and heard the gate clang shut behind him with a clatter of finality, and he heard the bolt shot noisily home.

He turned to the left and moved slowly away, his mind working rapidly. *The money is still there*, he thought, *in the car. There are four of them, Dinesen, Ricci, Buitoni, and one other, and they are all armed*, and he realised the impossibility of it all.

And then he nearly leaped out of his skin as he felt a light touch on his shoulder. He heard an urgent voice, Harry Pender's voice, saying: "Keep moving, they may still be watching you," and not stopping he felt, rather than saw, that Pender had moved out of the shadow of a clump of lilac hanging down from the high iron fence and was falling into step behind him, a few paces behind, a casual, disinterested pedestrian out for a stroll. He heard the low voice coming at him urgently:

"Go into the hotel—they're watching—then out again at the side door. See you in the passage. Hurry."

Not answering, he crossed the road slowly, his head sunk on his chest, and pushed his way through into the little hotel. He crossed quickly to the side door and out into the narrow street at the side of the building, and stood waiting, standing in the darkness beside a big delivery truck. He took out a cigarette and lit it.

In a moment he saw Harry Pender saunter across the road, then step hurriedly forward as he turned the corner. He came up urgently. He said: "Ian! Are you all right? I thought you'd had it."

Metcalfe said angrily: "What the devil happened to you? Where the hell were you?"

Pender said smoothly: "Keep your shirt on. There's not much time to talk. Mendels is on his way here with some friends. We'll get that box yet. Are you hurt badly?"

"Mendels? What happened? Where does he come in?"

"Are you badly hurt?"

"Hell, no. It's a clean flesh wound. What's this about Mendels?"

"Wait. Move over here to the corner—we've got to keep an eye on that gate. Keep your fingers crossed and hope they get here in time."

Metcalfe said irritably: "For God's sake, what's all this about Joe Mendels?"

Pender said: "Well, you told me to come after you if nothing happened in half an hour, so thirty minutes after you disappeared I started creeping up the stairs again to see what had happened to you." He grinned in the half-light. "From the sound of it, I rather imagined she was about to lose her virtue. Everything seemed under control, but I listened for a while to make sure; the door was shut, you remember, and while I had my ear glued to the panel, there was a shot loud enough to raise all Hades, and I heard you fall. That was the crucial moment; just as I grabbed the door-handle, I heard the 'phone ring."

Metcalfe said slowly: "I'm beginning to understand . . . what then?"

"Well, I'd actually turned the door-knob when I realised that she had picked up the 'phone. Obviously, if I'd have barged in, she'd have simply yelled for help at once, and that would have been the end of that. It was quite a problem." He said sombrely: "As a matter of fact, I almost assumed that you were dead. A gun-shot at such close range . . . I heard you fall . . . and there was something very . . . well, dead, about that noise. But she was talking on the 'phone, so my mind was occupied, anyway. It was obviously Dinesen. I heard her tell him to come over at once, and somehow I got the idea that he wasn't very far away. Then she said—and thank Heaven for that," he added, "'*No. Non e morto*,' so I knew you'd only been wounded, though I couldn't know how badly. The door was off the latch now, so I risked opening it an inch or so and I saw her pulling off your jacket and shirt and bandaging you up. She had the grace to look very pale and worried about it all, but I was equally worried—what to do? Obviously, Dinesen was on his rapid way there, and I rather hoped that he'd be alone, in which case I was going to wait till he was in the bedroom with the woman and then barge in and hold them both up. But then after a few minutes I heard him sneak in quietly downstairs, and I clearly heard him whispering to the others; he was posting them about the grounds." He went on with a grudging admiration, "I must say there's nothing wrong with his military training. He had one man at each door and another loose in the grounds to keep an eye on the car—otherwise I'd have taken the valves out of his tyres and we shouldn't now be praying for the others to get here in time."

Metcalfe said: "There are four of them—including Ricci and Buitoni. What about the servants? There don't seem to be any."

Pender shook his head. "Not as far as I could see. Can't think how or why she should be there alone——"

"She mentioned the servants to me, but nobody seemed to come running when she fired off my revolver."

"She may have been bluffing. Anyway, when Dinesen turned up, I sneaked behind the arch at the top of the stairs—he passed within a foot of me; I very nearly hit him over the head with my lead pipe—and wondered about reinforcements, which we were obviously going to need. So as soon as you and Dinesen and the Contessa had settled down to a jolly evening's entertainment, I beat it out of the kitchen window, sneaked round the house to the front, got right in among the bushes by the front fence, and signalled to Claire, who was still waiting at the bedroom window. Actually, not as easy as it sounds, with the garden full of thugs wandering about with sub-machine-guns. Put in some pretty nifty evasive action there. . . . Not knowing whether or not she could read Morse, I simply flashed a hopeful S.O.S. and a few minutes later, bless her soul, she appeared at the hotel doors. So I damn nearly broke my neck clambering over the iron fence unseen to all the thugs and sent her off to phone Mendels at once; to have him round up a couple of hefty friends and come right over—remember, he wanted some excitement? He ought to be here any minute now."

"What about Claire? Where is she?"

"Sitting in the car round the corner, waiting for Joe and watching the gates of the house. If that monstrous car of Dinesen's appears, we've got to follow it. I might say that I didn't know what your plans would be now; just thought it would be a good idea to have some help along. We obviously can't take the four of them alone; we've only got my revolver between us. Joe Mendels was the obvious answer."

Metcalfe nodded. He said: "If they get here in time. Meanwhile, suppose you get Claire to bring the car round here; I'd better keep out of sight. If Dinesen turns up, we'll have to follow, with or without the others. We'll leave Claire behind to watch for Joe—though how the hell he'll know how to follow——"

"He'll know the direction, that's all. But he should be here in a minute. Claire said he had a house full of guests and was bringing them all over right away. She said he sounded a little bit under the weather . . ."

Metcalfe groaned. He said: "I wonder who the hell his guests are; this is supposed to be top secret. A pitched battle in the middle of Rome with the Foreign Office and the State Department involved—the Colonel's going to love it." He said irritably: "There must be an easier way. . . . Go and get the car, there's a good fellow."

Pender moved off quietly. The little Fiat was parked outside the hotel, Claire at the wheel. He opened the door and got in. He said:

"Ian's all right; it was just a——" then broke off, conscious of the cigar smoke. He swung round in the seat. He said: "Good God! When did you get here?"

Claire said: "You haven't met, have you? Joe Mendels, Harry Pender."

Mendels said: "Glad to know you. Claire's been reciting all your troubles. Good to know Ian's all right —the moron."

Claire said: "There's a whole carload of help parked a hundred yards up the street, ready for work if required."

Mendels nodded. He said, a little thickly: "Some of the boys . . . we were having us a party. Some of them . . . I should say, some of us, are a little bit inebriated. Somebody's birthday."

Pender said quickly: "Who are the others, Joe?"

Mendels waved a delicate hand. He said: "Oh, just some of the boys . . . newspapers——"

179

"Oh no!"

"Not to worry, Harry. Soul of discretion, faithful to the cause. All Americans . . . don't even remember who's there. Will White, he's a writer of some sort; Gord Errol, sells automobiles; Ray Emery, he's an agency correspondent; and Pat Hinks, he sells liquor when he's not actively occupied in consuming it himself. Good bunch of boys. Pat was with me in O.S.S. during the war, and the others are left-overs from the army or the Marines or some such. You'll get on fine with them."

"Any arms?"

Mendels said hesitantly: "Well, you know how it is. Can't really expect us law-abiding citizens to carry arms, can you? But there might be a shot-gun or two lying about on the floor of the car . . ."

"Splendid!"

"And I seem to remember leaving my hunting rifle in the trunk some place. Know how many we're up against?"

"Four. Dinesen, your two Italians, Ricci and Buitoni, and one other. And the woman, of course."

Mendels was interested. He said: "So friend Ricci is here, is he? Looks like this might be the end of my Rome assignment."

Claire said: "But we still can't call in the police."

Mendels patted her knee affectionately. He said: "Who the heck wants to call in the cops? Not to worry, honey, let's us take care of this. You want I should whistle the boys up?"

Pender said happily: "Let's pick up Ian first."

It was nearly two o'clock when they heard the distantly resonant clang as the bolt on the big iron gates was pulled back and the creaking grill swung open.

The two cars were waiting round the angle of the dark passageway. First, the big Buick with Mendels at the wheel and Ian beside him and the two newcomers, Hinks and Errol, in the back, both slightly the worse for the evening's previous entertainment, quietly but argumentatively trying to sell each other their respective wares. Behind them, the little hired Fiat stood ready to take off after the bigger car, with Pender and Claire in the front and the two literary types tightly squashed into the back seat, vehemently arguing the respective merits of the novel and the newspaper.

Looking distastefully at the speedometer of the tiny car, Pender said unhappily: "We're going to be chasing a Maserati and a Buick—our top speed is probably round about fifty."

White stopped arguing. He said: "Not to worry, brother. That Buick of Joe's will catch any goddam car on the market. Ain't none o' them foreign cars can take off like that goddam Buick."

Emery said: "Wish I'd brought a camera. Might have got me some pictures."

Pender said: "Here we go."

The Buick ahead of them started up with a silent flurry of exhaust gases, and Pender stepped on the starter. They heard the distinctive roar of the Maserati round the corner as it pulled out of the drive on to the road, then opened its throttle on the highway. As the Buick swung round in pursuit, only its side-lights on, Metcalfe said:

"Keep well behind them, Joe. If they see us on their tail, we've had it."

Mendels said, a little complacently: "Not in this car, fella. We'll catch 'em."

"Nuovolari," Metcalfe said, "used to drive one of those things in the road races at a hundred and eighty miles an hour. Miles," he said, "not kilos."

"Oh, that's different. In that case, the sooner we catch them, the better."

Metcalfe said: "If we keep behind them till we're clear of the town—assuming, that is, that they *are* leaving town—and wait till we're on an open stretch of road, then we ought to be able to force them into the ditch and hold them up. We're seven to their four. If the Mancini woman is with them, they'll be all the less likely to start shooting. If it's going to come to a pitched battle, it must be well clear of the town. If the Carabinieri descend on the battle-field in time to catch us making off with the loot, then London is going to be very, very, embarrassed, to say the least. And it might easily come to that. Are you game?"

Mendels nodded. "I'll be happier if we've got away from that little Fiat. I don't think your Claire ought to be in this."

"I know. I was firm. Not firm enough. She said: 'This time I'm coming. . . .' You know the idea? *Once out of my sight and look what happens.* But they'll be safe enough in the rear car; it's your Buick that's going to cop it if there's any trouble."

Errol said: "Not to worry, Joe boy. Get you a new car first thing in the morning. Got just the thing for you——"

Mendels said: "Surely they'll be as anxious as we are to avoid an open fight. They'll see we've got two cars to their one." He said suddenly: "They've got the woman with them."

The long red roadster passed under a street light, a few hundred yards ahead of them. Through the three heads packed tight together in the back seat, the long blond hair of the woman in front was clearly visible.

Metcalfe said: "So much the better."

The column was moving fast now, the needle of the big Buick steady on fifty, the motor purring silently, scarcely audible. They were on a wide boulevard, a double row of plane trees breaking up the light of the lamps down the centre of the road, a dappled *chiaroscuro* of gently agitating design as they sped along.

Metcalfe said, staring out of the windows at the tall buildings alongside them: "If he keeps on this road . . . we're making for the Appia Antica by the look of it. Then where the hell's he going? Naples?"

"We'll soon see. Nice drive anyway. One of my favourite roads, the Appian Way. Built by the Censor Appius Claudius in . . . what was it? Three hundred and something B.C.? *Longarum regina viarum.* How's your classical education? It also has a more recent history."

"Uh-huh?"

"If I remember rightly, that's where most of the black-market boys used to make their collections during the occupation. Heck of a lot of military transportation changed hands along the Appian Way in the good old days. It's as good a place as any for a hold-up. Harry Pender know what he has to do? There are some pretty lonely stretches there."

Metcalfe nodded. "As soon as we stop them, he's to come up behind, stop the car; your two chaps'll jump out waving their shot-guns, and Harry stays in the car with Claire for a quick get-away if necessary. Your party keeps me covered; I do all the talking. If anybody starts giving any trouble, fire a couple of rounds over their heads. But for God's sake move fast if you have to—one of them's got a sub-machine gun."

"Do you think they'll fight?"

"Dinesen—no. I don't think he'll try open warfare. After all, we've been friends for a long time. It's the others I'm worried about."

Mendels nodded. "Right. Ricci's the one to watch; he's got too much to lose. That's where the trouble will be, if any. Of course, he doesn't realise you know who he is; he may be just as anxious not to get embroiled with the local law, because once they get their hands on him, that's the end of Signor Ricci. Anyway, we'll be ready for them."

The imposing yellow stones of a ruined gateway passed over their heads, dimly lit by yellow lights and white in the gleam of the rising moon.

Metcalfe murmured: "A fascinating place, Rome."

Mendels nodded. "The most fascinating country in the world. I love it," He glanced at the dashboard clock. "Two-thirty," he announced. On the back seat Pat Hinks leaned forward and held out a pocket flask.

He said: "How's the bullet-riddled body, Mac?"

Metcalfe took the flask. He grinned in the darkness. He said: "How's the prospect of a fight?"

Hinks said: "Never did look to see if these shot-guns are loaded, but we sure are. You set 'em up, Mac, I'll knock 'em down." He said: "That's pretty good liquor you got there, Mac. Guaranteed three months old. You don't figure on dying on us before the night's out?"

Metcalfe said: "I'm fine. This is the closing adventure."

Hinks shook his head sadly. "Pity," he said. "Pity. I sure like a nice funeral once in a while. Nothing like a good funeral with plenty of liquor. . . ."

On the open road the cars were moving faster. The

faint green lights of the dash showed the speedometer nearing sixty, then as Ian watched, the needle crept up to seventy, lingered there, then moved to seventy-five. Their headlights were on now, the bright white beams flooding the road ahead of them.

Rome was soon far behind them and they saw the pale white gleam of the moon on the water as they tore past the marshes and into Terracina, braking fiercely as they entered the tiny ancient village by the sea, then shooting ahead again as they swung out of the public square and on to the main road again, lurching madly as they took the little hump-backed bridges too fast, keeping their eyes always on the rear lights of the roadster far ahead.

Mendels muttered: "One thing to catch up with that guy; something else again to overtake him."

They saw the distant bulk of the fortress prison at Gaeta as they speeded through Formia and on down the coastal road, shooting past the night-bound lorries on the cool tarmac, the tall trees of Campania guiding them like an arrow as they shot down the highway. They sped through Capua, deserted and silent now, over the harsh iron bridges, and hurtled into the blackness ahead of them. Metcalfe was worried.

He said: "At this speed, he'll soon see we're on his tail."

Mendels nodded. "Uh-huh. If he hasn't already found that out. The night traffic on this road is pretty fast though. . . . Caserta coming up. Does that mean he's headed for Naples after all?"

But Caserta was on them and past them in a few moments. Pat Hinks said sleepily: "Don't they have speed cops in this part of the world? We took that main street at nearly seventy. We O.K. for gas?"

Mendels nodded. He was sitting up straight and alert

at the wheel, his sharp eyes fixed with an attentive immobility on the distant reach of his headlights.

They flashed through Maddaloni, a village in darkness and peace, and swung off the road at Nola. The Maserati turned into a side-road and seemed to slow down slightly. The needle on the speedometer of the big Buick held steady on sixty, its pale green glow faintly luminescent in the darkness.

Mendels said: "Dark countryside. No towns of any size around us. And twenty miles to the nearest village. What do you say we take him now?"

Metcalfe said: "Ready when you are."

The distance between them slowly lessened.

The Maserati was a constant half-mile in front, its twin rear lights close to the road, steadily holding the centre. Then it began to slow down. They dropped to fifty and held it, and then to forty, and for a few more miles the pace did not change; the shadows of the chestnut trees and the high hedges moved past them more sedately, and the imposing majesty of a ruined aqueduct, tall and graceful and stately, its ancient stones covered with moss and creeper, stood out in awesome simplicity against the night sky close beside them. The cars had slowed down again; they were holding thirty-five.

"What's he up to?" Mendels asked.

"Looking for a turning?"

In the back of the Buick, Errol was leaning forward, his elbows on the back of the front seat, staring fixedly at the car ahead of them, closer now. He said suddenly: "They're on to us, Joe."

Mendels did not answer. They sat in silence watching the roadster. Its five occupants were facing insistently ahead of them, studiously ignoring the car behind. Mendels said at last: "You've got something there."

"You think so?" Metcalfe asked.

"We've dropped from seventy-five to thirty-five in the last few miles. He must be wondering why we don't overtake. That being so, one of them, at least, is bound to look over his shoulders once in a while just to say what the hell. In an open car? A guy always wants to know what's holding up the fellow behind him."

Metcalfe grunted. He said: "Well, we're giving Harry a chance to catch up. Any sign of him?"

Errol swung round and watched through the rear window. He said: "Yeah, he's there. Probably busting his guts out, but he's there."

Metcalfe turned to Mendels. He said: "Well, shall we take them?"

Mendels nodded. Over his shoulder, he asked: "You guys ready?"

There was a clatter in the back as they sorted out the shot-guns. Hinks said cheerfully: "Well, what d'ya know? They're loaded yet. Let's go!"

Mendels swung the Buick into the centre of the road and pushed his foot down. The great car surged silently forward, and Metcalfe momentarily felt the pain of the pressure in his side. He felt the rush of cold air as the windows came smoothly down at the touch of a button, and he saw the blue gleam of a shot-gun barrel over his right shoulder, and he felt the tenseness in the atmosphere as the distance between the two cars shortened. In their headlights, the Maserati was suddenly brightly lit, low and red and gleaming. Dinesen was clearly visible at the wheel. There were two hundred yards between them, then a hundred, then fifty. Then, in an incredibly brief instant, they were running side by side on the narrow, winding road. Metcalfe switched on the spotlight and directed it full on to Dinesen's face. Leaning close against the open window, the pain in his chest acute in the excitement, feeling the blood pulsing in his wound, he shouted:

"Pull over!"

His words were half lost in the rush of wind, and he shouted again: "Pull over!"

Dinesen's face was set. This was no surprise to him. Metcalfe realised at once that he was ready for them. He saw him staring at the shot-gun barrel, and saw, or fancied he saw him glance briefly but comprehensively at the car itself, as though measuring its power, and then his right arm shot out and pulled the woman beside him (her face showing excitement rather than alarm) down into his lap, shielding her head with his body. At the same instant, with a sudden supercharged roar, splitting open the relative silence of the night, its exhaust spitting fire, the Maserati shot forward, leaping ahead like an angry beast of prey.

Mendels thrust his foot hard on the floor and swung the wheel smoothly round. The polished arc of the Buick surged forward toward the roadster, and the crash of metal on metal jarred their ears, a rending, tearing, crushing sound. Then the Maserati, Dinesen fighting the wheel, its tyres screeching, swung clear to the centre of the road, careened over to the wrong side, righted itself, then shot ahead of them, a rear mud-guard broken and noisily trailing, banging clumsily on the pavement, sparks flying as it struck again and again.

Mendels swore and Hinks shouted gleefully: "Geronimo!" in a drunken exaltation. They saw one of the men in the back of the roadster tugging savagely at the broken fender, sprawled across the body of the car the others, white-faced, staring at them over their shoulders. The fender came off and clattered noisily on to the road, and they felt their wheels flatten it and kick it into the ditch, and Mendels said thickly: "All right, hold tight everybody," and the Buick took up the chase.

They sat silent for a moment, Metcalfe deep in the bitterness of his thoughts, Mendels intent on the road slipping with incredibly silent speed under their wheels, holding the centre, driving with smooth and careful skill as they moved into the eighties, purring effortlessly along behind.

He said at last:

"Nothing much between here and the sea. What then?"

Metcalfe said gloomily: "God knows. We'll never catch that Maserati."

Mendels said: "Don't know why we didn't pull that off. We should have done, you know."

Metcalfe said bitterly: "It's about time we had a stroke of luck. One damn thing after another. And at this speed, we're bound to lose the others."

"There's one thing," Mendels said. "I may be wrong, but we seemed to hit him pretty hard. Could have damaged his gas tank or one of his rear tyres. Guess we'll have to start praying again. If he gets a blow-out at this speed, he's going to be in real trouble."

They were doing more than ninety now, rubber screeching as they rounded the gentle curves, the tail lights of their quarry far in the distance, dim.

Metcalfe said: "It's nearly three o'clock. Three more hours to daylight. If we don't catch them before then, we've had it. And once he hits the town, we'll lose him." He said savagely: "You see what I mean? It's the same every time. We get within half an inch of him, and he wiggles clear again. And now—three hours to daylight and we're as far away as we ever were."

Mendels said: "If we do catch up with him—maybe it's a pretty big *if*—if we do, this time we'd better start shooting. Either that or call in the police."

"No." Metcalfe shook his head decisively. "This has got to be kept unofficial. At all costs." He said irritably: "Can't you get a bit more speed out of this crate?"

Mendels grinned. He said mildly: "Just under a hundred. Can't do much more on this road; but then, neither can he. We still might catch him. And this time we'd better start shooting. A round of buckshot into his gas tank, if we can get close enough, might make him see the light."

Metcalfe said: "First catch your hare . . . and don't forget that damned machine pistol they've got. A burst of that in our faces at speed won't do us any good."

The Maserati was a long way ahead now, its lights mere specks on the long straight road. Metcalfe said: "Two miles or more; we'll never catch him." And then he shouted: "Look out! He's turned off the road!"

Mendels peered ahead. He said: "Where the devil is he?"

He glanced briefly at the odometer. He said: "Two miles, was it? Watch the clock; we'll pull up."

They sped into the darkness, slowing down now. Metcalfe, watching the digits ticking up on the odometer, called: "A mile and a half . . . a mile point seven . . . five . . . point two. Here we are. Two miles. It was here somewhere."

They stopped the car. Errol said: "Take her to the top of the hill and we'll get out and have a look."

They crawled forward slowly, lights extinguished, to the top of the rise. They stopped again and got out, straining their ears in the silence.

Mendels said: "He's put his lights out, but if he's moving we'll hear him."

Metcalfe nodded. He said: "In that bus of his we'll hear him ten miles away."

There were only the night sounds of the country. The soft, damp air was cool on their faces. The lights of Naples were yellow and smudged far away to the north and the soft rush of the sea noises surged softly up in the silence as the breeze caught the sibilance of the surf far below them. There was no sound of the Maserati.

Mendels said, whispering: "He can't have gone on ahead?"

Metcalfe shook his head. He said: "At ninety miles an hour? Without lights? No, no. I don't even believe he's turned off. We should hear that engine of his from hell and gone. He's lying low somewhere. Waiting for us to go on."

"But why? He was gaining on us. What made him stop?"

Metcalfe shrugged. He said: "Your guess is as good as mine. Out of petrol? That damaged tyre? Afraid of the daylight? Don't forget he can't be sure we won't go to the police. Listen!"

They strained their ears in the darkness. The clouds broke in the sky and flooded them with a soft luminescence. They watched the shadows creeping across the fields below them. Hinks was leaning against the side of the car. He said softly:

"Holy cow! What'n hell's that down there?" Pointing.

Metcalfe followed his gaze. Below them, to their left, the lovely, silent stones of a dead city lay placidly at the foot of the great mountain that rose mightily above them, at once a shield and a poised sword, its crater top eloquently mouthing a threat of disaster as it stood sombrely outlined against the silent sky, the nebulous, wispy clouds clinging to its tip as though loathe to leave the spectacle of the fearful fires within it, hesitant, delicately poised and silent spectators. The stones were smooth and white and still.

He said briefly: "Pompeii. The exotic past."

They stood staring down at the ruined city. Then out of the silence, as the wind swung round momentarily, they heard the noise. It was a clatter and a rumble and an insistent commotion. They listened for a moment, and Metcalfe said:

"No. That's no Maserati. More like a lorry."

Then the lights appeared on the road to the north, twin dim specks in the distance, and as they noisily approached he said suddenly:

"Good God. I'd forgotten all about them. It's Claire and Harry in the Fiat."

They stood waiting till the little car drove up, steam hissing from its radiator. Metcalfe said:

"Switch off, for heaven's sake. We're listening for Maserati noises."

Pender grinned happily. He said: "All right. But I hope she'll start again. We burst a few blood-vessels getting here."

He patted the bodywork affectionately; he said: "But we made it." They struggled out of the tiny car, stretching their cramped limbs.

Claire said: "What's happened? We saw you hit him. And then we rather dropped behind."

Metcalfe put his arm around her shoulders. He said quietly: "He cut his lights just about here; we think he's lying low and waiting for us to go on."

Hinks said: "I've got some hooch in the car. What say we have a party?"

"Then why don't you take the cars on," Claire said,

"and we'll all wait here and listen. We're bound to hear him start up if he's within a few miles of us. Then come back after a short while."

"Not a bad idea." Metcalfe turned to Mendels. He said: "What do you say, Joe? You and Harry take the cars on for a few miles to flush him, then come back?"

Mendels nodded.

Claire said anxiously: "How do you feel? Having any trouble?"

Metcalfe smiled down at her upturned face in the moonlight, a lover standing beside her. He shook his head gently. "Fine," he said. "I feel fine."

Pender said: "Suppose he starts up the moment we've gone, and we wait fifteen minutes before we turn back? He'll have the hell of a start on us again."

Mendels moved to the trunk of the car. He said over his shoulder: "One thing they taught us in O.S.S. Never start an operation you can't finish for want of equipment. Should have a Verey pistol here some place. Can't say we're not well equipped. Here!"

He handed Metcalfe the pistol and two flares. He said:

"Of course, it'll give the game away at once. But I don't figure that's going to make the heck of a difference, under the circumstances. Only way we can find him is bring him out into the open."

Metcalfe nodded. He said: "Attaboy, Joe. O.K., Harry? Better take Claire along with you. As soon as we signal, beat it back like the bats out of hell." He added: "We sit by the side of the road and wait. Quietly, huh?"

Hinks nodded solemnly. He said: "Just let me get my luggage."

He took a bottle from the back of the Buick. He said

7* 193

softly: "Gotta have my samples along. Might meet a customer." He pulled out the two shot-guns as well.

They took up their positions at the edge of the road, close in by the trees. The two cars started up and moved slowly off, the big Buick silently, its lights bright on the road ahead, the little Fiat limping noisily and dimly along behind.

As the clatter died away in the distance all was silence. Metcalfe sat close under the broad and friendly foliage of a chestnut treet, staring out at Pompeii's pale beauty in the moonlight below. The others were shadows merged into the bushes. Somewhere above him an owl hooted. Somewhere to his left he heard the soft *plop* of a pulled cork. Momentarily the smell of rye whisky was on the air.

The wound in his side began to throb again. He thought of Claire as he waited in the cool silence.

Chapter Twelve

THE two cars had travelled for fifteen miles and twenty
minutes when they came to the village. The square,
inelegant stone-and-stucco houses interspersed with red
brick sat glumly and darkly astride the road, out of all
keeping with the soft and felicitous countryside around
them, dull and dirty and uninspiring. There were few
trees to break the monotony of the masonry. In the
village square (just a sudden and angular widening of
the main road) the lights of a single café were burning.

Pender said to Claire: "Wait a minute." He pulled
to the side of the road and braked to a stop. He said:
"Sit tight; back in a minute."

He rasped the hand-brake on, slipped out of the car,
and walked across the road to the café. Beyond the
swing door a buxom peasant woman was wiping the
marble counter-top with a damp rag. Bottles of wine
were ranged on the shelf above her, in straw casing,
brightly-labelled, weird-shaped, glowing and bulbous,
reflecting a sparkling coruscation of colour. The mirror
behind them was smeared and fly-specked. In a back
room a gramophone was grinding noisily, and at a table
in the corner four men were playing cards, a pale
young woman in black sitting sleepily and without
interest beside them.

Pender said cheerfully: "*Buona sera, signora. Un
biancho, per piacere.*" He sat at one of the tables.

The woman stopped her cleaning and brought him
the wine. She put a tumbler and a half-litre flask on the
table and stood beside him, idly straightening the table-

cloth. Under her loose black dress, her breasts were big and free. She pushed a lock of hair from her face with a gesture of absolute femininity, implying at once a weariness and softening, a yielding and a resignation.

Pender said affably: "We lost our friends—in a Maserati. You didn't see them go by here a few minutes ago? Or hear them?"

One of the card players looked up, a labourer, thin-faced and weatherbeaten. He said:

"A Maserati? The long one?" His black eyebrows were raised almost to the low line of his hair, his fore-head heavily crinkled. He said again: "The long one?" —gesturing with his hands, long and low.

Pender said quickly: "That's the one. Has it gone through? When? How long ago?"

The woman nodded her head. The man said approvingly: "A fine car, the Maserati. Don't see many nowadays, eh? The taxes, eh? In the old days ... Maserati, Alfa-Romeo, Ferrari, plenty of them in Rome. Naples too. Plenty of them. Nowadays ... no more money. Government take it all, eh? *Eh, gia.* A fine car, the Maserati."

Pender said: "How long ago? Did you see it?"

He raised his eyebrows another half-inch. He said: "*Ma cosa vuol' dire?* I don't understand. Did I see what?"

Pender said patiently: "Have you seen my friends' car go through on the road outside here—a few minutes ago? A Maserati?"

"A Maserati?"

"Yes."

"No. Hasn't passed here. But I know the Maserati well. There's always one up at the filter-beds." He turned to his companions again. He said: "You know the Maserati—*ah, che machina!* Used to drive one myself

196

once. Long time ago, in Palmanuova. *Eh, gia.* I was a chauffeur. Drove a Maserati for a certain Weiss, a Swiss; he had two of them. . . . The Duke of Aosta had one too. Didn't know I was a chauffeur, did you, eh? Well . . . a long time ago——"

Pender said: "If it had passed here, would you have heard it?"

"A Maserati? *Per Dio!* At twenty kilometres one hears them."

The woman beside him nodded. She said: "No, signore. Here, nobody passes. We are in the country here. Two hours and more, no cars on the road. Only the local people here—*gente di paese*. And this time of night everybody sleeping. Except these worthless ones who play cards all night."

Somebody said: "*Ma . . . stai zitta . . .*" and Pender finished his glass of wine. He laid fifty lire on the table and stood up. The woman gave him his change from the pocket of her apron, counting the ragged notes carefully on to the table in an untidy bundle. She said: "No cars have passed this way, signore, nothing."

Pender went outside. The Buick had pulled up behind the tiny Fiat. Mendels stuck his head out of the window. He said: "What gives?"

"Just wanted to check up. No Maserati passed. That means it's certain they're behind us. Seems pointless to go any further. What about turning the cars round and waiting for Ian's signal?" The yellow glare of the café was harsh and bright across the street.

Mendels said: "I got an idea. Why not leave that heap of yours in the village here, and all of us go back quietly in my car; no lights. Just sneak back up to them. They'll never see us against the trees, wherever they are. We can pull into the side of the road when the moon is out and move along when the clouds cover it.

Then we're all ready to take off after them as soon as they show themselves."

Pender said: "Uh-huh. Makes more sense than sitting here, anyway. If Ian signals, it's still going to be more than ten minutes before we can rejoin him; with ten minutes start, we'll never see hide nor hair of them. Let's do that."

He went back to the Fiat and opened the door. He said to Claire: "Change of plans. We're going back in Joe's car. Leave this here and pick it up later." He helped her out of the Fiat, and they climbed back in the Buick, all sitting together on the front seat, Claire in the centre and Pender by the door, his thin body twisted round so that his left arm lay along the seat at the back of her shoulders.

Mendels turned and smiled at Claire. He said: "Not tired yet of this wild goose-chase?"

She shook her head. She said: "You don't know Ian as well as I do. He'll get that box of banknotes if it takes a life-time. When we've all given up, he'll still be chasing it. And one day he'll get it. Maybe not tonight. But he'll get it, you'll see." She said: "Perhaps I'm biased. I suppose I am. But I still say he'll win. He always does."

Mendels looked at her shrewdly, then turned the car slowly in the wide and open square. He said softly: "Do you love him?"

She nodded. She said: "Yes. Very much."

"Marriage? Or is that none of my business?"

She smiled. "One of these days, I expect."

"He's a lucky guy. I guess he knows it."

They started moving slowly back in the direction from which they had come, moving slowly. The lights extinguished, the great motor silent and smooth, scarcely a vibration marring the stillness, like a ship on calm water, the clouds dark and sombre against the patches of lighter moonlit sky, and the mountain ahead of them rising up ponderous and awful, its open mouth gaping greedily at the heavens, the mantle of shrubbery at its feet a mere unbroken cloak of darker substance which they knew to be vines and bushes and hedges and cultivated patches and, further on, tall dark trees which thrust their appealing fingers into the sky, in prayer to the volcano, in fearful supplication to the gods of the fires below. The clouds cleared from the wide moon and the land was suddenly bright. They lumbered into the side of the road, on the black verge, close against the trees, waiting in the shadows for the darkness to come again, the engine softly idling, silent. They crept slowly forward again, then stopped once more, the still and fragrant Italian countryside, the loveliest on earth, soft and quiet and cool around them, not even the noise of a lorry on the main road far to the east ever drifting up on the slight wind to them, nothing to disturb the serenity of the night. The tall trees stood out dark and splendid against the sky. There was something eerie in the darkness.

Mendels said, speaking softly in the stillness:

"Strange how the noises of day fit a man into his environment. Twelve hours from now, either direction, cars and lorries and bicycles and people; ships and airplanes; and all the visible paraphernalia of progress. If you can call it progress. But here . . . now . . . in the darkness . . . this is the cradle of civilisation. Civilisation was born here. It spread right across the world, and it started here . . . right here. The Romans used to camp here, at this very spot. The Greeks before them and the Etruscans before them. They left their marks all around us: Capua—a capital city before Rome was built; Naples—'the New City,' a mere two thousand years old and more; Herculaneum, Surrentum, Cumae, Posidonia, Pompeii. I tell you, the world was born here—it's all around us, in this small circle. Would it really surprise you to see a legion of troops in armour pass by here, with us sitting like some strange gods come to visit an ancient civilisation? A legion of soldiers in *Sagum* and *Cassis*? Their heads would be bare in the breeze, and they'd be carrying their helmets slung from their shoulders, and they'd be armed with short sword and dagger and maybe a lance as well. Would it surprise you? It wouldn't surprise them. They'd think we *were* gods, come down from Vesuvius to watch them. We'd be nothing but a portent, an augury. We'd be linked with chicken entrails and made to prove that Nero was, or was not, going to win this or that battle. That's what they'd take us for. And how do we know they're not right? By jimminy, look at it: Capua—there it is, just over the hill, still a thriving city. Boats still pulling in to Posidium. There's Pompeii right beside us. How the hell do we know . . ." He said: "Did Pat leave one of those bottles on the back seat? I need a drink."

Pender swivelled round and searched for a while. He found a bottle of rye in one of the side pockets. He said: "We're in the wrong century. The world was a . . . simpler place then. I almost said, 'better.' Not sure I wouldn't have been right."

Claire said: "They had the games in those days. Thumbs down and off with his head. Listen to the crowd cheering."

"Well? We have some beautiful bombs."

"They threw Christians to the lions."

"And we kill off a million people a year with our shiny new automobiles."

"They had practically no medicine."

"And practically no income tax."

Claire laughed. She said: "We could keep this up all night. There goes the moon again."

They pulled quietly on to the road in the darkness once more.

Mendels said: "It's hard to realise how much a couple of thousand years means. You can take a drink in the streets of Pompeii from lead pipes put down twenty centuries ago. They had forced air heating in their baths, just like we have in our houses back home today. They fought each other for public office just as we do, and they all tried to get out of paying their taxes. They even got drunk just like us. I tell you, it was only yesterday . . . Twenty centuries? My father's father's . . . say it sixty times and you're right there." He was drinking neat whisky out of the bottle, holding the wheel steady with his left hand. He said: "I'm not worried about the Romans; pretty solid guys, I guess. So are we. But what about all that stuff in between? Nineteen fifty-five and here we are slipping along among the towns they built three, four, five hundred years before Christ. O.K. But where's all that history in between? What about King Arthur and Kubla Khan and Theodosius and . . . and . . ."

Pender said: "Come to that, what about Snow White and Uncle Tom Cobley?"

Mendels handed the bottle over to him and sighed. He said:

"Yeah, I know. I drink too much." He said to Claire: "You think I drink too much? Too many friends like Pat Hinks. Hell, he's never sober. But a great guy. A great guy."

Claire said: "Top of the next rise."

"Already?"

"Pull into the hedge and you'll see."

They slowly came to a stop abreast the rise in the road. Metcalfe was waiting for them. He said softly: "Thought it was you. What happened?"

Pender said: "We came to a café and checked. Fifteen miles up the road. No sign of them. And no side turnings. *Ergo*, they're here. Thought we might as well come back quietly. No turning off this road all the way back to Nola. And we know they passed through here. Nothing happening here?"

"Nothing. Not a damned sound." Metcalfe sounded worried. He said, speaking in a whisper: "There's not a single turning off this road. If they haven't passed the café ahead, then for God's sake they simply must be here somewhere." He turned and stared down the road into the darkness behind them, straining his eyes and his ears. He said anxiously: "We didn't pass a single turning. He *must* be on this road."

Mendels said: "It's more than forty minutes since he stopped. Either he's got the heck of a lot of patience or he isn't here."

Metcalfe said angrily: "But where's he going? That's the point. Is he just trying to get clear of towns in case we go to the police? There's nothing down this way—nothing." He said to Claire: "What about those reports? Anything in the files to indicate an interest for him down this way? A house, a farm, a boat perhaps?"

Claire shook her head. She said: "He's got a house at Rapallo on the Riviera, and this place in Rome; as far as we know, nothing else. Not in Italy, anyway. A boat's unlikely, because this frantic race was a last-minute effort; he'd have had no time to lay on a meeting with it. Unless that was all pre-arranged and he was coming down here in any case." Her eyes strayed out to sea, staring away at the wide silver of it, far to the west and below them. She said: "I'm inclined to agree with you. He's still lying low here somewhere."

Pender said: "Three hours to daylight. Does he realise that we daren't touch him except under cover of night? Is he waiting for the sun to come up and the traffic to start so that he can drive off under our noses and laugh at us? He must know we can hardly hold him up in broad daylight. Is that it?"

Metcalfe said miserably: "I don't know. I just don't know. Damnation! He was right at this spot when his lights went out. He must be here . . ."

Pender said: "Where are the others?"

"Scattered about under the trees. We're spread out over about half a mile or so. What do we do now? Just wait?"

Claire said: "We could walk a mile or two in each direction and look for a side turning, just in case——"

Mendels said, shaking his head: "Look for them if you like, but there's no side turning. Know this part like the palm of my hand. Used to go hunting quail up on the mountain there, then cut down this way to the sea for a swim. Used to do a lot of fishing round here too."

Metcalfe said urgently: "Down to the sea? From Vesuvius? Then there is a side track of some sort?"

"No," Mendels said: "sorry. It's just a footpath. Runs along the New Excavations at Pompeii. The workmen use it as a short cut to the road——"

"Could a car get along it?"

"Not a hope in hell. It's just a couple of feet wide—over the fields and into the vineyards. Nothing but a footpath up to the wine press and the main road. It's the old Roman track from the filter-beds, actually. But you couldn't get a car along it. Not a hope in hell."

"Not even a small one?"

"Not even a bicycle. There's even a stile of sorts to keep the cattle in."

Pender said suddenly: "What was that about the filter-beds?"

Mendels said: "The footpath—crosses the main road, then goes on up to the filter-beds. The Roman ones. Rather interesting, actually. Used to supply Herculaneum with water from the mountain, filtered on the lower slopes. Only been excavated a few years. What's on your mind?"

Pender said: "This might be the stroke of luck we want. It's a long shot . . ." He hesitated.

Metcalfe said: "Well, go on. What is it, for God's sake?"

Pender said slowly: "In the café down the road . . . I asked about a Maserati. One of the workmen there . . . no, it can't be. . . . But, well, one of them said there was often a Maserati up at the filter-beds . . . is it too much to hope for? Are there so many Maseratis about?"

Mendels said: "Was a time when every young blood in Rome had one, but they're a bit scarce nowadays. Did he mention the colour?"

"No. But he said '*quello lungo*'—the long one. In other words, the roadster."

Mendels said: "By jimminy . . . by golly . . . the Mancinis! Isn't there a Casa Mancini in Naples? A wine merchant?"

Metcalfe said: "No idea. But what about it?"

"They make a white wine called Aminian."

"Well?"

"Aminian is a sort of *Lagrima Christi*—it's made from grapes grown on the lower slopes of Vesuvius. One of the most famous wines in the world. The name at least goes right back to Pompeii. Does that add up? A Mancini vineyard and a Maserati roadster—both near the filter-beds."

Metcalfe said, puzzled: "But how the devil does he get up there?"

Mendels shrugged his shoulders. He said: "Damned if I know, brother. But we'd sure as hell better get up there. What do you say?"

Claire said quietly: "Makes sense, Ian."

Pender agreed. Metcalfe said: "All right, let's risk it. I'll go and bring the others in. But I still think——" He broke off.

There was a deep rumbling noise ahead of them, suddenly a low-throated roar, the thrumming, smooth pulsation of a powerful engine. Then headlights switched brightly on, no more than a few hundred yards ahead of them, flooding the road and the grass verge with a white brilliance. At once the rumble swelled to a sudden roar and the car leaped out of the shadows and on to the road. It swung sharply to the south and roared away, its sudden din a mockery of their whispers.

Metcalfe swore loudly. He shouted: "The car, Joe—turn the car round." He said angrily: "Filter beds! Filter-beds indeed!"

Mendels started the engine, raced forward to the edge of the road, backed up, shot forward again, backed almost to the ditch, forcing his gears, not caring about them. The red lights of the Maserati disappeared as the car swung round the bend and they heard the muffled sound of it far in the distance.

Pat Hinks came running up, panting hard, limping with unaccustomed running, the others behind him. He said: "Jesus, Jesus . . . it was right beside me and I didn't see it—fifty yards away, on the other side of the road . . . under the bushes. Jesus . . . I didn't see a goddam thing till he put his lights on."

Metcalfe shouted: "Into the car, quickly! We'll still catch him." He said irascibly: "Three more hours to daylight. We've got to catch him——"

Hinks said: "Wait . . . wait——"

Metcalfe said, man-handling him, pushing him towards the Buick:

"Get your breath back in the car—no time to lose . . . are the others all here?"

Hinks said again: "Wait . . . wait—there was only one guy in the car."

There was a sudden silence. Mendels said softly: "So."

Metcalfe said: "Only one? Are you sure? How can you be sure?"

Hinks said: "Hell, he was fifty yards away . . . less maybe. I was sitting down under a tree, low down. As soon as he put his lights on, I could see him clearly. Little guy with short black hair, pale thin face. I lay doggo so he wouldn't see me. He looked over his shoulder as he turned on to the road. Clear as daylight. I see good when I'm liquored up, and I'm sure as hell liquored up right now."

Mendels said: "That's it, then. The others have taken the footpath up the mountain. That guy Dinesen's nobody's fool. The filter-beds again. Only he doesn't know that we know."

Ian said quickly: "With the car as a decoy. He'll expect us to follow it."

Mendels said: "That guy's got brains." He jumped quickly out of the Buick. He said softly: "Hey, Gord? Want to take the car and follow?"

Errol slipped quickly behind the wheel. He said, grinning: "Want me to catch him?"

206

Metcalfe said quickly: "Get after him, let him lose you."

Mendels stepped back. He said: "Step on it, Gord. See you."

Errol switched on the lights and the big car shot soundlessly away. They stood watching it gathering speed, and then it had turned the corner and was gone.

Metcalfe said soberly: "They can be as much as forty minutes ahead of us. Or would they have just moved off?"

"No, I don't reckon so. Plain enough what's happened. He drove the car into the bushes and parked; then they all took the track up the mountainside on foot—all except one man who stayed with the car. His job was simply to lead us away from here if we looked like staying too long. He must have seen us come back and figured that we were going to search the area. Got scared we might find him, and took off, leading us away as per instructions. Good planning. The others get clear while one man leads us all over southern Italy."

"So they'll be on their way to some hide-out. And they'll imagine we're all in the Buick chasing him. How far to these famous filter-beds?"

"Three miles or so—a bit less, maybe. We can take a short cut through the town."

"The town?"

"Pompeii. The footpath is about half a mile further up. If we strike across country at a dog-trot, we might even catch up with them—we can cut off quite a corner by moving in a straight line. It's only fields. Easy enough to cross."

Claire said: "They're sure to be carrying the money-box with them. Should slow them down a bit."

Mendels grinned and said: "Some money-box!"

Metcalfe said: "All right, let's go. Joe and I in front, Harry and Claire fifty yards behind, the others fifty yards behind them. Quite an army. We're up against Dinesen, the Contessa, Ricci, and one other—four all told."

Pender said, "If we find them——"

"We'll find them. I can feel it in my bones. Let's go."

Mendels said: "You'd better take the rifle. Harry's got his revolver. Pat and I will take a shot-gun each. That makes three weapons in the advance party, only one with the rear. O.K.?"

Metcalfe said happily: "O.K."

They set off across the fields.

The moon was high above them when they came to the broken wall of Pompeii. Mendels said to them, whispering: "The track is about a couple of hundred yards or so to the right. If we go straight through the city and join it beyond the Vesuvius Gate, we can save another few hundred. Chances are they're making for the outbuildings in the vineyards which lie a little to our left—ahead of us. We'll get on to the Strada di Stabia, go straight on for half a mile through the centre of the town, then come out at the Gate on the north-west. It's another mile or less to the beginnings of the vineyards. Down this way."

Walking quietly, whispering, relaxing their pace after their heavy hurrying across the fields, they clambered down the steep bank to the excavations, dropping on the cobbled street below them. The dry limestone rubble dribbled down lightly after them. The stones of the ancient paved road were square-cut and gently rounded at the top, sloping unevenly towards the centre.

There were cypress trees growing along the verges, sparse and dark and sombre in the half-light, and the dim outline of a slender archway, supporting nothing but its own elegance, lay close beside them on their right, the round white moon high above it. They turned left towards the Stabia Gate with its flanking bastions, and Metcalfe paused for a moment to stare at the heavy vaulted archway with the great square stones beside it, creeper-covered and eroded. A heavy fragment of broken pilaster lay at his feet, a solid trunk of carved and fluted stone; it was covered with a dark and intertwining creeper, imprisoned by a black tentacle from the soil which fingered its insidious way across it and bound it triumphantly to the earth, a co-agency of the terrene violence that had hurled the stonework there. The angry labours of the volcano above them had overthrown these mighty handicrafts with an upheaval of infinite disdain, and the earthy ashes and the dust had covered them; and now, the black vines creeping out of the corrupted soil were gathering over them once more, conspiring to hold them there . . . and man was digging them up again, once more cutting away the weeds, breaking away the tufa, setting the monuments up again, a testimony at once of his pride, of his folly and of his obstinacy. And still the volcano rumbled its displeasure. He said softly: "Twenty centuries ago . . ." The dead stones were cold and silent and spacious around him.

They turned into the main road, moving silently over the rounded cobbles, avoiding the central ruts cut by a thousand Roman carts and chariots, and moved slowly forward, the ruined walls of the Gladiators' Barracks close beside them by the Covered Theatre, the antique stones stretching far out, across to the Forum and the Old City, with its little shops and bakeries and wine-presses and markets and its temples. Temples, he thought, temples everywhere—to Apollo, to Isis, to Jupiter, Juno and Minerva, and to Venus. They came to the Baths and glanced briefly down the Street of Abundance, with its wine-shops and its long-dead restaurants and its earthen jars precariously balanced in groups against the walls, still patiently waiting the service of the two-thousand-year-old young slave who would carry them off to be filled. . . . Here, he thought, they would have been eating and drinking, joking and chatting, some of them sleep-drunk on the potent Vesuvian wines, some of them fondling the girls in the brothels, some selling their wares, calling their trades, or beating out their copper pots and pans, or weaving their baskets or fulling their clothes; some strolling the streets down to the public square . . . when the sudden hail of pumice-stone descended upon them. They would have stared up at the towering mountain above them in accustomed alarm as the first huge explosion re-sounded through the air and sent the cinders and the steam and the rocks and the dust high, high up above them into the red sky, to hang there for a moment in awful magnificence before raining mercilessly down upon them, crushing them, smothering them, burning them, burying them. . . . They walked on quietly, not talking, moving in silence.

Mendels suddenly touched his arm. He stood there silent in the shadows, pointing. With his delicate, aquiline features and his high, wide forehead, he could have been an Etruscan noble standing at the pillared doorway of the Baths, indicating the way to the Temple with an expressive gesture. His clothes were an anachro-nism, out of harmony with the spirits about them.

He said softly, his voice no more than a breath: "Sh . . . there they are."

They moved quietly under a portico, the great grey, stone pillars solid beside them, brick-topped, vine-covered. He said softly: "Over by the cypress tree."

There were four of them. They were clearly visible against the skyline to the right as they came from the north-eastern borders of the New Excavations, moving slowly towards the main cross-roads of the town. Dinesen and the Countess were ahead, her hair gleaming bright in the moonlight. Behind them, one of the Italians was carrying the tin box on his shoulders, hoisting it like a Neapolitan porter, using his back and one shoulder to support it. In the rear, the other man was following them, the machine-pistol loosely held in his right hand. They were perhaps five hundred yards ahead, moving across their line of direction, coming in from the right.

Metcalfe felt the triumph in him reaching complacency, and said to himself, *This time we've got them.* He ran softly back and whispered to Pender, his mouth close in to his ear:

"Nip back and get the others; have them join us, but not to make a sound." The temptation to cough was almost insupportable.

Pender nodded and slid into the shadows. He moved like an animal, no sound or sight, suddenly gone in the stillness. They crouched in the darkness and watched and waited, staring across the open spaces that once were houses, across the tops of ruined walls that once were twenty feet high, through the broken gaps that had once been a great and prosperous city.

Dinesen's party came closer. They were moving down the Strada di Nola now, at right angles to their own direction still, coming into the same street on which they crouched waiting in the darkness. They were moving quietly, but without fear of discovery.

Mendels touched Ian gently. He whispered: "Shall we challenge them at the corner?"

Metcalfe shook his head. He was thinking, *We should have left Claire behind; they've got that damned machine-gun.* He said softly: "Wait till the others get here. This time we'll make sure of it."

Mendels nodded. Dinesen and the woman reached the corner. She sat down on a millstone and touched her foot with her hand. They could hear them talking quietly now, an indistinguishable murmur of sound carried across the intervening space. The moon was high and bright, the shadows of the ruins falling sharp and well-defined about them. The woman stood up and pulled her coat closer about her. Dinesen stood close beside her, staring into the shadows behind them. They heard him say, quite clearly, speaking Italian: "*Come on, come on; it's not far now. Come on; we're nearly there.*" He said something to the woman and they heard her laugh, standing still and lovely in the moonlight, and Metcalfe looked down at the hand that had touched her breast, remembering the animal nakedness of her, her white skin soft and lucid, still paining him with its urgency. Her flesh still burned in his hand, and he held his palm out into the moonlight, watching the oblique shadow of the doorway strike it. And then Pender and Hinks and the others came running up silently, and he saw that Hinks was carrying his shoes slung round his neck by the laces, and he shrugged off his disquiet and laughed softly. He put out his hand and touched Claire's cheek and she turned quickly and smiled at him. Hinks whispered thickly, his breath smelling strongly of whisky:

"What's the plan, General?"

Metcalfe whispered: "We'll wait till they move off, then Harry, Emery and White will cut round the back, get ahead of them and cut them off. The rest of us will follow them, then close in from both sides. You stay here and reinforce the main party." He whispered: "Look after Claire for me, will you?"

Mendels said: "They are certain to be making for the Gate. That's at the end of this road—about four hundred yards up. It's the shortest route to the filters now. If so, then—— There they go now."

They watched the party ahead turn the corner and move towards the Vesuvius Gate. Mendels whispered quickly: "Turn left at the corner, take the first street on the right, run like hell, and you'll come to the water cisterns at the end of the road—you'll be moving parallel to Dinesen and not more than twenty yards away from him on the other side of the wall. The cisterns lie right beside the gate."

Metcalfe said: "Get weaving. Let them get within a hundred yards of you, then call out to them. We'll answer from behind them to show them that they're surrounded. They won't be so anxious to start a fight. Now beat it. Not a sound."

Pender nodded. He signalled to the others and they moved off, running silently ahead. They watched them slip into the shadow of an overhanging balcony, and then they were gone. Mendels whispered: "It'll take them two minutes to get into position. I think this time you've got them."

Ian said: "This time we've got them." He said to Claire: "Stay here with Pat, close in to the left of the road. Joe—you take the right. As soon as Harry shouts, I'll take centre and answer him."

Moving from doorway to arch, from pillar to niche, keeping close to the side of the road, darting quickly and silently across the patches of moonlight, stopping in the shadows to watch and to listen, they slowly closed the distance between them.

They could clearly make out snatches of conversation now. They heard someone say: "... until the car gets back ..." and Dinesen's voice, clearly, "If he smashes my car up ..." and then the woman's voice suddenly, cold and quick and urgent, saying:

"There's someone ahead of us."

Metcalfe swore as he froze in the shadows. Dinesen and the others were suddenly gone; only with difficulty did he see that they too had moved instantly and silently into the shadows, all of them moving at once, well trained, then not moving, but being part of the shadows, the shadows of stone and brick and marble and occasional foliage. Metcalfe stood stock-still too, part of another shadow, and only the silent majesty of a ruined, deserted, long-left town was about them, its silent stones peaceful, quiet, still, empty; nothing moving, the pillars and corniced friezes standing about and above them in absolute ageless immobility. Then they heard the sharp, subdued click of a bolt slipping into place, and they knew that one of the Italians—was it Ricci?—was holding the Beretta at the ready, threatening the shadows, held steady in a vicious hand, its ventilated barrel menacing the emptiness, its polished walnut stock gripped tight against a cold and pounding heart. The gun was an emblem. They knew that without it there stood a coward and a weakling, a frightened, hunted thing of flesh and bone and shaking nerve; but with it, there was a powerful, savage animal, a giant.

In the silence, it seemed they must have gone. The space where they had stood was empty; nothing moved. Metcalfe could almost hear his watch ticking. Then Pender's voice, clear and loud, called out to the darkness. He said, raising his tone, not shouting, speaking clearly, coldly:

"Come out, Dinesen. We're all round you." Metcalfe stepped into the road, holding his rifle loosely, feet wide apart, filling the road with his bulk in the moonlight, his moon-shadow dark and oblique and long on the cobblestones, feeling the sudden excitement throbbing through him, a sudden fear and exaltation. His wound was bursting again in his chest. He called out clearly:

"We're all round you, Dinesen. We're all armed."

Then Mendels moved out into the light, and then he saw Pender and Emery and White rise up like ghouls out of the shadows at the end of the road, disclosing themselves in the distance on the other side of the space where Dinesen had stood.

For a long moment there was no answer. Then, unexpectedly, one man stepped out into the road ahead of them. They heard the rapid clatter as the gun started firing and the whine of the bullets as they ricochetted off the ancient stones and spun away towards the mountain in the distance, cutting viciously through the foliage, and White and Emery and Pender dropped out of sight again as suddenly and as startlingly as the clay figures in a circus booth, ducking away from the sudden danger whining over their heads and chipping angrily into the cistern behind which they sheltered, and even as they disappeared they heard Dinesen roar, a violent bellow of savage anger:

"Don't fire, damn you! Ricci, you fool!"

They saw him leap into the centre of the road and seize the gunman by the shoulder and swing him round and they heard the sharp sound as he struck him savagely on the side of the head, and they heard the gun clatter to the ground and saw Ricci fall on top of it, falling forward on to the cobbles, and they started moving forward, a collective action, unrehearsed, instinctive. They saw Dinesen move quickly back to the shadows and lug the big tin trunk from the shoulders of his companion, and they heard him shout: "*Di qua, this way; over here, di qua!*" and saw him jump on to the low wall of the Fullery at the side of the road, shouting again: "*Di qua! Presto!*" standing for a moment tall and gaunt and angular against the sky; and as they started running, openly, not hiding any more, Metcalfe saw Ricci stumbling to his feet and the gun started firing again, straight at them this time, at close range, the bright red-yellow flash spurting out of its barrel. spitting at them. Out of the corner of his eye he saw Pat Hinks lunge in front of Claire, pushing her to the ground, shielding her with his body, lying across her, and he looked across at them and called: "Are you all right?" And then he threw the rifle to his shoulder and looked into the spitting flames, dropping to the ground and firing at the same time, knowing that he had missed, and then, above the clatter of the gun, there was suddenly the sharp single report of a pistol, a sharper, more precise sound, and the gun stopped chattering. He saw Dinesen still standing on the low wall against the sky, the pistol in his hand, and he saw Ricci slump forward to the ground and knew that he was dead and that Dinesen had killed him; and then Dinesen called out:

"Is anybody hurt?"

He did not answer. He dropped his rifle and ran quickly across the road to Claire and dropped on one knee beside her and said:

"Are you all right, darling?"

She said: "Yes, I think so," her voice unsteady, and then she choked and started crying, shaking horribly,

216

and he saw that Hinks was lying still and quiet on top of her and that his wet, warm blood was coursing on to her shoulder.

Mendels was suddenly beside him, crouched on the ground, saying softly over and over again: "The bastard, the bastard, the bastard," saying it over and over again as though there were comfort in it, and then dragging Hinks clear and turning him over and staunching the pumping blood with a pocket-handkerchief.

Claire was sobbing and wiping at the blood, and he helped her to her feet, not finding the right thing to say and therefore saying nothing, holding her trembling body tight against him. He saw the silver pocket-flask gleaming white at his feet. The sudden intrusion of fear and of violence, unexpected but now known to have been inevitable, was cold about them. Metcalfe shivered.

Claire said: "He . . . he was . . . trying to shield . . . me. Is he dead?" And he said: "No, not dead." She stood shivering for a moment and then suddenly stopped and knelt down beside Hinks and started opening his jacket and pulling at his shirt, and Metcalfe helped her.

Mendels said gently: "I'll be back in a minute."

He walked quickly up the Strada di Stabia to where Ricci lay. The single shot that Dinesen had fired had broken his neck and passed through his throat. He had been killed, Mendels thought savagely, thinking of Hinks throwing himself in front of Claire, like a wild animal, through the neck. *Bring them down quickly with the neck shot, then they can't do any more damage.* He stopped and picked up the Beretta, examining it with distaste. He thought, *Back home in the old days he would have used a Thompson.* He slipped the magazine out and dropped it into his pocket, then ejected the shell from the breech and pocketed that too. He stood staring disconsolately about him for a moment or two, wondering what to do about Hinks, staring into the pillared Fullery with its concrete tubs and washing tanks and its flat, smooth paving-stones. Somewhere through there, Dinesen and the others had vanished. He went to the deep well nearby, pushed aside the heavy wooden cover, and dropped the Beretta to the bottom. It fell with a clatter to the dry stones and rubble nearly a hundred feet below. He threw the magazine and the single round from his pocket after it. The dull scraping thud of wood on stone as he replaced the cover was the only sound that broke the silence. He stared for a while into the darkness that had covered Dinesen, wondering about him, his agile mind turning the problem over.

He looked to the east and thought the sky was getting lighter. He wondered what to do about Hinks.

Chapter Thirteen

MENDELS came back to where they crouched beside
the wounded man. They had opened up his clothes and
disclosed the wounds, and Claire was working on them
carefully. A bullet had entered the back just above the
shoulder-blade; it had apparently twisted on the bone
and come out at the base of the neck, pursuing the
frequent unlikely path. Another—or perhaps it was the
same one—had gouged a deep furrow at the back of
the head, from below and behind the left ear up to the
top of the skull, and the blood had soaked into the
shoulder of his jacket. There was a lot of blood.
They had staunched the alarming flow from the
neck with a pad and bandages torn from a shirt. His
face was pale in the moonlight; his body was limp and
motionless.

Metcalfe said: "He's all right so far; but we've got to
get him to a hospital. A doctor, anyway. And the
sooner the better."

Mendels said: "The nearest 'phone is . . . what—a
mile or so away. There's a garage up on the road above
us. Might even be able to get a car there to run him
into town."

"Bullet-wounds will take some explaining."

Mendels nodded thoughtfully. He said: "There's a
guy at the Embassy. . . . What about Dinesen?"

Metcalfe hesitated. He said at length: "I've got to
go after him, of course. Suppose the American con-
tingent drops out and takes care of Pat? You've done
your share. This isn't even your quarrel. If Pat . . .

219

What do you say Harry and I go on and leave you to it? Claire could stay with you."

"We can't drop out now. Not after this."

"Someone's got to get help for Pat."

"All right. If the others are willing. . . . Suppose Will stays here with Pat and Ray goes off to find a telephone. I could then join up with Ian and Harry. Pushing the baby on to you boys, but . . . what do you say, Will?"

White grinned cheerfully. He said: "Might be better if I go fetch help. If Ray gets too near a 'phone he might suddenly remember he's a newshawk."

Emery said: "Yeah? Can you talk Italian?"

"Well, I can say '*Buon giorno*' as well as the next guy."

"And how you gonna get a doctor down here by saying *buon giorno* on the telephone?" He announced: "This guy's pretty good at languages. Why, in France, he even learned to say '*Voulez-vous coucher avec moi?*' How you gonna get a doctor to come to Pompeii at four o'clock in the morning by saying, '*Buon giorno. Voulez-vous coucher avec moi?*' Answer me that, will you?"

"Well . . ."

"You stay here with the corpse. I'll go get help. Where's this telephone at?"

Mendels said: "Come with us to the road, then turn left down the hill for about half a mile. It will be closed up, of course. You'll have to do a bit of hollering to get them out of bed."

"Best hog-caller this side of the Ozarks."

"And forget the agency for a moment, will you?"

"Sure . . . I know. Top secret. Yes, General. Certainly, General."

White said: "What do I say if the police show up?"

"They're not likely to. If they do, play dumb. Ricci and another guy were shooting it out, and you two got in the way. We're chasing the other guy—but send them in the opposite direction." He said to Metcalfe: "How does that sound?"

Metcalfe nodded. He said: "Fine. But I agree with you; they're not likely to have heard the shooting. I suppose we'd better have a story ready, just in case. What were we doing in Pompeii in the first place? At this time of night?"

"We're tourists. Out driving along the highway to see Vesuvius by moonlight. Decided to take a look at Pompeii."

"Where's our car?"

White said gleefully: "Gone to buy us some sandwiches and a bottle of Chianti. Kinda hungry."

Metcalfe said: "It'll do. I think perhaps Claire had better go along with Ray——"

"No." Her face strained and white, Claire spoke decisively. She said: "I'm coming along with you."

Ian looked across at Mendels and caught his eye. He said: "All right. I don't like it, but . . ."

He took off his jacket and laid it carefully across Hinks's chest. He stood looking down at him for a moment. He was still and pale and quiet in the moonlight, but breathing steadily now, the blood no longer flowing.

He said heavily:

"We've been lucky. The second casualty tonight. . . . Another half-inch and either of us would have been dead. Are you sure you want to come on?"

Mendels nodded. He said: "But I'm not happy about Claire."

Standing still and straight against the yellow stone-work and the black cypress trees, slender and lovely in the grey light, looking across the darkness to the mountain, Claire said: "They're up there, somewhere. On Vesuvius. As long as the Mancini woman stays with them . . . I'll drop out when she does. As long as she stays, I will."

Metcalfe took her by the arm, letting her feel the pressure of his fingers on her flesh. They left Will White with Hinks squatting down beside him in the shadows, rolling up his coat to make a pillow under his head, staring at him anxiously, but knowing that the worst was over for him, waiting for him to recover consciousness and say thickly, *Where the hell's my bottle of rye?*; knowing that this would be one of the great stories to tell the folks, already dreaming up the embellishments . . . *must have been about twenty of them . . . sure, we took off after them, just me and Pat . . . never had but one shot-gun between us, and brother, that tommy . . . little Italian tommy, they call it a Beretta . . . and Pat says, The hell with it, Will, let's go get 'em . . .* knowing that soon now they would be laughing and joking about it, all the folks thrilling with vicarious excitement. *Sure, in a place called Pompeii, a sort of ghost town . . . no, honey, nothing to do with the gold rush. . . . You never hear tell of Pompeii? Well, Pat and me . . .* He investigated the flask, and found with satisfaction that it was still more than half full.

Mendels said: "Over here, they must have gone through there," pointing to the open walls of the Fullery. "We know where they're making for, more or less, but do they know that we know?"

"We can search the whole of Pompeii and never find them if they want to lie low. There are a thousand places here they could hide in. In one of the houses . . . it would take us a week to search every one."

Mendels nodded.

Metcalfe said: "If we assume they're going up to—say the Mancini place, wherever that is, near the filter-beds? Will they know that we're going there too? Or will they imagine that we traced them here simply by following them after we found the Maserati?"

"They'll think we followed them. They can't possibly know that we've found out about their hide-out. We're not even sure ourselves. All we know is that they have some sort of interest up near the filters. They can't possibly know that we know that."

"Then let's take a short-cut again. Let's make straight for the vineyards."

Mendels agreed. He said: "The only advantage we have lies in knowing—or in thinking we know—where they're going. With only one trump in the hand, we'd better play it for all hell. If we can find the spot they're making for . . . Hell, what are we wasting time for? Let's get up that goddam mountain."

They walked quickly and quietly along the Strada di Stabia, not stopping, and out at the Vesuvian Gate, the vineyards ahead of them on the gently sloping hill, rising faster now, steeper with every yard they went, the soil rich and black beneath their feet. Pushing laboriously forward they came to the first scattered vines, slung low on carefully spaced wires, the heavy grapes ripely bunched and cool to the touch with the cold dew of the volcano's morning. They plucked at the fruit as they went along, tasting the icy flesh with sensuous pleasure, feeling the golden-cold of the rich, sweet succulence, the bunches pregnant and heavy. They stumbled along the length of the fence, then came to a copse of young hazel trees, speckled and spindly, and turned right again, facing toward the summit high above them, looking up at it distantly. Moving on and on, they came at last to the road, a wide track of levelled earth covered with loose gravel, little used, that ran from left to right across them, high hedges on both sides dividing it from the surrounding vines and the fields and the boscage. They stumbled across the ditch and stood panting on the roadway.

Mendels pointed to the left. He said: "Down the hill, half a mile or so . . . the garage is on the left. You'll have to wake them up. You know Doc Sarrat at the Embassy?"

Emery nodded.

"Ring him up at his house—the Embassy will give you his number; tell him to come on out in a car and pick Pat up. Ask him to keep quiet about it till I can get a chance to see him and explain. Tell him I'm on a job; I'll get in touch with him when I get back. He'll need a stretcher to move Pat on to the main road at the Maritime Gate—that's about as close as he'll be able to get in the car. O.K.?"

"Sure. How about you fellas?"

"We'll be up at the filter-beds. Know where they are?"

"Nope."

"Another mile or so up this track. You can't miss them. We'll be sneaking around the vineyard there. You might look us up afterwards. If not . . . see you back home."

Emery said briefly: "See you." He walked quickly down the hill.

They crossed the road and took the footpath again, Metcalfe and Pender and Mendels and Claire, forcing their way through the thick shrubbery, pushing aside the supple saplings and planting their feet firmly on the steep and narrow path, slipping over the massive roots

of chestnut trees and pulling themselves up by the lean
and delicate hazel shoots, slithering steeply, panting
hard. The narrow trail grew steeper and steeper and
they paused frequently to rest, looking behind them at
the great bay incredibly far below them, with Pompeii
still unclouded and clear and unbelievably lovely in the
foreground.

Mendels said, breathing hard, looking down at the
white stones far below: "If the doc can get there before
daylight, he can get Pat clear before the trippers start
arriving."

Metcalfe was looking up at the withers of the volcano;
the sky showed a broad grey patch, light-tinged with
red, a band of opalescence hanging low along the
mountain, the first rays of distant light seeping up in the
east. He said:

"And Ricci?"

"That's their worry. I can feel no regrets for Ricci.
I'm afraid. They'll soon find out who he is, and nobody's
likely to tell them what happened. Ricci is now strictly
a matter for the police. It's only Pat we need worry
about." He said softly: "Poor Pat. . . . Let's get
going."

"Any idea where to?"

"Half a mile to the beds. Tired?"

Claire said: "How's the chest?"

"I'd forgotten all about it. Daylight soon. Then
what?"

They pulled themselves slowly, laboriously upward.
Claire said, fighting for breath: "If they've come this
way with that tin-trunk on their shoulders, they can't
be very far ahead of us."

The trunk. The old officers' uniform box, as much a
part of the army as the Sam Browne or the swagger
cane, had become an emblem, a symbol, a cipher. It

was the epitome of their work, the essence of their being. It was no longer a question of righting a wrong or the completion of an undertaking; it was the acceptance of a challenge, perhaps, but no more than that. This box was a device, an uncompleted paragraph that had begun in the militant Ethiopian hills, with guns firing and powder bursting in red-lit grey clouds, with tired and ragged red-eyed men far from their homes and their lovers, inescapably and without hope caught up in the involution of the battle, standing fearful among the white rocks and the black clods and the green thorns under the sweating heat of the blue sky, far, very far away, plucked out of their own particular environments, removed from the comforting proximity of the lamp-post on the corner, and gently placed instead on a lonely, distant mountain where savagery and violence were rife; it had begun with fear and greed and murder. It was the essence of their purpose; a battered green tin-trunk, stamped "H. J. Hewitt, Major, K.A.R.," buried for more than a decade, and fought for across two continents. It was ahead of them at last, and close.

Metcalfe squinted at his watch in the darkness and saw that the time was slipping by. His mouth was dry from the exertion, the wound in his chest throbbing gently with every step. Musing, they came at length to a sudden widening of the track, an abrupt flattening of the terrain, an unexpected clearing, a wide and level place of grass and soft shrubbery, edged with dark and sombrous forest, the heavy trees confining their vision to the wide space about them. The moon and the morning sky were bright on the unexpected water, square concrete lakes, great rectangles of pale blue water spread before them like a cold, wet floor of blue mosaic edged in stone. Further to the left, the vineyards began again. Close beside them was a small cluster of wooden buildings, roofed with ragged sheets of tin, ramshackle, broken-down, dilapidated. They looked like the outbuildings of a small farm. They appeared to be quite deserted. Beyond them was a long and low building of whitewashed stucco, a roof and three walls and a floor, open on the fourth side; it was a sort of garage. They walked over to take a look at it, peering around them into the shadows as they moved. All was silent.

There was an old Bianchi saloon parked against one wall, a square-bodied car of some antiquity, but well preserved and polished; it was the kind of car the *padrone* would keep down at his vineyard to tour the groves in, a farm car that would lurch ponderously but with dignified and unrestricted ease over the rough mud tracks and the gravel paths. Beside it there was a space for another car, and the oil drippings of the missing vehicle were faintly visible in the partial shadow. There were two spare wheels in the darkened corner. Metcalfe took out his flashlight and examined them; they were fitted with racing tyres and he read aloud the inscription on the hub-caps: "Maserati". He said softly: "We're here. I wonder if they are?"

Claire said: "We must still be behind them even if we came in a straight line; did they hear us coming, I wonder? We weren't very quiet. Yet there's a car there if they wanted to get away from us."

Metcalfe moved to the back of the garage and played the light over the Bianchi. One of the front doors was open; close beside it was a foot-pump. He reached up and felt the bare electric light bulb that was hanging over the centre of the adjacent bench; it was still warm to his touch, only recently switched off. He shone his light around him. There was a work-bench with some odd tools lying on it: a screwdriver, a couple of spanners, a dismantled carburettor, a large and rusty wrench, an axe. On the floor were two cans of petrol; these had just been pumped out of a large drum which stood on a wooden stand against the wall. He ran his fingers along the exposed plunger of the pump, it was cold and wet.

He heard Pender call softly and saw him coming forward in the half-light, pushing a struggling body ahead of him. It was the other Italian. Pender said, grinning:

"Found him trying to sneak away into the woods from behind the building. He had a pistol. Don't think he ought to be trusted with it."

He was holding the emaciated little man by the arm and the scruff of the neck, a wretched, abject, trembling fellow.

Metcalfe asked: "Buitoni?"

"*Si, signore.*"

"What are you doing here? Where are the others?" Buitoni looked up at him fearfully. His scanty hair was short-cropped, recently shaved. His weasel eyes were sharp in his thin, high-cheeked face. He said, stammering:

"They told me . . . they told me to fill the tank of the car, signore. . . . There was . . . signore, I had nothing to do with the shooting; it was Ricci only, and then when Signor Dinesen shot him . . . I was afraid. . . . I swear to you——"

"Where are the others?"

"I do not know, signore . . . I know nothing. I am a poor, unfortunate——"

Metcalfe said grimly: "Do you want to go back to prison?"

"*Per Dio*, signore, the Carabinieri . . . please, signore, I have nothing to do with all this——"

"Where are the others?"

Buitoni hesitated. He said: "If you would let me go, signore . . . I do not want to go back to prison. . . . I want to forget all this and go home——"

Metcalfe said: "Our quarrel is not with you. Where are they?"

Buitoni said, whining: "They promised me a lot of money, signore. They said when it was all over . . ." He said uncomfortably: "I am a poor man——"

"You're wasting my time. Where are they?"

"Perhaps . . . perhaps in the long room, signore."

"The long room?"

"The wine store"—pointing—"or perhaps they went to the forest. They told me to get the car ready and they went away. Then I heard . . . I heard you coming and I was frightened, so I put out the light and hid, but this signore found me . . ." His voice trailed off miserably.

Metcalfe said brusquely: "All right. Go now. Get away from here. If I set eyes on you again——"

"But the money, signore? They promised me——"

Pender shoved him into the open. He said: "Get weaving, chum."

The little man hesitated for a moment, looking from one to the other fearfully, then suddenly moved away, hesitated again, then turned and ran. They watched him till he disappeared among the trees.

Mendels said pleasantly: "Franconi, Ricci, Buitoni —all accounted for. The odds are getting better."

Metcalfe said: "The long room."

"Worth while immobilising that car?"

"Not worth it. If he tries to make a break, we've got him."

Pender said: "The long room might be any of these buildings. Which one first?"

They stood together hesitant. Pointing, Metcalfe said: "That one."

It was the obvious choice. Among the broken-down outhouses, set a little apart, was a small square building a little better than the others. It was not a house exactly; it was a hut verging on the dignity and permanence of a cottage, the kind of place in which a foreman would sleep and work during the grape harvest. There were tubs outside, dumped lazily against the wooden door. The plank door itself had a cut wooden latch and a hole had been bored in both the door and the jamb to hold a chain and padlock. The chain was hanging loosely down; the padlock was gone. Metcalfe pointed the fact out to the others, silently. Beside the door there were two windows, both covered with slatted wooden shutters, once painted and now scarred and blistered and worn.

They walked round it quietly. At the back there was another window similarly darkened. The high roof was steeply pitched and well tiled in squares of red terracotta, the eaves widely overhanging. The walls were of crudely finished planks, and down one side there was a wide verandah with an earthen floor, roughly furnished with a bare pine table and a bench. A box of empty wine-bottles stood in one corner. Metcalfe picked out a bottle and shone his light on the label. It read, in neat black and gold print: "*Casa Mancini. Vino vecchio di Pompeii Amian, 40 Massime Onorificenze Esposizioni Mondiali.*"

He said softly: "If they're anywhere here, they'll be in this building."

Mendels was standing close beside him, his head cocked a little on one side, seeming to sniff the air with a delicate nostril. He said: "What makes you so sure?"

"There's the padlock missing from the door; *somebody's* inside. But most of all—this is the only building here that could be defended," he said grimly: "if he wants to make a fight for it."

"Uh-huh. Then they can hear us talking, anyway. What are we being so quiet about?"

Metcalfe went to the wooden door and tried the latch. It was free, but the bolt was fastened on the inside. He rattled it loudly and called: "Dinesen?"

There was no answer. Sure of himself, knowing that he could not be wrong this time, he called again:

"Dinesen? We're coming in."

He put his foot against the door and pushed. The planks held. He drew his knee back and thrust out his foot again, harder and more savagely, kicking with the under-side of his foot, the whole weight of his body behind the blows, kicking again and again at the flimsy door until it gave, splintering noisily on the inside.

Mendels said: "Fine thing if there's a peasant inside."

Metcalfe shook his head. He said: "If there is I'll buy him a dozen new doors."

He said to the others: "All right. Stand back."

He threw the great weight of his body into the damaged door, forcing his angry shoulder into it, grimacing with sudden pain at the forgotten wound in his chest, then drew his leg back once more and thrust his foot forward ferociously. The door flew back on its damaged hinges, crashing back and into the wall by the window, a sudden sharp splintering of woodwork sounding as he fell forward clumsily into the room, springing quickly to his feet and standing clearly framed in the dark aperture.

Mendels called, urgently: "Be careful, Ian."

Metcalfe grunted. Holding his rifle loosely, easily, confident now, feeling once more at ease with his problem, he walked to the window and threw back the jalousie, and a faint grey light seeped in, a pale pastel light of greys and daybreak colours, a mixture of the white of the moon and the red of the eastern sky and the cold *grisaille* of the clouds over the volcano, bringing coldness with it, a freshness of breeze off the grapes and with it the smell of the mountain bush. The sky outside was light, a suffusion of greys and reds and the soft tint of Italian peach-skins. Framed in the open window, the volcano reached up to the dark night sky above, only the flanks standing clear and sharp against the soft, light colours of the morning behind them.

The single room was empty. It was cheaply furnished with tables and chairs and rickety cupboards and there was an old iron bedstead, a coarse, striped mattress lying on it, and two demijohns stood against the wall, a coil of rubber tubing hanging on a nail above them. Along one side was a steep stairway leading up to the loft above, a stairway of steps without balustrade, leading up to a trap-door in the ceiling, to the loft where the wine would be stored, a hasp and heavy padlock on the underside; but here again the padlock was missing. Metcalfe grinned to himself. He said aloud: "The last lap."

He walked quickly up the steep staircase and tried the trap-door. It was fastened from above. He pushed his back against it and felt it give slightly, then fall heavily back into place. He fancied he heard the sound of rattling bottles.

He called out to Mendels, filled with a new confidence: "They're here all right." He said: "Dinesen? No good hiding, my dear fellow. It's undignified."

There was no answer. Above him, standing under the peaked roof of the loft, staring down at the trap-door heavily weighted with cases of wine, his revolver drawn, tall and gaunt and angular and suddenly very tired, Dinesen stood in silence. He watched the heaving of the trap-door under its precarious load and wondered if it would hold. The Contessa was seated on the green tin-trunk beside him. He raised his eyes to her and she nodded, her pale-blue courtesan's eyes sombre and troubled.

He said: "Ian? Can you hear me?"

Metcalfe, standing below him on the stairs, separated only by the heavy planking of the ceiling and the floor of the upper room, stopped short. He said, consciously keeping the jubilation from his voice: "Aha. Well? After all this time?"

Dinesen said, speaking quite clearly: "Ian? I warned you before. I will shoot if necessary. Make no mistake Ian. I will shoot if I have to." His voice was taut and sharp.

Metcalfe said: "There are four of us down here, and there are more coming. You haven't a hope in hell."

"No? Look at the sky. It's nearly daylight. It's time we understood each other. If the police find us here, shooting it out, then I shall be in a stronger position than you; I've no benighted Colonel on my back to worry about diplomatic relations. You can't afford to have the police on your track, and you know it."

"And neither can you."

"Precisely. This is between the two of us. No outsiders. No law. And that means it has to be decided within the hour, because very soon the labourers will start arriving. What are you going to do then? Half a hundred hefty peasants—employed by *us*. How's that going to fit in with your plans?"

"By the time they get here, we shall have gone."

"You think so? Do you really believe I can't hold this place for an hour? That's all I have to do, hold it for one hour, no more. And make no mistake—if I have to, I shoot. Don't make me kill you at the last minute. Give up and go back to London."

"At your first shot, we open fire too. We're well armed, Dinesen."

Metcalfe heard Claire sob. He said angrily: "Don't be a fool, man. You're beaten. Hand over that box, if only for the sake of the women."

Clear and loud, the Countess's voice came through the barrier between them. It was harsh and cold and brittle. She said, speaking in Italian: "Take your English girl and go back to Rome, Signor Metcalfe. Rome is the place for lovers; not Vesuvius. This is a violent mountain, signore. Go back to Rome."

He said pleasantly: "I'm sorry, Contessa." He called: "I'm coming up, Dinesen."

Dinesen pointed his revolver down at the trap-door and fired. The bullet crashed through the lowest wine-case with a violent shattering of broken glass, splintered its way through the heavy planking of the floor and embedded itself with a savagely dead and final sound into the steps of the stairway. A sudden strip of white where the bullet had splintered the wood of the ceiling highlighted the argument. Another shot followed the first and another, the three explosions close together and sounding almost as one in the confined space. Swearing loudly, Metcalfe dropped quickly back from the stairway, crouching close against the wall, gripping his rifle tightly.

He called out: "An hour to go? You can't make it, Dinesen; I'll have you out of there in ten minutes."

Dinesen did not answer.

Metcalfe walked across to the doorway. He said to Mendels: "He's right, you know. If he holds out till the countryside gets here, we're done for. Once the peasants start arriving, if nothing else happens, he can just walk out of the place. He knows it, and he knows that we know it too."

Mendels nodded. He said: "There's only one answer, of course."

"Yep."

Claire said: "What's that?"

Metcalfe said: "Burn him out. It's the only thing to do. Set fire to the place and force him to come out. If we start a gun battle here . . . well, we can't see them and they can't see us. Seems a bit silly to blaze away into space hopefully; liable to hurt the wrong people. I'll put a bullet through Dinesen's heart any day, if only for the sake of Pat Hinks. But he's got a woman with him . . . makes a difference, whether we like it or not. So we burn them out."

Claire said: "What happens then? What about Dinesen?"

Metcalfe shrugged. "Not interested in him. But I want that box. And I'm going to get it if I have to blow up Vesuvius for it."

Mendels said: "There's gas in the garage. A can of *benzina* to start things going." He walked away towards the garage, leaving Ian and Claire together by the broken doorway, staring into the relative darkness of the long room with its musty air still hanging about them in the stillness.

Metcalfe muttered: "An hour? We haven't got an hour. The *paesani* will be here at any minute now." He put his arm around her, holding her tightly. He said: "We've been up all night. Tired?"

"No."

"Scared?"

She shook her head. She said: "Not scared. A little . . . worried. All this started so . . . so easily. It was a simple safari in Africa. There was no thought of fighting among friends . . . of shooting each other down in cold blood like this. Those shots were not meant as a warning. He couldn't even see you. He might have killed you. I was frightened then. A few weeks ago we were all together in London, good friends. And now . . . all this over a box full of money. It's more than frightening—it's . . . it's revolting. What's happened to all our values?"

"I know. But it's a matter of principle now. We're so close . . . if he gets away with it now . . . he mustn't. That's all there is to it; he mustn't get away with it. It's become too important. Its importance has, well, it's got blown up to abnormal size by the trouble we've had. I know; I grew out of fighting for principles a long time ago. I used to have ideals, I suppose, before the war. But this . . . don't you see, it's Hewitt, it's Major Hewitt's . . . well, his vindication. He was killed in the very early days of the war, when we all still had our ideals. This is the last chapter of something that was started when we all thought quite differently. He started it, and I've got to finish it for him. And perhaps we haven't changed so much. I don't know. . . ."

"Is it worth killing for? Again?"

Metcalfe hesitated. He said: "I won't kill anybody; I promise you that. Not even Dinesen. Have you still got a soft spot in your heart for him?'

"No. Not any more. I didn't expect this of him. I always thought his lack of scruples was . . . well, just bombast."

"Perhaps it was once. I think perhaps this has changed him. As he said himself, the stakes are too damn high. When the opportunity arises . . . when you see something you suddenly want, if it's big enough . . . " He said moodily: "If it's desirable enough, it's very easy to forget your scruples and your decency. It's very easy to say, 'The hell with it.' Something you want badly enough . . . even if you never realised before the opportunity arose that you had ever wanted it. Then once it starts, the strong man takes it to its logical conclusion regardless of the obstacles. Dinesen's a strong man, that's all. Perhaps I even envy him, in a way."

Claire was inspecting him shrewdly, her fine eyebrows widely arched, her eyes steady and restful, her Madonna-look hiding a woman's brain and a woman's knowledge, remembering Harry Pender crouched in the darkness by the creeping vines of the tall iron fence, '*She shot him but he seems to be all right; she was kneeling on the floor beside him, bandaging him up . . . get on the 'phone to Joe Mendels, tell him we want help, as much help as he can get, in a hurry, there's no time to lose. . . .*' She thought of the beautiful Italian woman, the lovely creature with no scruples.

She said, smiling at him: "If it's any consolation, it's you I love. Not Dinesen."

He kissed her quickly on the mouth, feeling the softness of her lips, then broke roughly away. He said: "Let's get on with our bonfire. But first, we'll find some cover."

Mendels came back from the garage with two cans of petrol. He said: "Pour it all over the floor inside. You and Harry cover the front of the house. I'll take the back. O.K.?"

"O.K." He said to Claire: "In here. Keep your head down if anybody starts shooting."

She nodded and crouched in the angle of a small outhouse, her heart beating fast, conscious of the tension about her, sensing the potential disaster.

Metcalfe picked up the cans of petrol, slinging his rifle over his shoulder. He knelt on the floor of the empty room with its bare wooden furniture, and unscrewed the cap of one of them. Taking out a handkerchief, he soaked it in the petrol and laid it on the floor, in line with the doorway, standing the cans beside it. He put a match to the handkerchief and watched it flare brightly for a second, watching the black smoke swirl heavily up to the ceiling. He stepped quickly to the door and called out:

"Dinesen? Your last chance to come out. We're setting fire to the hut. Come on out!"

Listening carefully, he heard an oath from upstairs, then the angry sound of Dinesen's footsteps as he strode to the trap-door and thrust aside the wine-cases, tumbling them savagely on to the floor. The trap-door was thrown open, and Dinesen stood there obliquely framed in the opening, tall and thin and gigantic in perspective, his feet apart, his revolver in his hand.

He said angrily: "Don't say I didn't warn you."

He raised the revolver and Metcalfe stepped quickly back as the shot sounded. The handkerchief on the floor was still burning brightly beside the petrol tins. He drew back from the door, stepping into the open space and said: "Well, here we go."

Sighting his rifle quickly, not waiting, he fired two rapid shots into the petrol tins beside the little fire. For a moment nothing happened; then the leaking petrol caught with a soft *whoosh* and the fire spread along the wooden floor. For a moment it flickered patchily, and then there was a sudden explosion as the bulk of it caught and the cans went hurtling across the room, splashing their burning contents as they landed, spattering the timbers with a drench of liquid flame. Standing a few yards back, Metcalfe felt the heat of it as the smoke billowed out of the doorway and the windows. It was red and orange and vivid and vicious, brightly flaming as the fire licked angrily and triumphantly at the long-dry timbers till they caught, then seeming to move on from post to post in rapid succession; it was a live thing, seeming to make sure each adze-hewn post was in flames before moving on to the next.

They watched as the fire spread with astonishing rapidity, noisily crackling. Claire stood half exposed in her protective corner, staring sombrely at the holocaust spreading so fast and so noisily, wondering about the two people in the upper room. Metcalfe was waiting grimly in the open space in front of the door, his rifle at port across his body, his face set, Pender standing watchfully beside him. At the back of the building Mendels crouched behind an earthen bank, staring at the upper window, his shot-gun ready, waiting. The sky above was light now. It was not yet daylight, but the pastel shades had spread to embrace the skies above them; only in the west was it still dark. They saw the wooden shutters of the building catch, and crackling uproariously the flames swung up the outside of the walls, licking erratically at the planking.

Inside the building, upstairs in the loft, coughing at the smoke seeping through the plank floor, feeling the heat of the creeping fire below and about them, Dinesen and his mistress stood hesitantly together, angry, frustrated, glowering with an impotent rage as vehement as the flames themselves. In one corner the floor was already aflame; the heavy pitch-soaked cross-member was burning savagely, the heat glowing off it with appalling intensity. In a few minutes the whole floor would go.

Dinesen took up the tin-trunk. He took it by the handle and slung it across his broad shoulders with his left hand, heaving its great weight up with no effort, standing atop the furnace with his plunder on his shoulder and his gun in his hand. He said briefly, coughing in the smoke, his eyes red and smarting, brushing angrily at the smoking air, his face begrimed and sweating, breathing heavily:

"There's not much time. We'll run for it. Follow me into the woods. . . . If we can hold them off for another half-hour . . . God damn it, half an hour is all we want. . . . Are you ready?"

She nodded, standing beside him with defeat in her bearing, staring fearfully at the flaming stairway, her hand to her throat, her hair loose about her face. She said: "I'm ready."

They took the stairs at a rush. The flames were bright and hot about them as they stumbled down two at a time, choking, groping blindly for the open doorway, Dinesen leading, the Countess close behind him. He fired two random shots as he came into the open, the smoke-tears in his smarting eyes blinding him. He felt the sudden cleanliness of the air and knew that he was in the open and fired again blindly, and then Metcalfe hit him.

He was standing at the door, gulping in great breaths of fresh air, peering hazily through the smoke, seeing the towering bulk of Metcalfe standing no more than a few feet away from him, and he raised his revolver and squeezed the trigger, not caring now, careless with the intemperance of desperation; and then Metcalfe threw up his rifle and thrust it out with both hands, flinging it from him forcibly, thrusting it forward and diving to the ground at the same time. The barrel struck Dinesen squarely across the shoulder, jolting to a painful end of its short journey in the crook of his neck, driving the air out of his body; and as he went down he felt Metcalfe's powerful arms around his knees and toppled heavily over, knowing that in the moment of pain and breathlessness he had dropped his gun and that the tin-trunk was heavily athwart his body. He twisted round and struggled to his feet, moving fast with the instinctive reaction of the desperate animal, feeling Metcalfe clawing untidily at his shoulders, dragging him down, and he drew back his fist and drove it hard into his face, seeing him roll over backwards on the ground, feeling again the sudden surge of hope; and then there was a scream behind him and he turned and saw the heavy timbers crashing down in flames, saw them before he heard them, conscious only of the scream, seeing only the woman on the floor clawing at the air with one arm, dragging herself forward through the fire and screaming, and the timbers crashing down about her and the sparks flying and the smoke billowing, and the appalling heat surging out from the building; and he staggered forward into the flames and took her by the shoulders, pulling her forward desperately to the door, kicking away the heavy burning timbers, lugging at them with bare hands, tearing the burning clothes from her body, pulling her out into the open, where the day was white and the air was clean; and he lifted her up in his arms and carried her, struggling with her, limp and fainting and tearful, her long hair singed, her clothing burned and torn, the soft smooth skin of her streaked with grime, her lissom body limp and exhausted, stumbling forward into the freshness of the morning.

He felt the cold on his face again and looked up, breathing heavily through the smoke, the hot fire close behind him. Metcalfe was facing him, silently waiting. His hair was tousled and there was a trickle of blood from his nose. Mendels stood beside him, half-smiling, neat and still elegant, holding his shot-gun lightly. Pender stood a little to one side, his revolver levelled and steady. Claire was a solitary figure in the yellow dawn behind them, watching them apprehensively. He saw that the battered green tin-trunk was at Metcalfe's feet. He stood for a moment staring at them. Nobody spoke. The day was all about them now, the air cool and moist, the first bright yellow beams of sunlight streaking along the profile of the volcano, lighting the vines and the fields and the dark-green trees with a new and brighter aspect.

For a long time he stood there watching them, breathing heavily. Then he moved forward slowly, saying nothing. Metcalfe and Pender and Mendels moved aside and let him pass in silence. Metcalfe stared down at the still beautiful face of the woman in his arms as he moved between them. Her eyes were closed, her features relaxed; her breast was gently moving.

They watched him carry her to the old Bianchi and lay her gently, lovingly, on the padded leather seat. He climbed in heavily beside her and started the motor. A moment later, the car pulled slowly out and turned into the wide mud pathway. It lumbered heavily forward, then disappeared among the shadows of the trees; the dense green foliage framed it darkly for a moment, and then it was gone.

Mendels, elegant and unruffled and debonair, staring after it into the distance, spoke softly.

He said: "The Ethiopian gambit; checkmate."

Metcalfe fumbled in his pocket for a handkerchief, not finding one. Claire handed him a square of lawn from her handbag; he smiled at her as he dabbed at the blood under his nose.

He said: "Somebody give me a hand with this bloody trunk. Let's go."

[P.T.O.]

Also by ALAN CAILLOU

The World is Six Feet Square

Large Crown 8vo   12s 6d.

THIS is an escape book, and a prison book, and makes first-rate reading in both capacities. Alan Caillou and his small party, forming a deep-penetration patrol, were captured by the Italians in the Western Desert.

In *The World is Six Feet Square*, the author relates, with fidelity and zest, the strange story of their adventures from that point onwards.

"Something very much out of the ordinary run"
Times Literary Supplement

"This book is a record that arouses admiration, raises many a smile, and shows a fine sense of the dramatic."
Manchester Evening News

"An intelligent and unusual book this, full of good reading."
Punch